Disney

Tangled
The Series...

The Write Story

By
NEW YORK TIMES
Bestselling
Author

Jimmy
Gownley

Illustrated
by

Veronica
Di Lorenzo,

Federico
Mancuso,

Rosa La
Barbera,

and
Caroline
LaVelle
Egan

Colors
by

Anastasia
Belousova

and
Chintsova Yana
Konstantinovna

Random House 🏠 New York

Lettering by Chris Dickey

Designed by Kurt Hartman

Edited by Lauren A. Burniac and Holly Rice

and Managing Editor Cathryn McHugh

Published in the United States by Random House Children's Books, a division of Penguin Random House LLC, 1745 Broadway, New York, NY 10019, and in Canada by Penguin Random House Canada Limited, Toronto, in conjunction with Disney Enterprises, Inc.
Random House and the colophon are registered trademarks of Penguin Random House LLC.

rhcbooks.com

ISBN 978-0-7364-3849-0 (trade)—
ISBN 978-0-7364-9024-5 (lib. bdg.)

MANUFACTURED IN CHINA

10 9 8 7 6 5 4 3 2 1

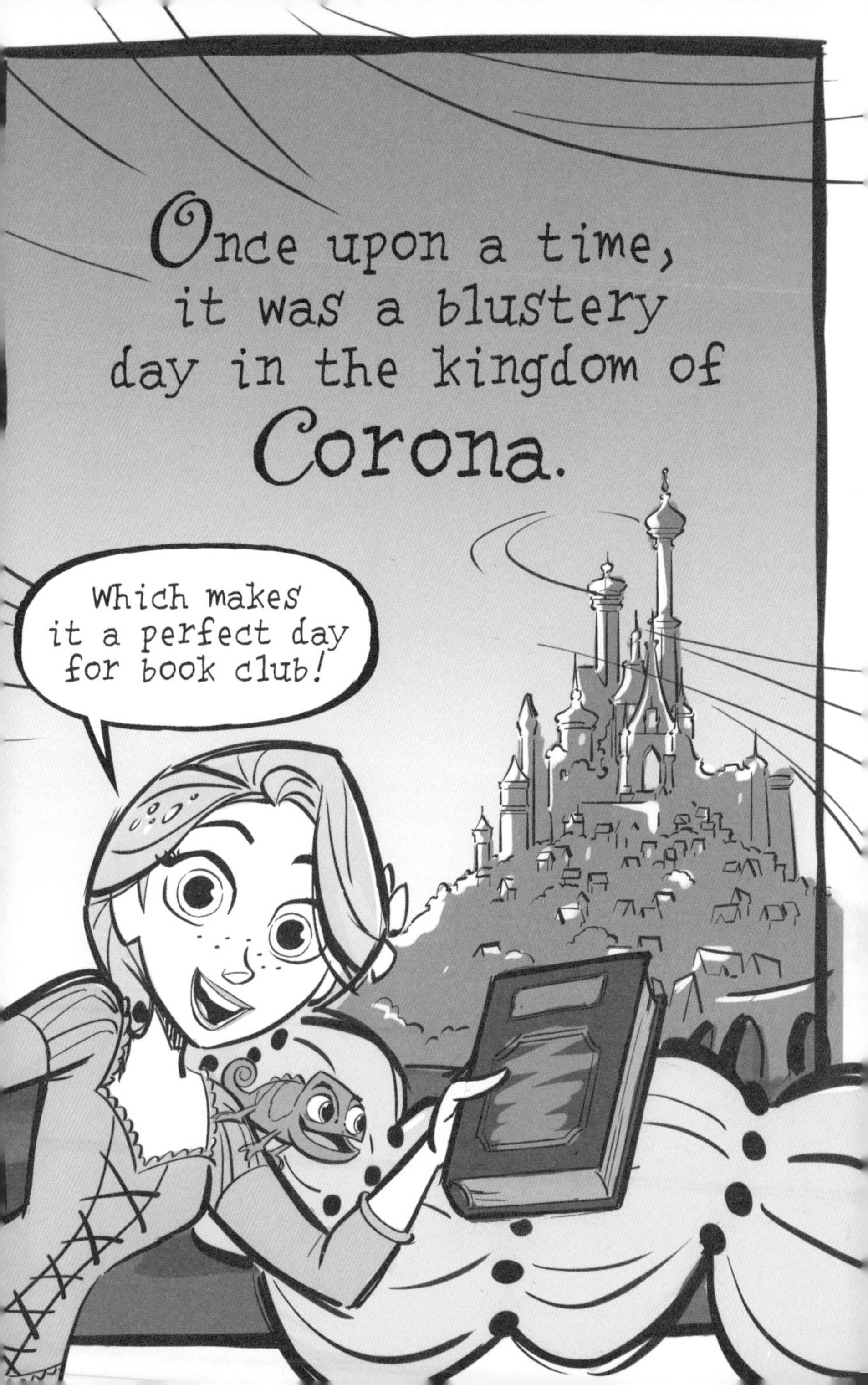
Once upon a time, it was a blustery day in the kingdom of Corona.
Which makes it a perfect day for book club!

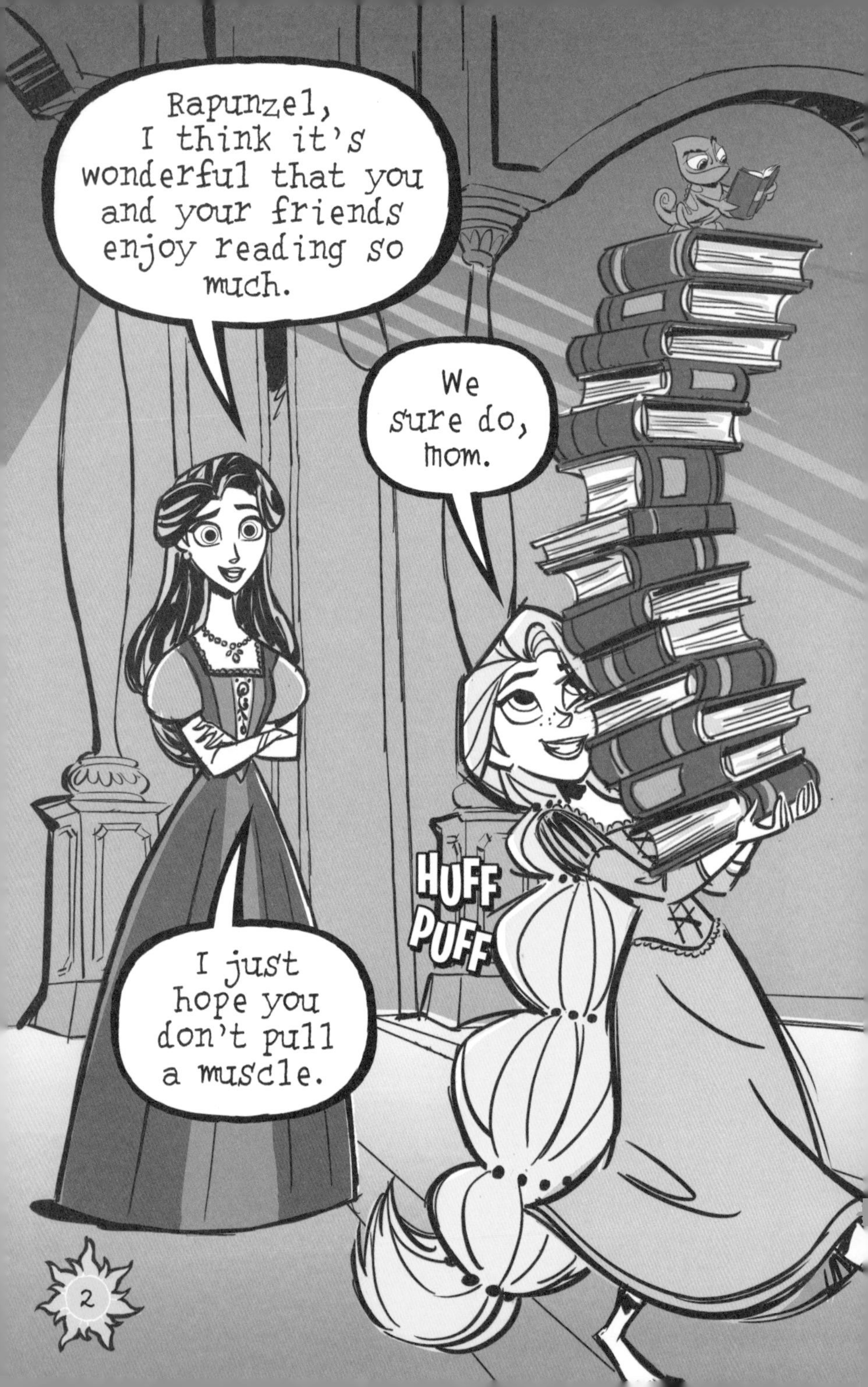
Rapunzel, I think it's wonderful that you and your friends enjoy reading so much.
We sure do, mom.
I just hope you don't pull a muscle.
HUFF PUFF

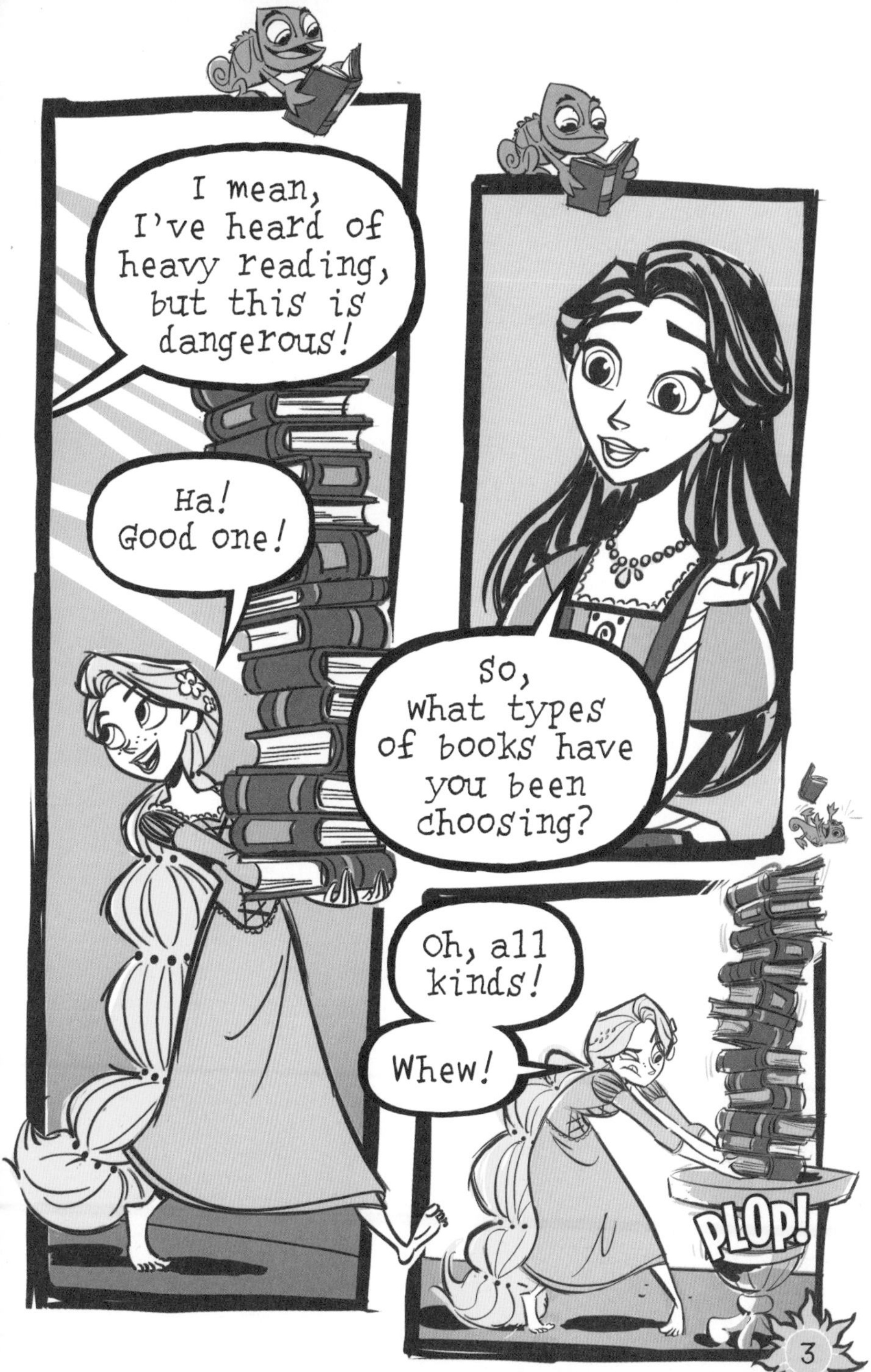
I mean, I've heard of heavy reading, but this is dangerous!
Ha! Good one!
So, what types of books have you been choosing?
Oh, all kinds!
Whew!
PLOP!

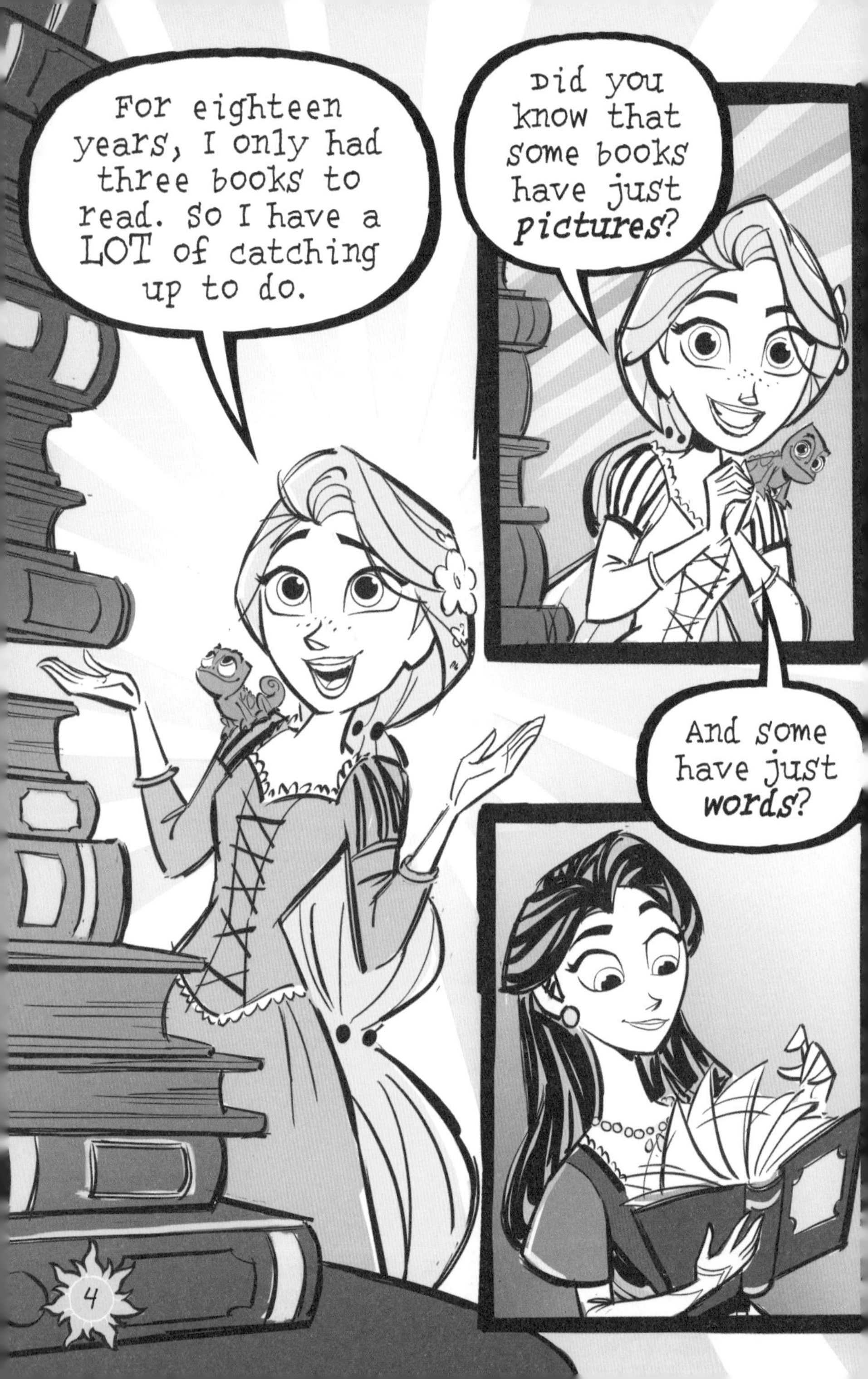
For eighteen years, I only had three books to read. So I have a LOT of catching up to do.
Did you know that some books have just *pictures*?
And some have just *words*?

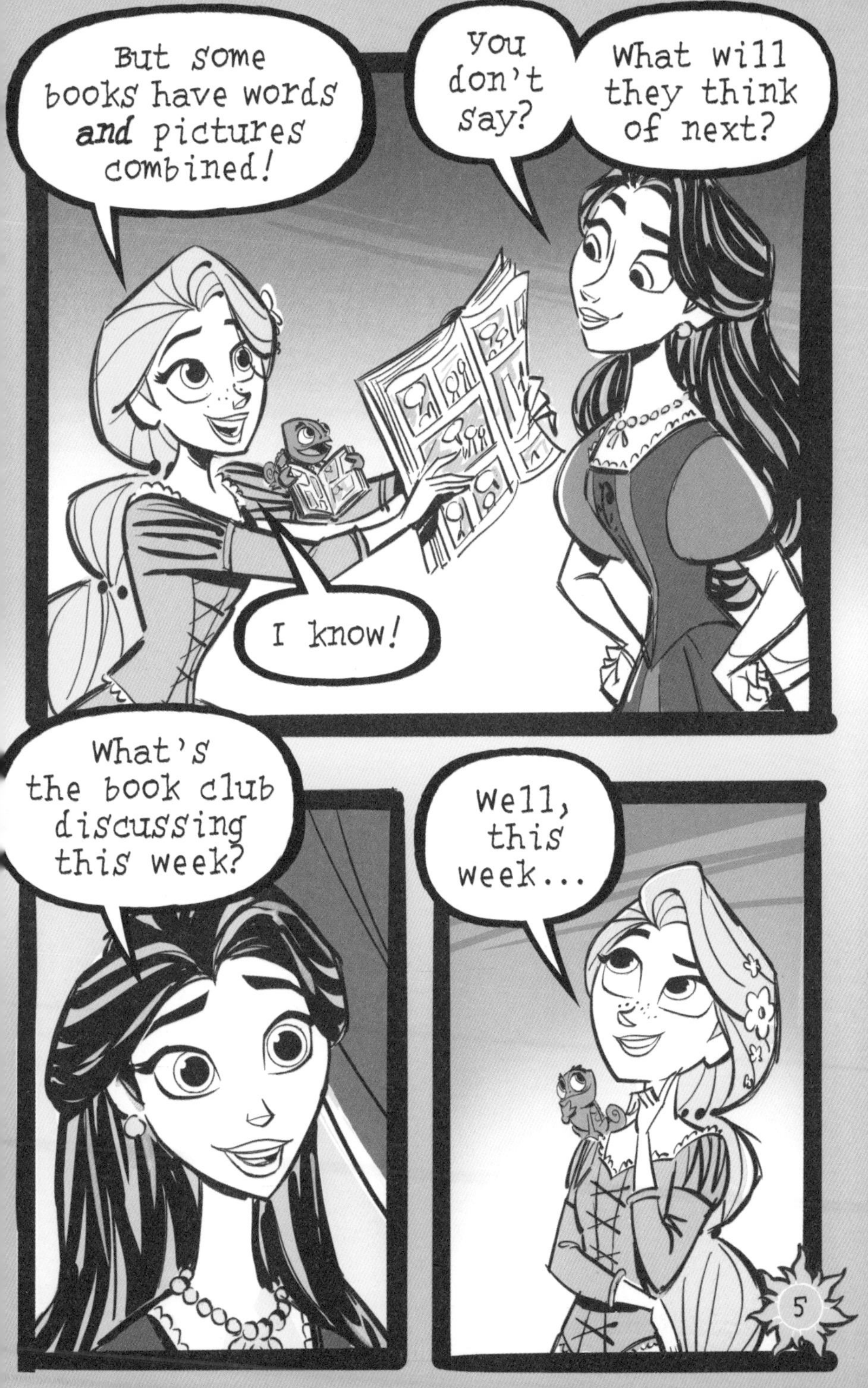
But some books have words **and** pictures combined!
You don't say?
What will they think of next?
I know!
What's the book club discussing this week?
Well, this week...

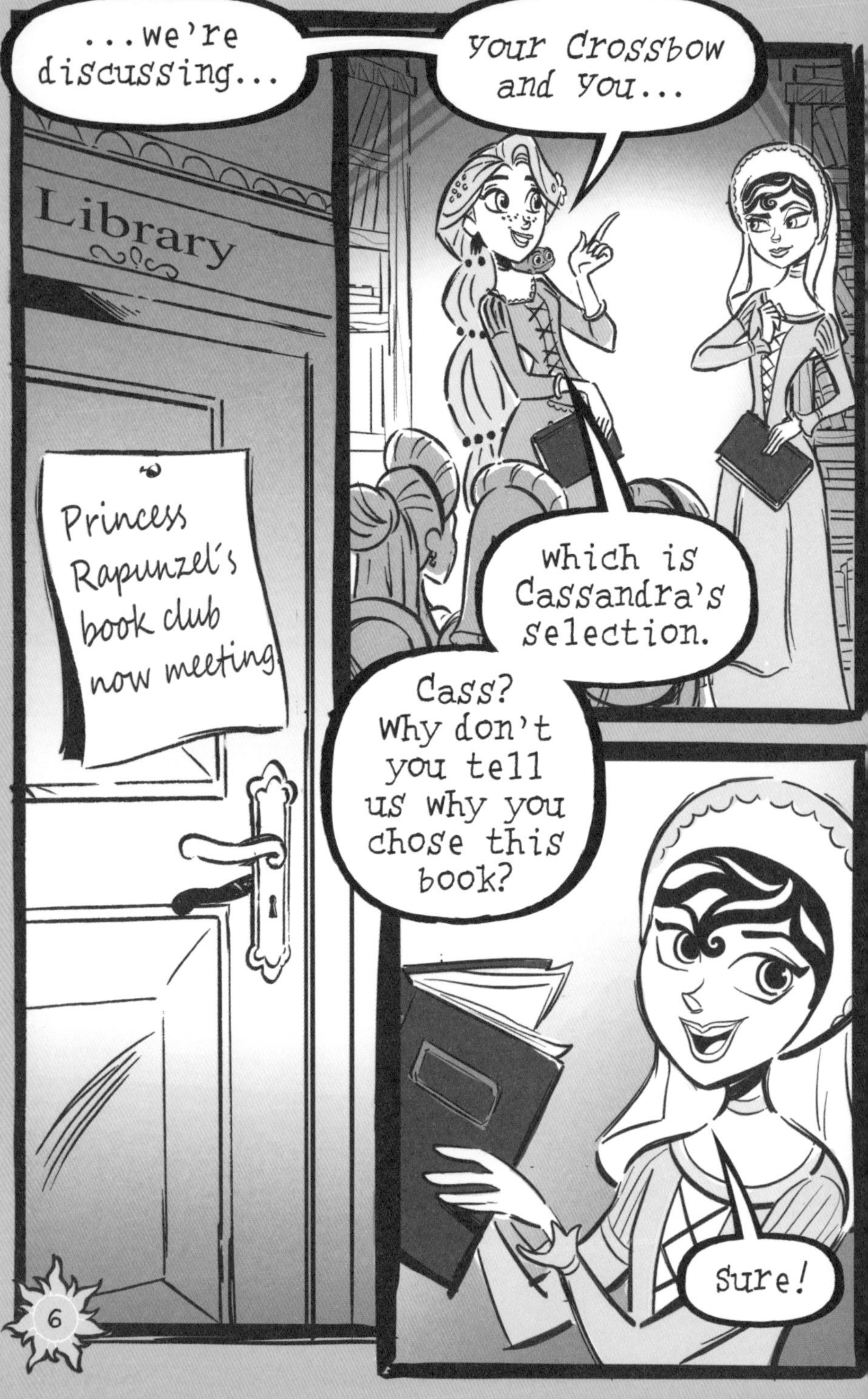
...we're discussing...
your crossbow and you...
Library
Princess Rapunzel's book club now meeting
Which is Cassandra's selection.
Cass? Why don't you tell us why you chose this book?
Sure!

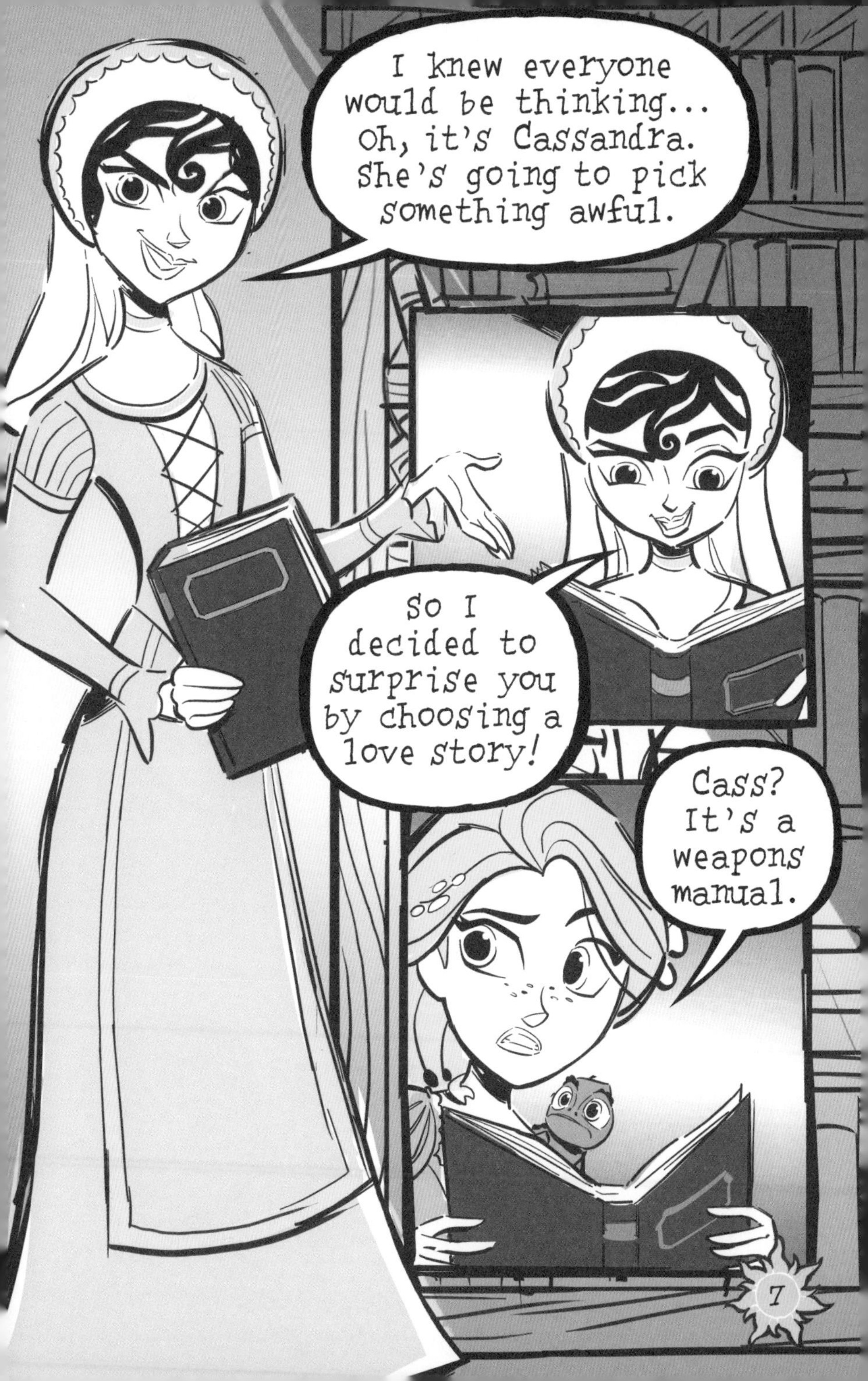
I knew everyone would be thinking... Oh, it's Cassandra. She's going to pick something awful.
So I decided to surprise you by choosing a love story!
Cass? It's a weapons manual.

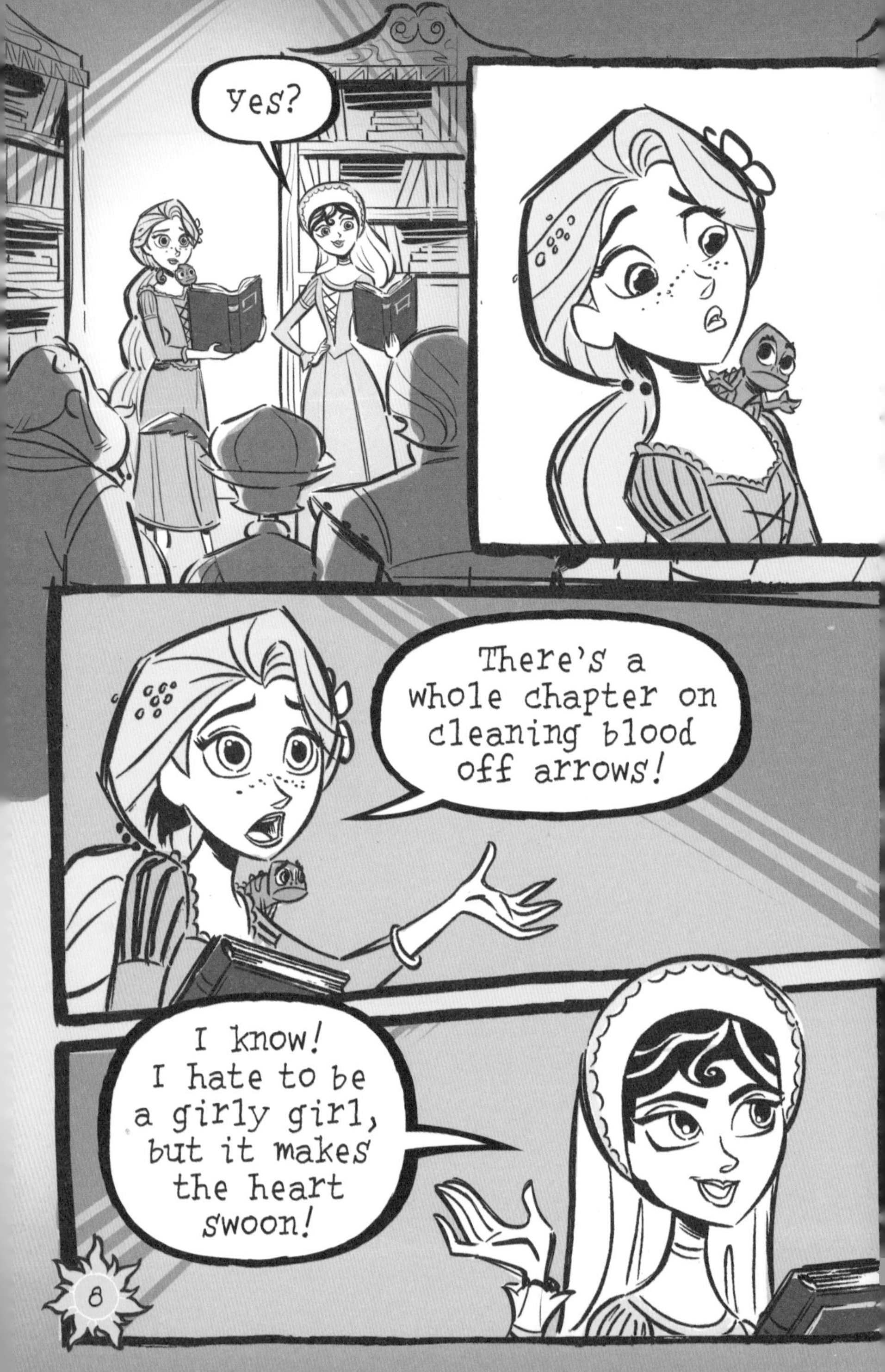

yes?
There's a whole chapter on cleaning blood off arrows!
I know! I hate to be a girly girl, but it makes the heart swoon!

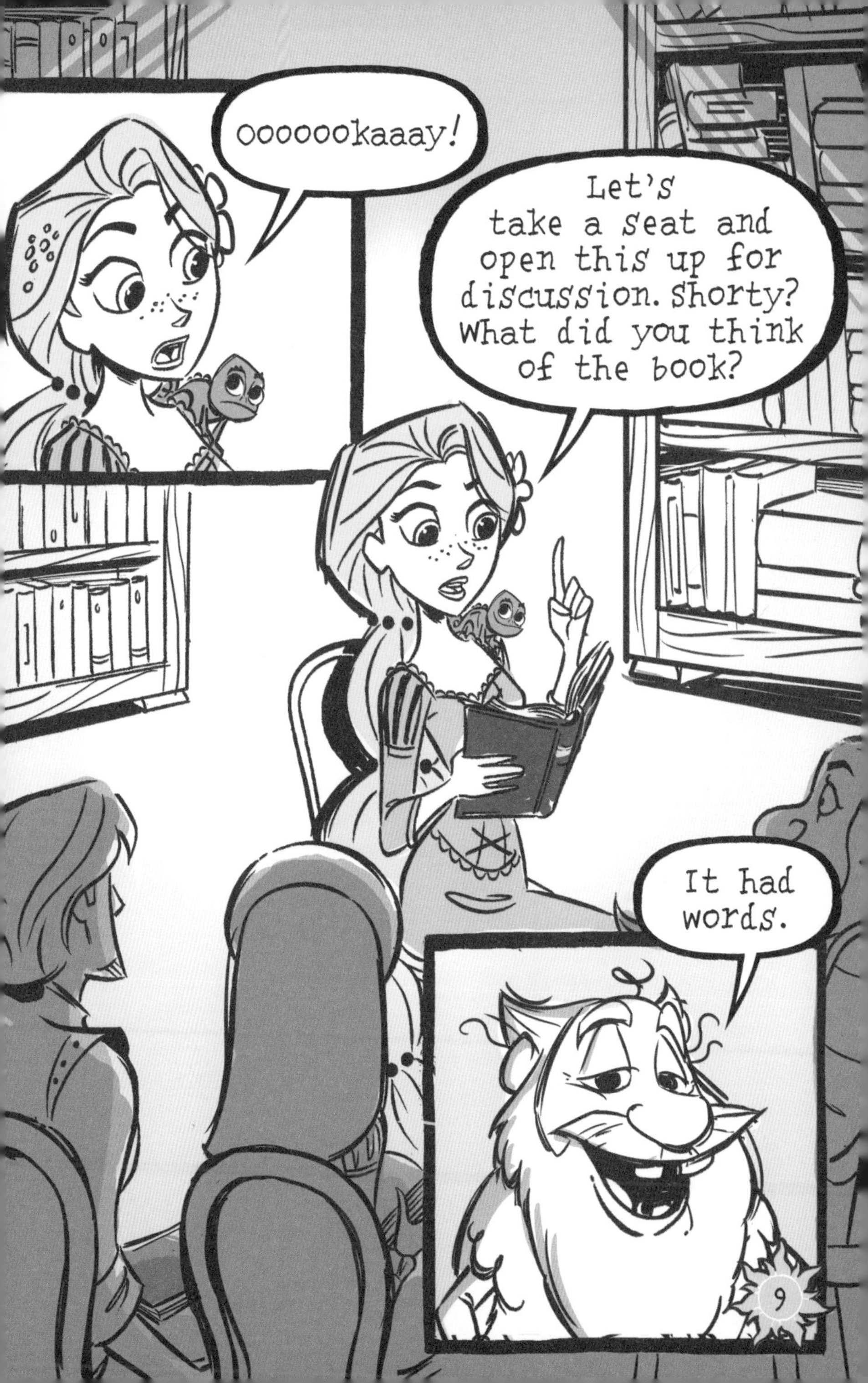
Oooooookaaay!
Let's take a seat and open this up for discussion. Shorty? What did you think of the book?
It had words.

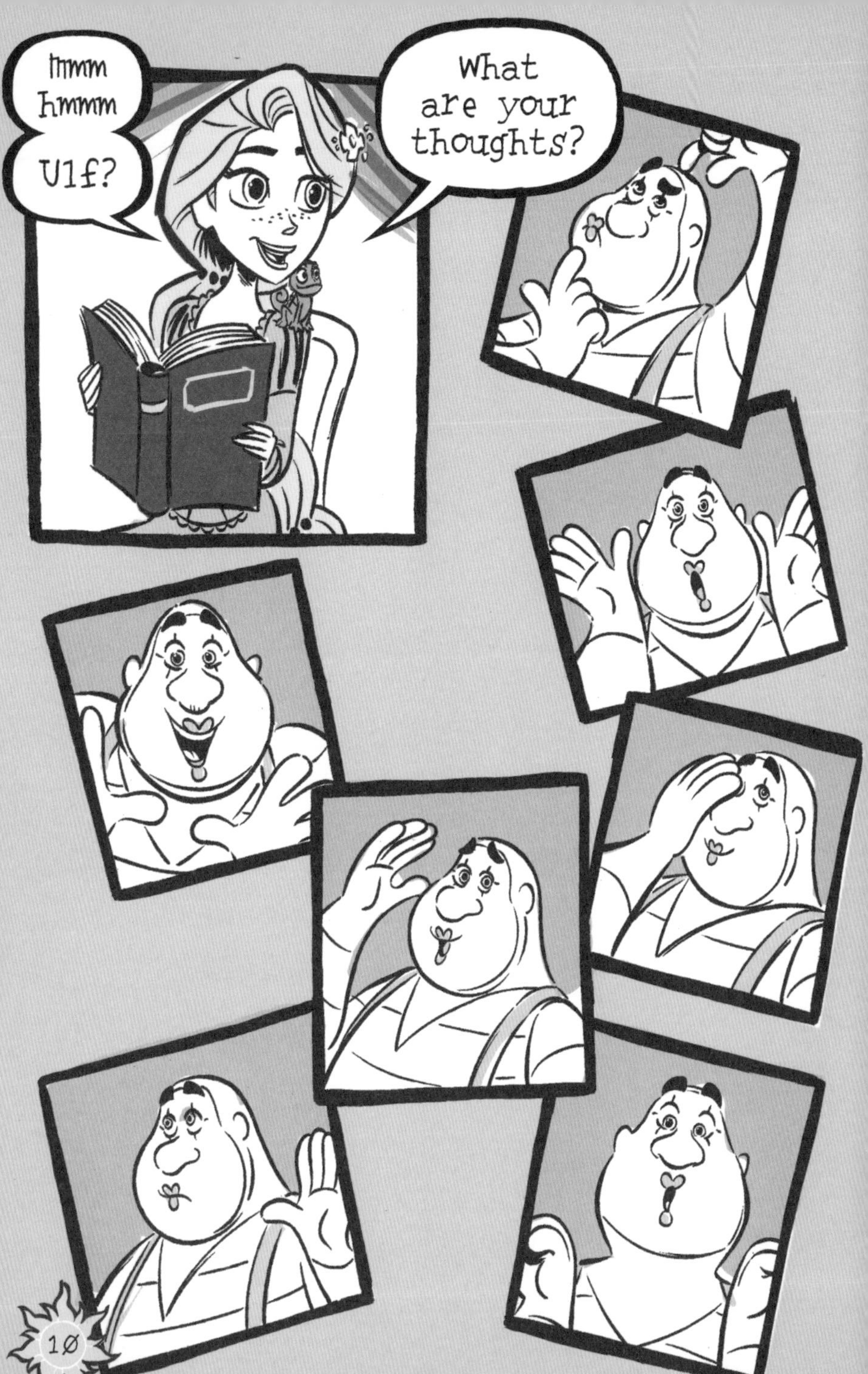
hmmm hmmm
Ulf?
What are your thoughts?

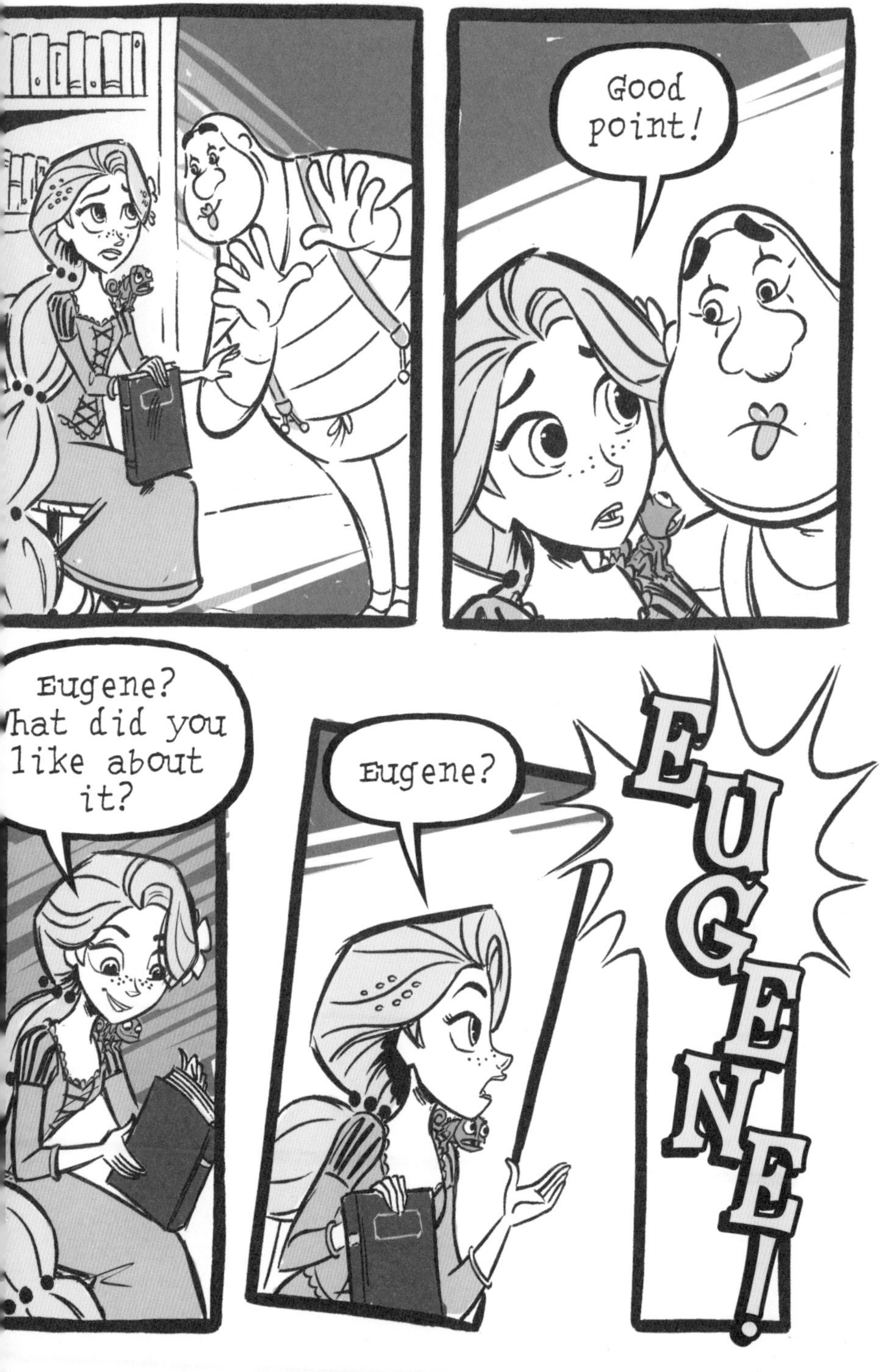
Good point!
Eugene? hat did you like about it?
Eugene?
EUGENE!

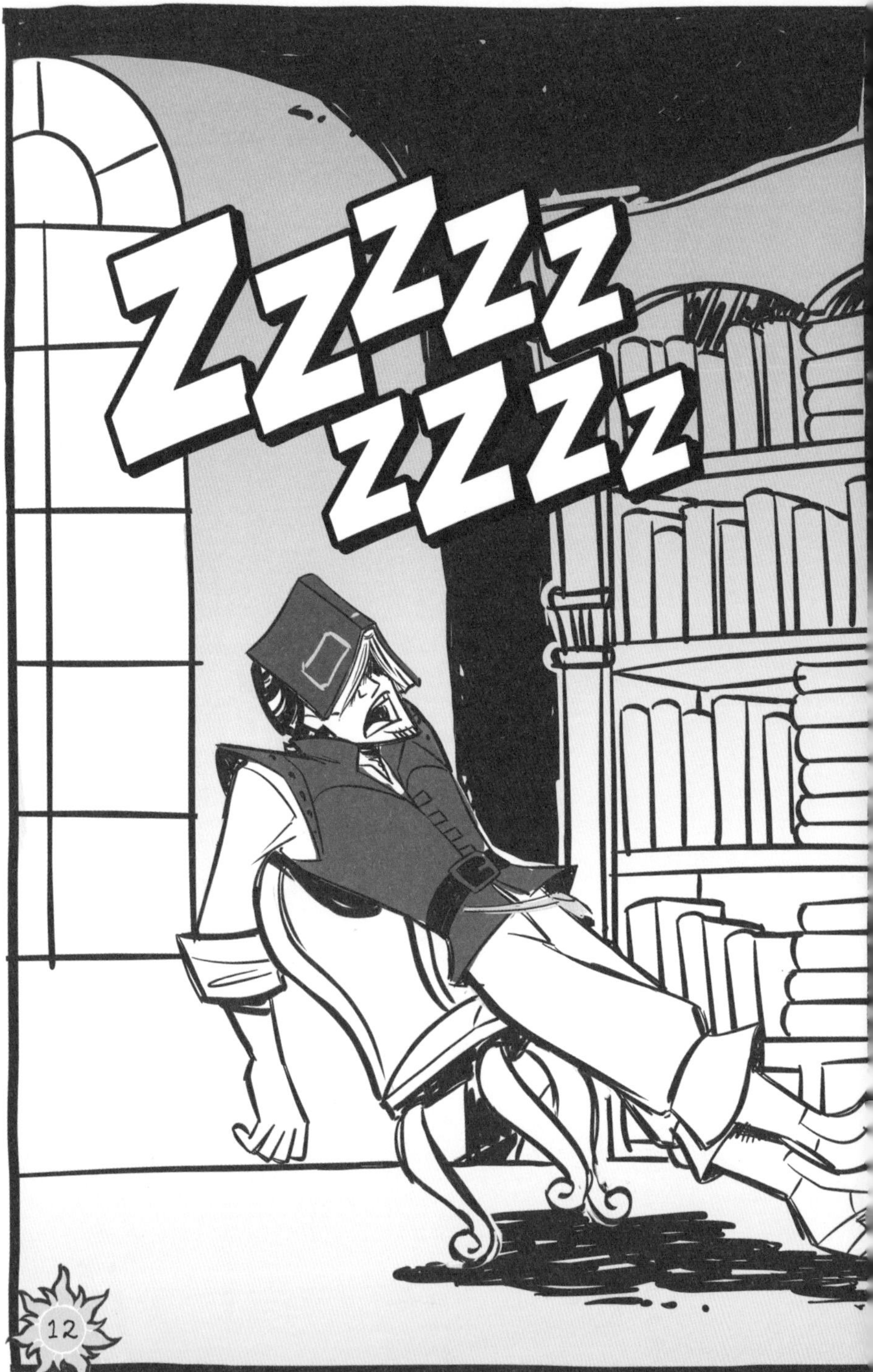
ZZZZZ
ZZZZ

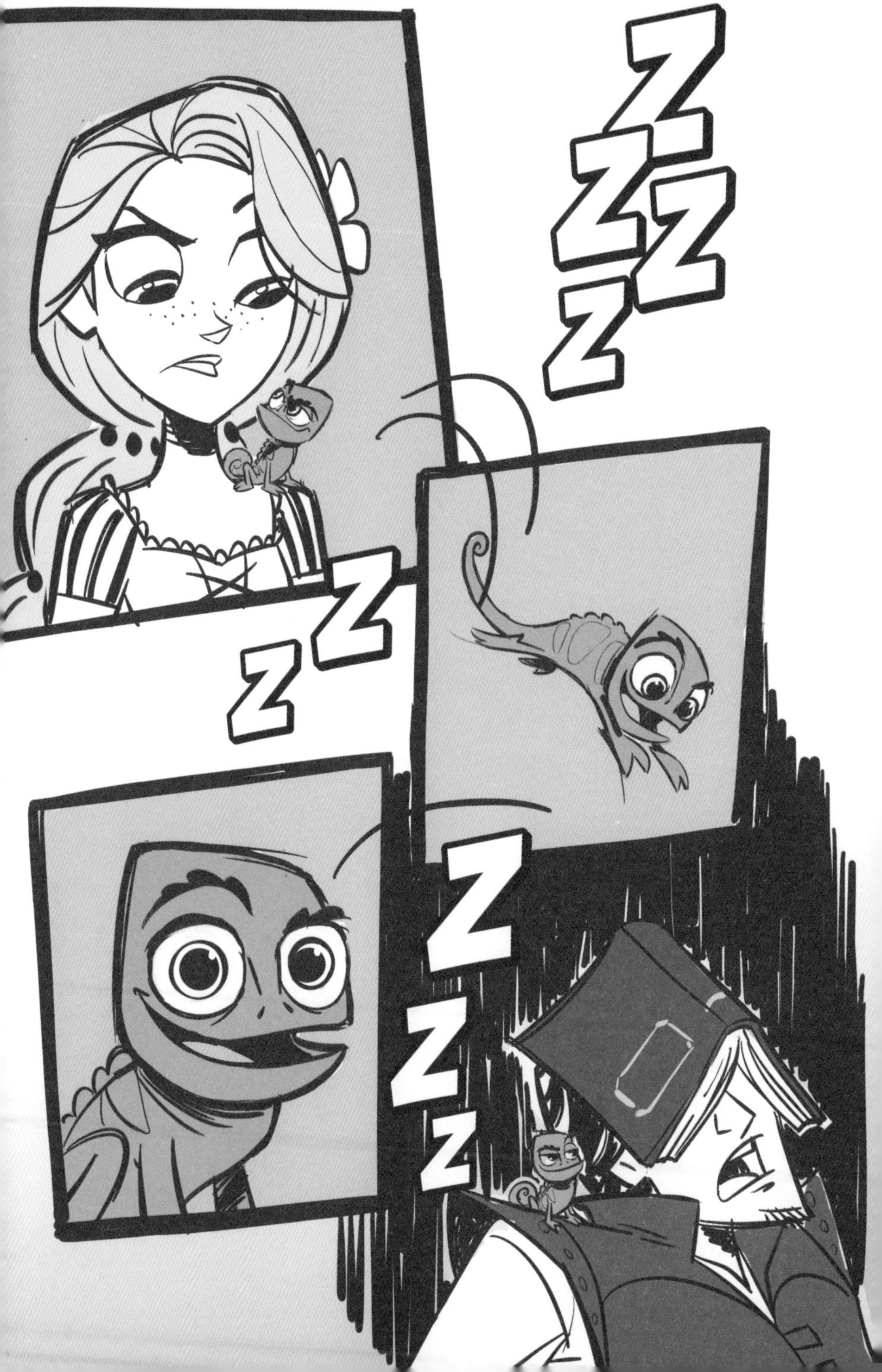
ZZZZ
ZZ
ZZZZ

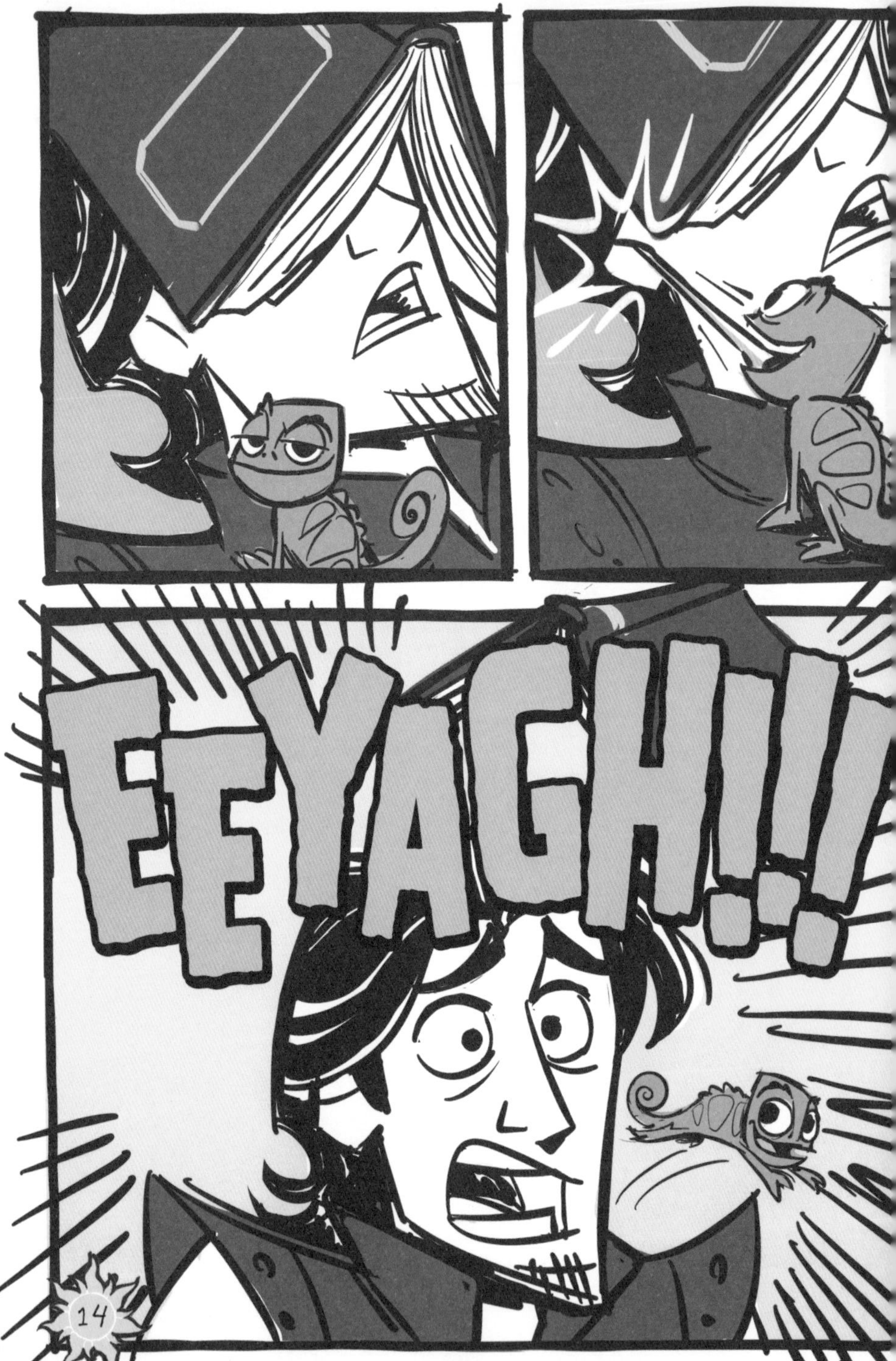
EEYAGH!!!

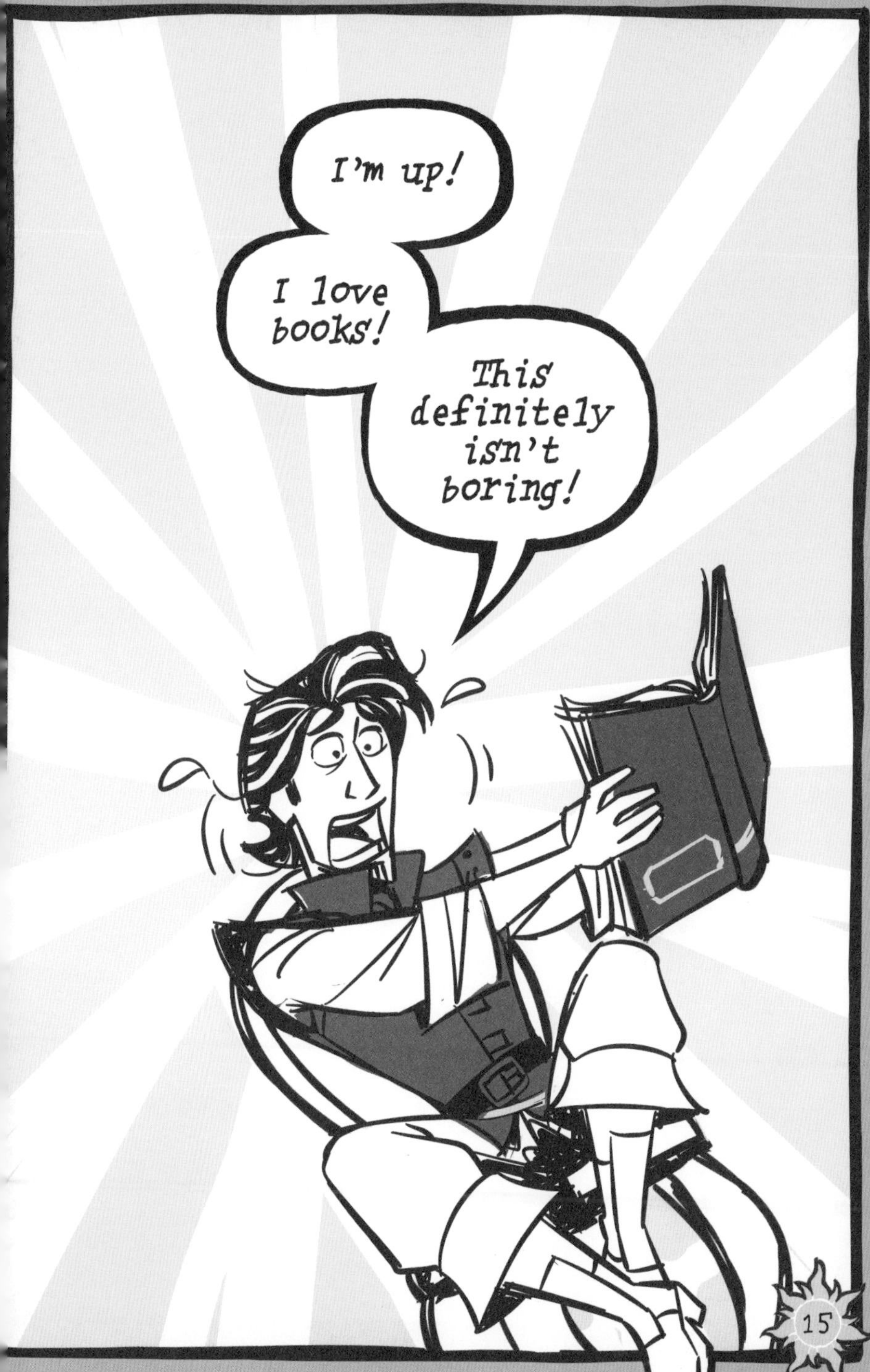
I'm up!
I love books!
This definitely isn't boring!

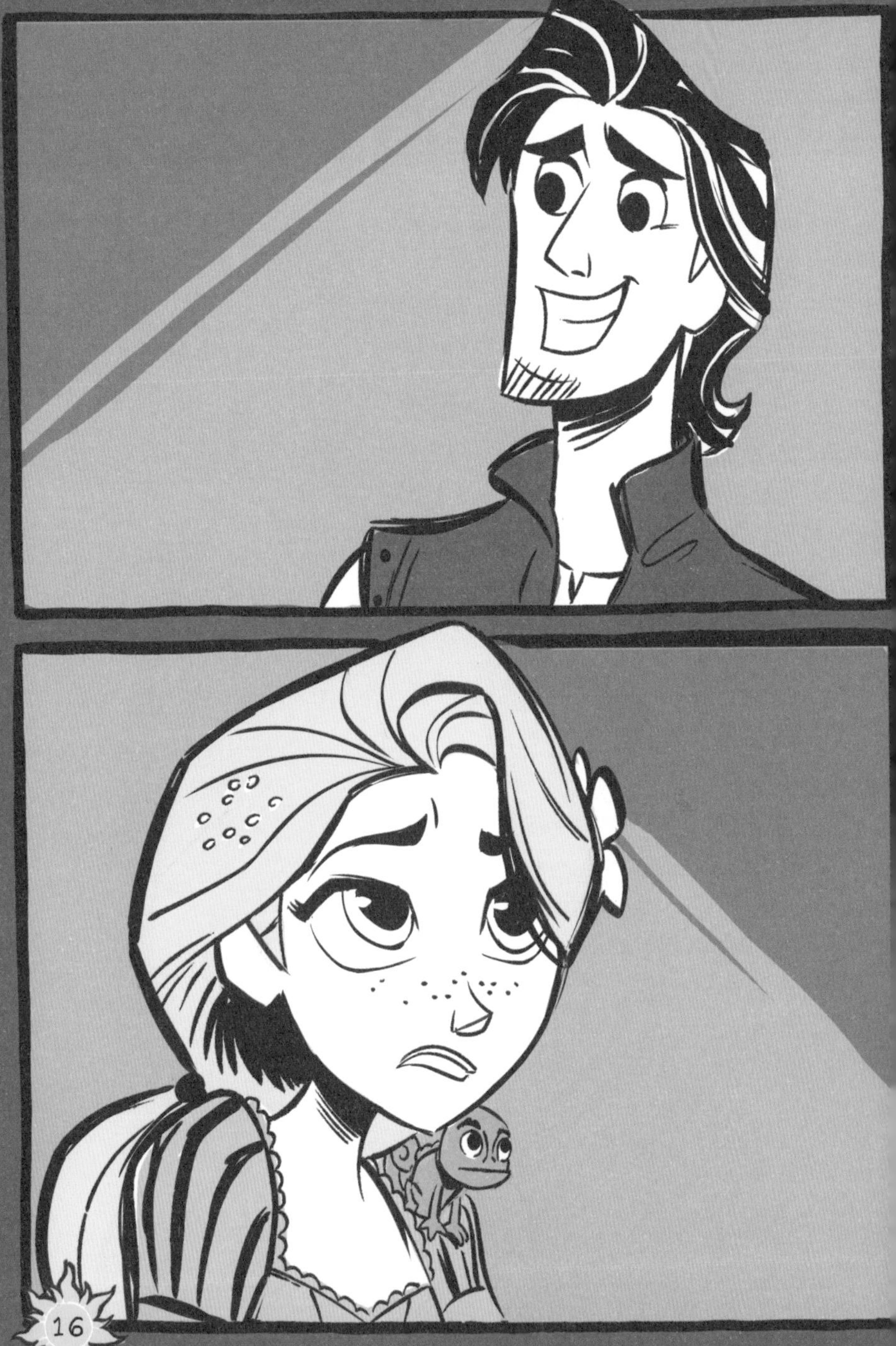

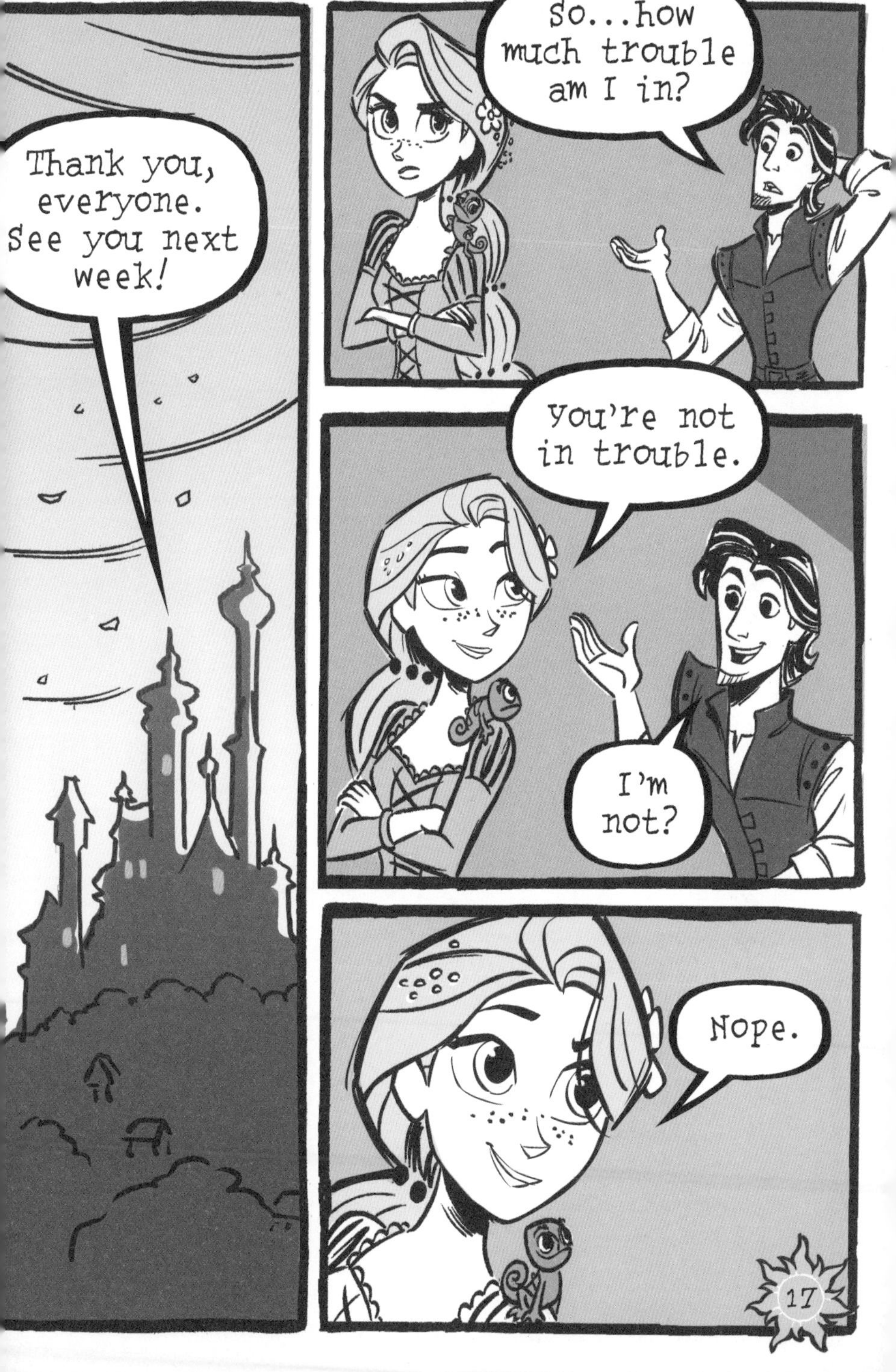
Thank you, everyone. See you next week!
So...how much trouble am I in?
You're not in trouble.
I'm not?
Nope.

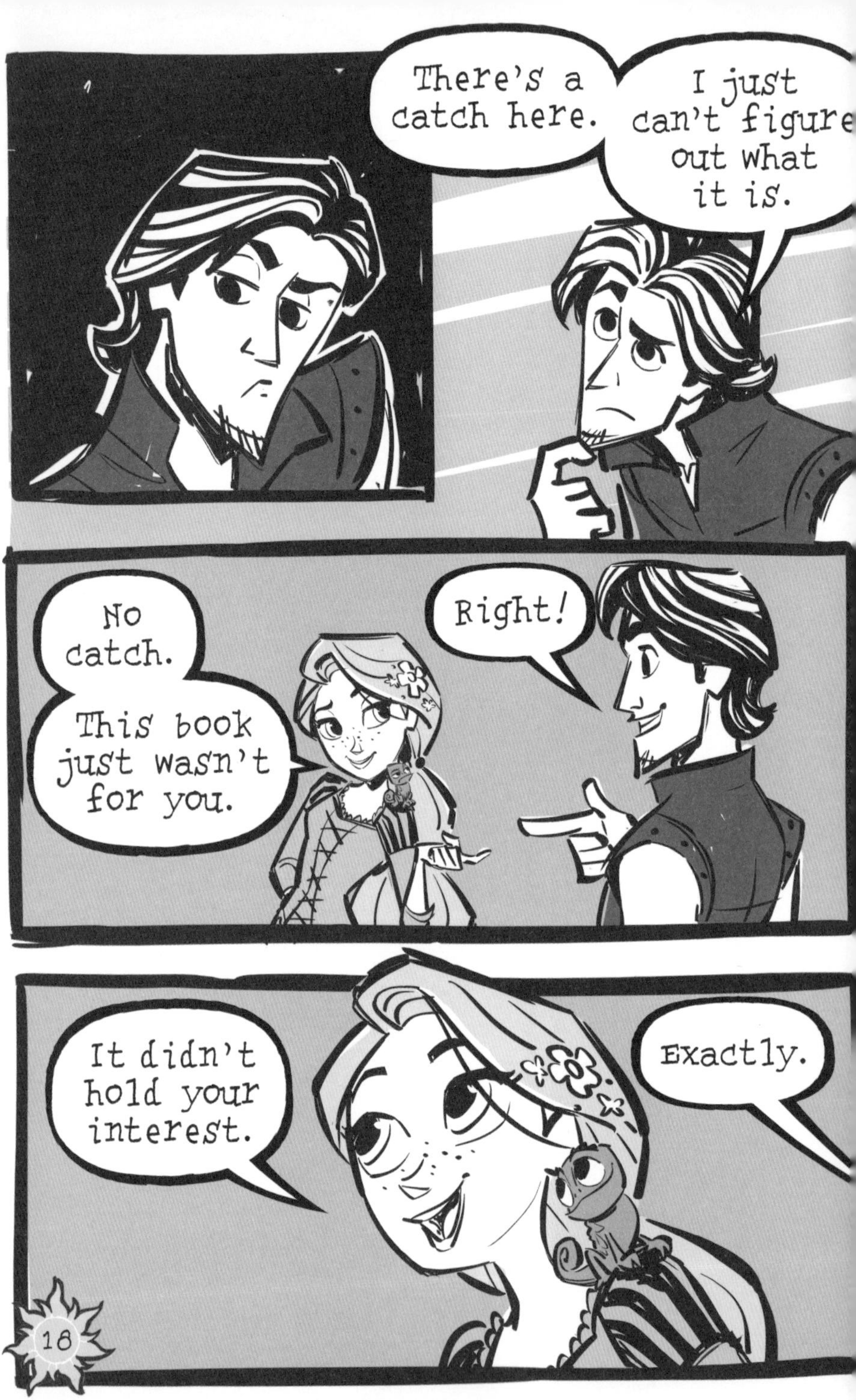
There's a catch here.
I just can't figure out what it is.
No catch.
This book just wasn't for you.
Right!
It didn't hold your interest.
Exactly.

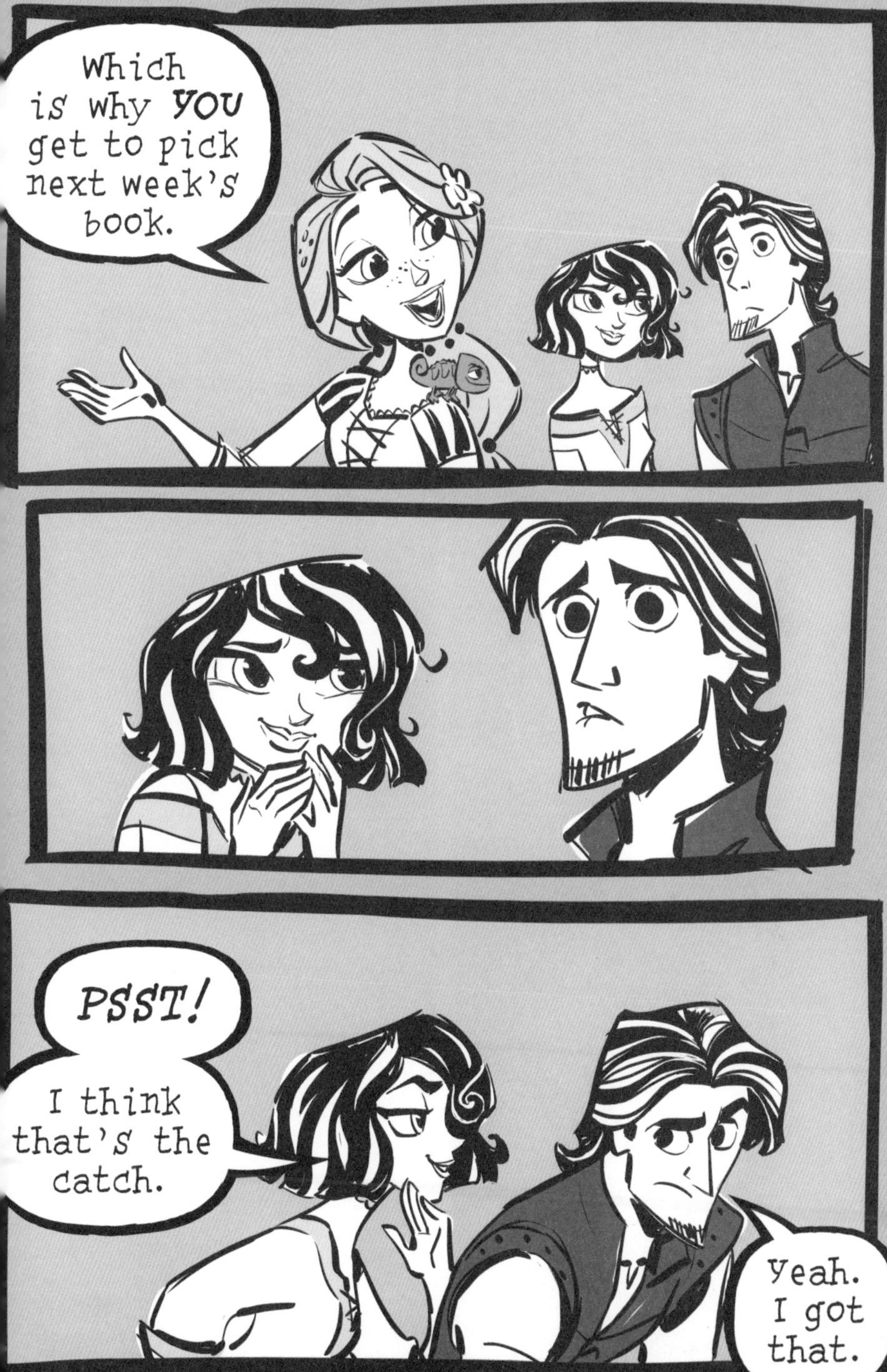
Which is why **YOU** get to pick next week's book.
PSST!
I think that's the catch.
Yeah. I got that.

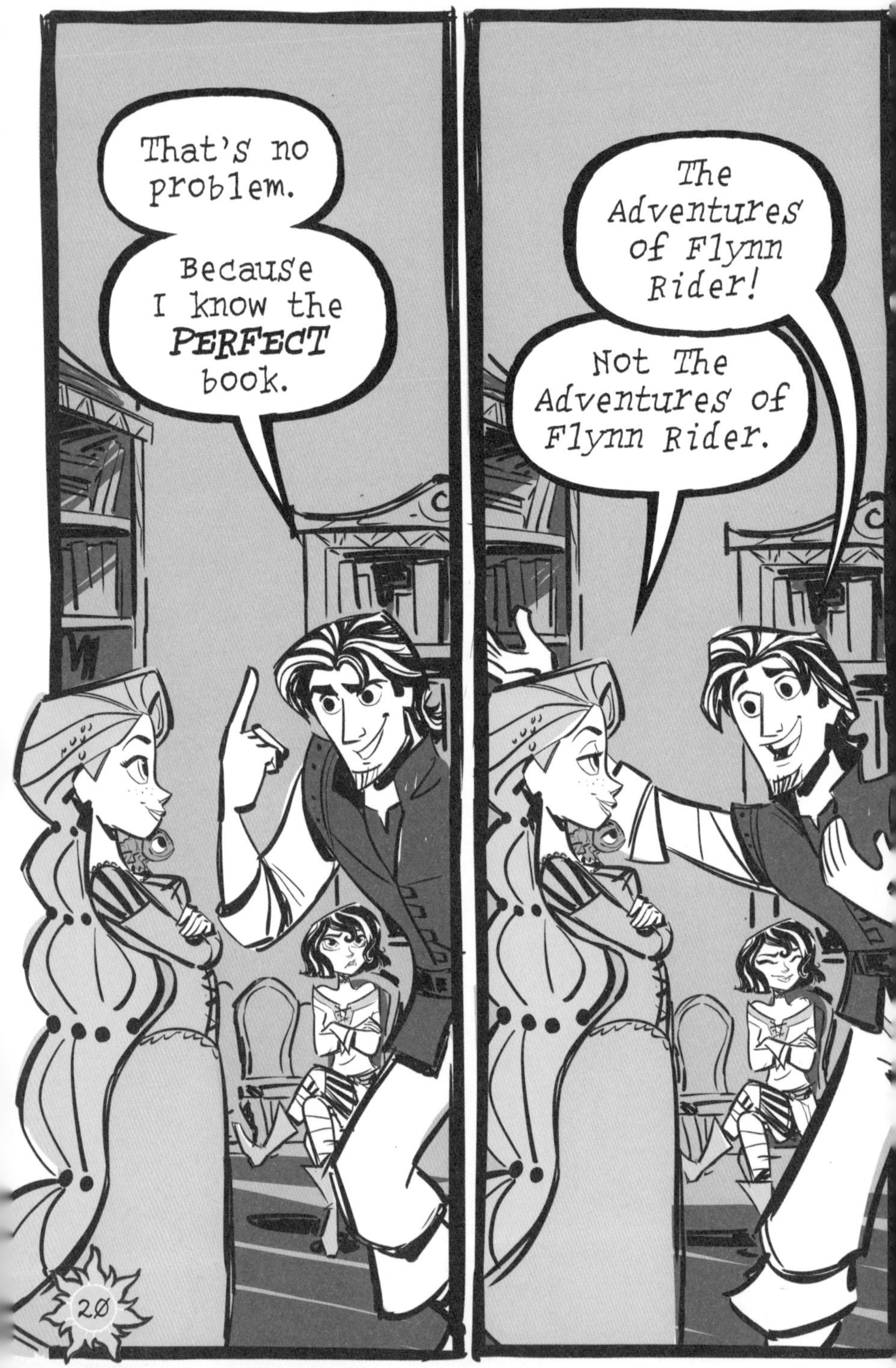
That's no problem.
Because I know the PERFECT book.
The Adventures of Flynn Rider!
Not The Adventures of Flynn Rider.

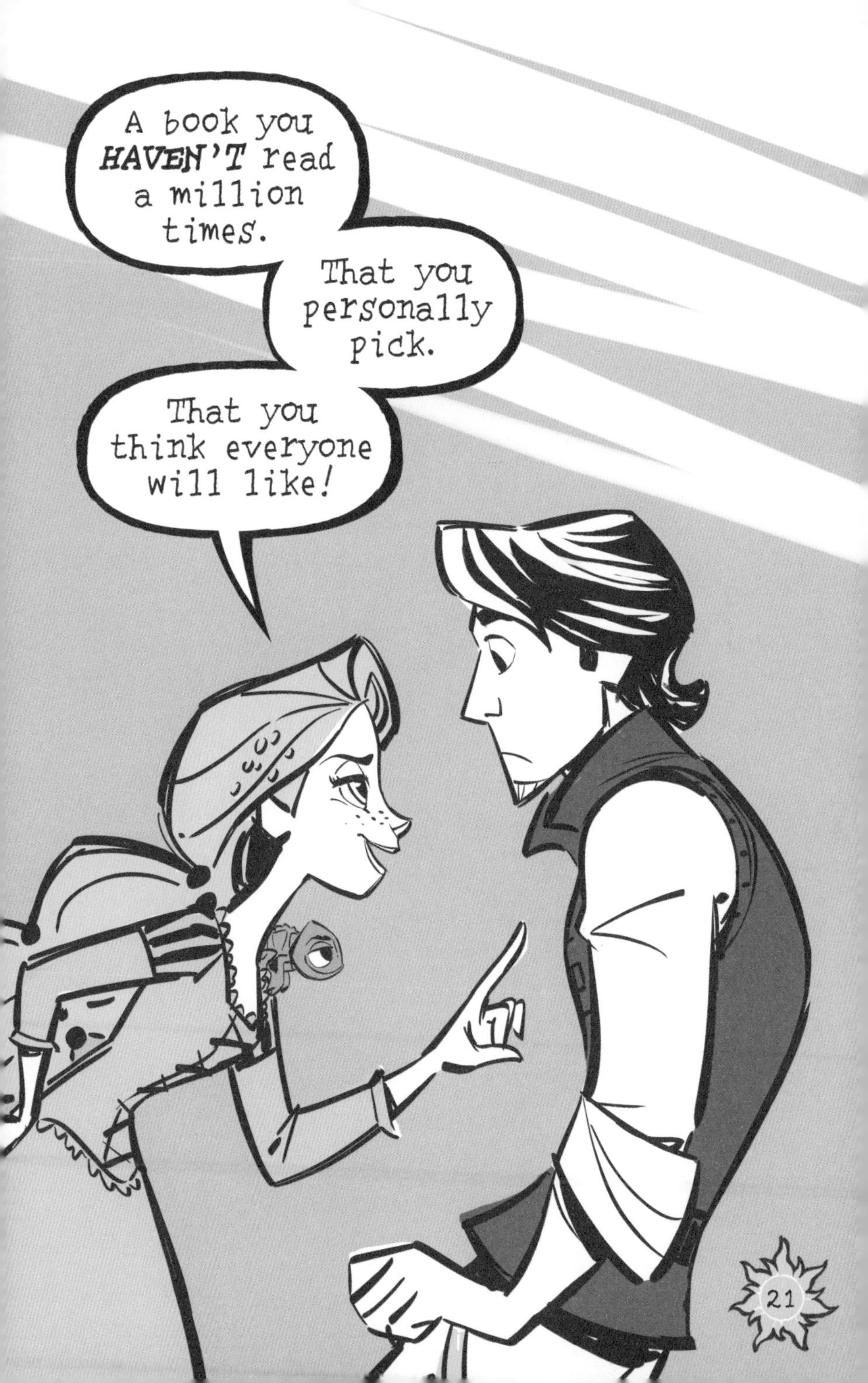
A book you **HAVEN'T** read a million times.
That you personally pick.
That you think everyone will like!

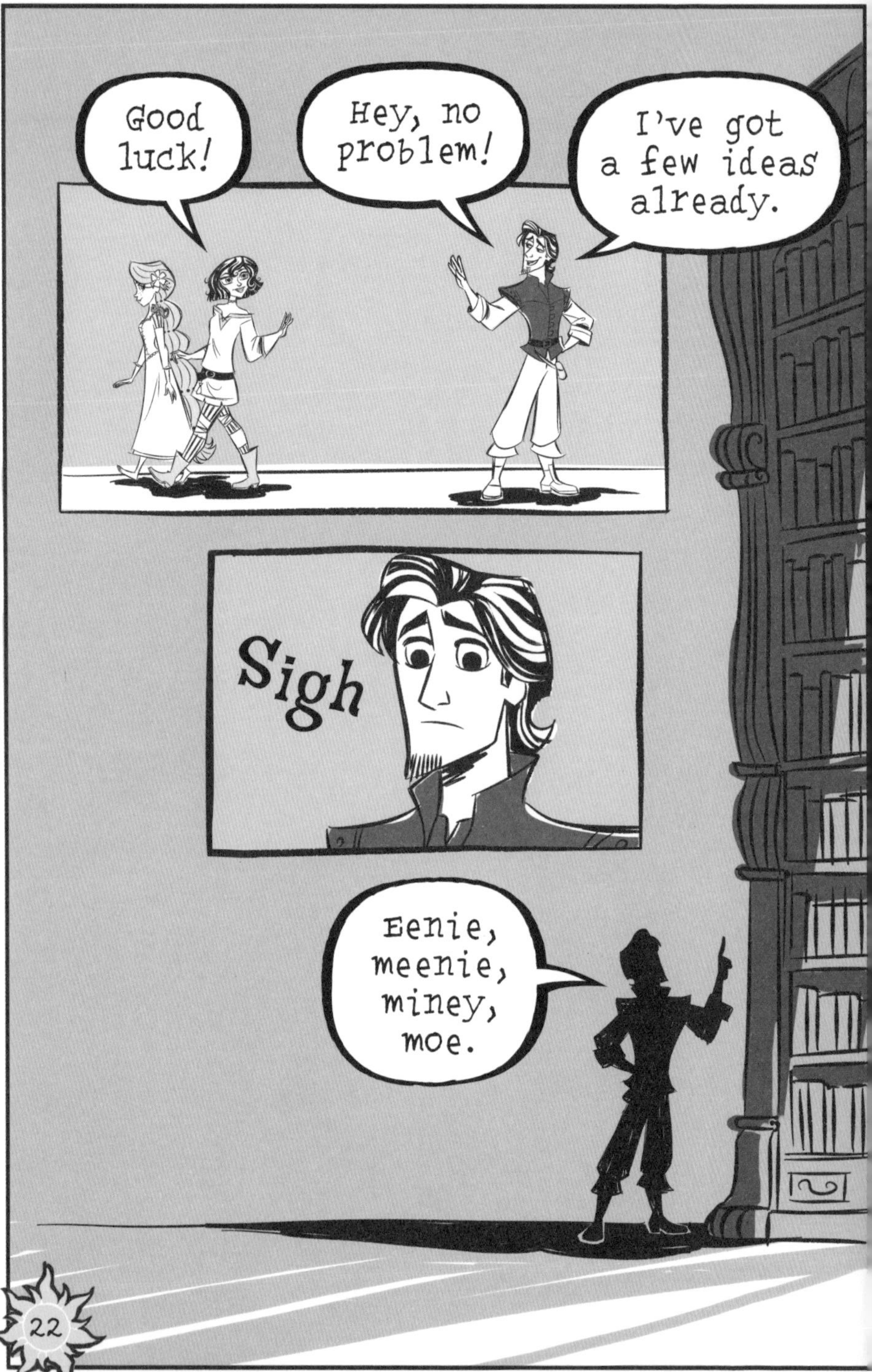
Good luck!
Hey, no problem!
I've got a few ideas already.
Sigh
Eenie, meenie, miney, moe.

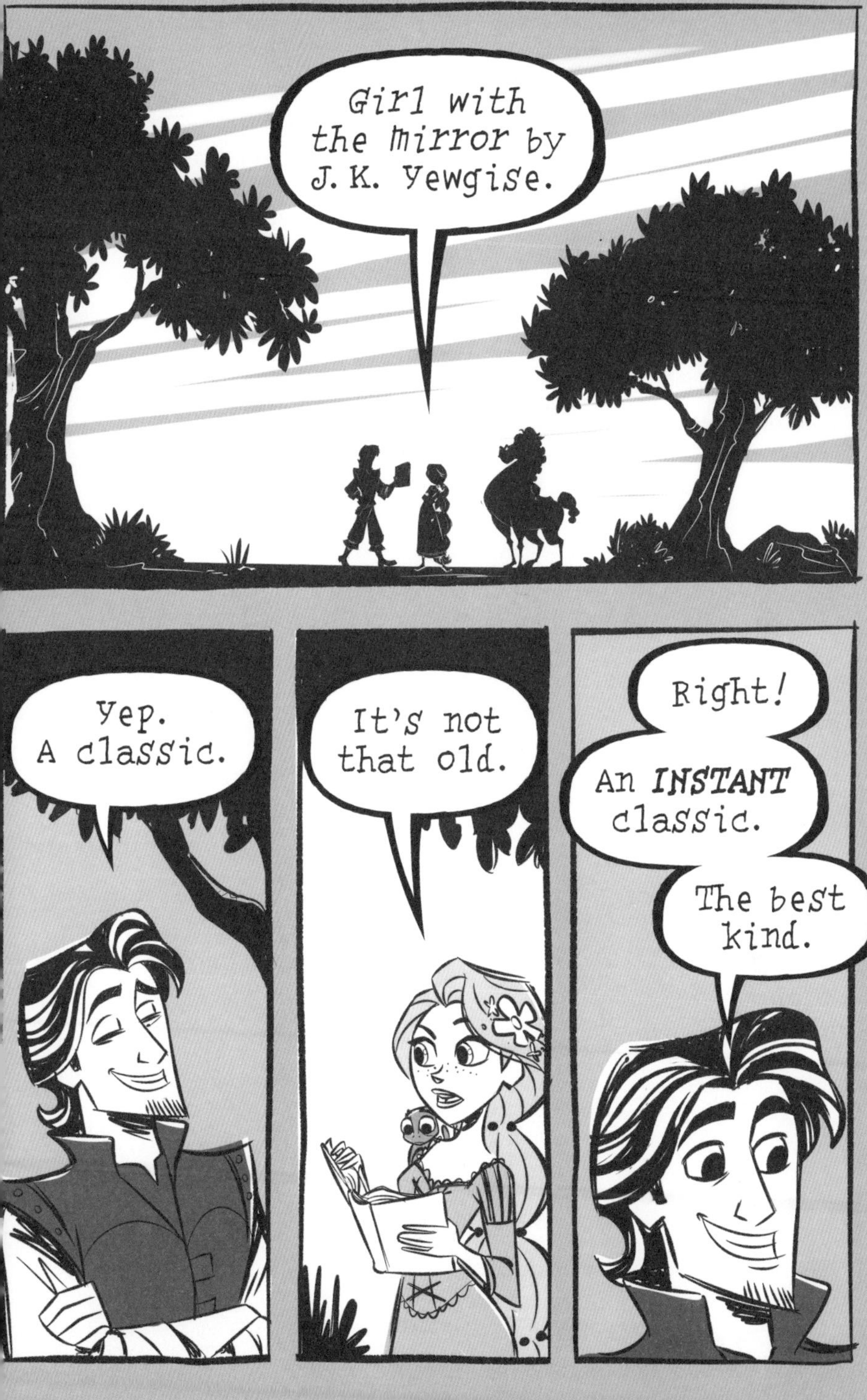
Girl with the Mirror by J. K. Yewgise.
Yep. A classic.
It's not that old.
Right!
An INSTANT classic.
The best kind.

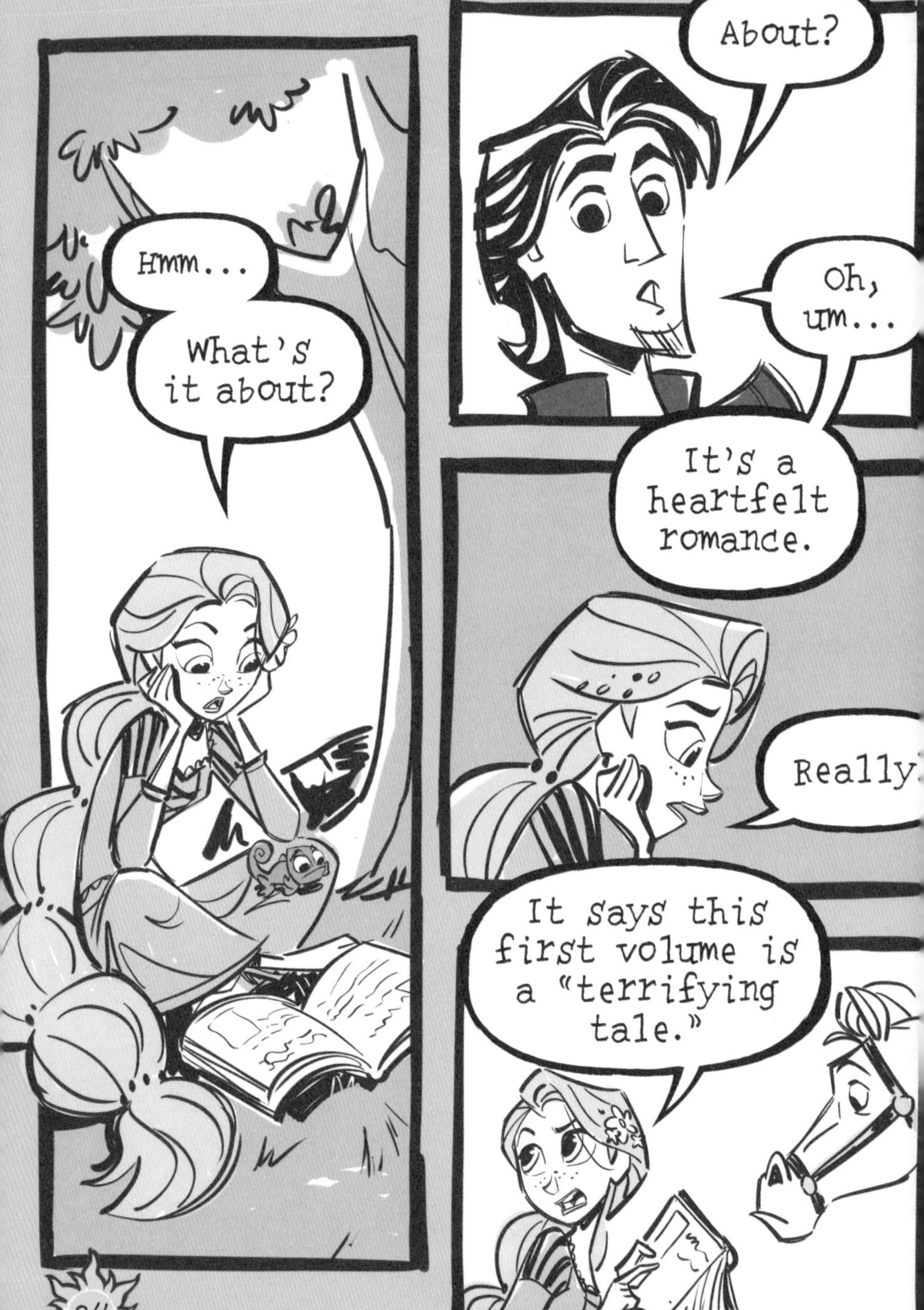
Hmm...
What's it about?
About?
Oh, um...
It's a heartfelt romance.
Really
It says this first volume is a "terrifying tale."

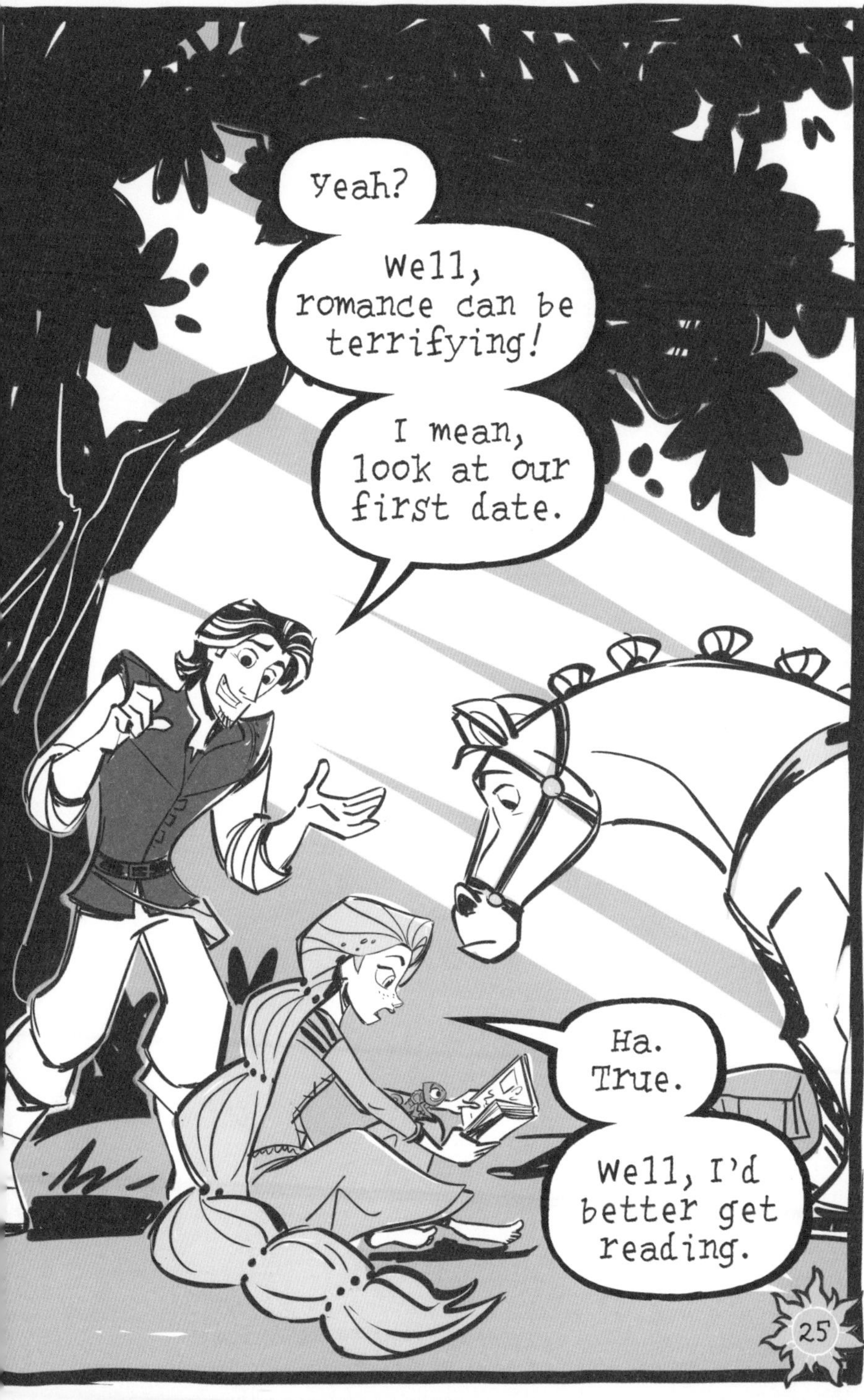
Yeah?
Well, romance can be terrifying!
I mean, look at our first date.
Ha. True.
Well, I'd better get reading.

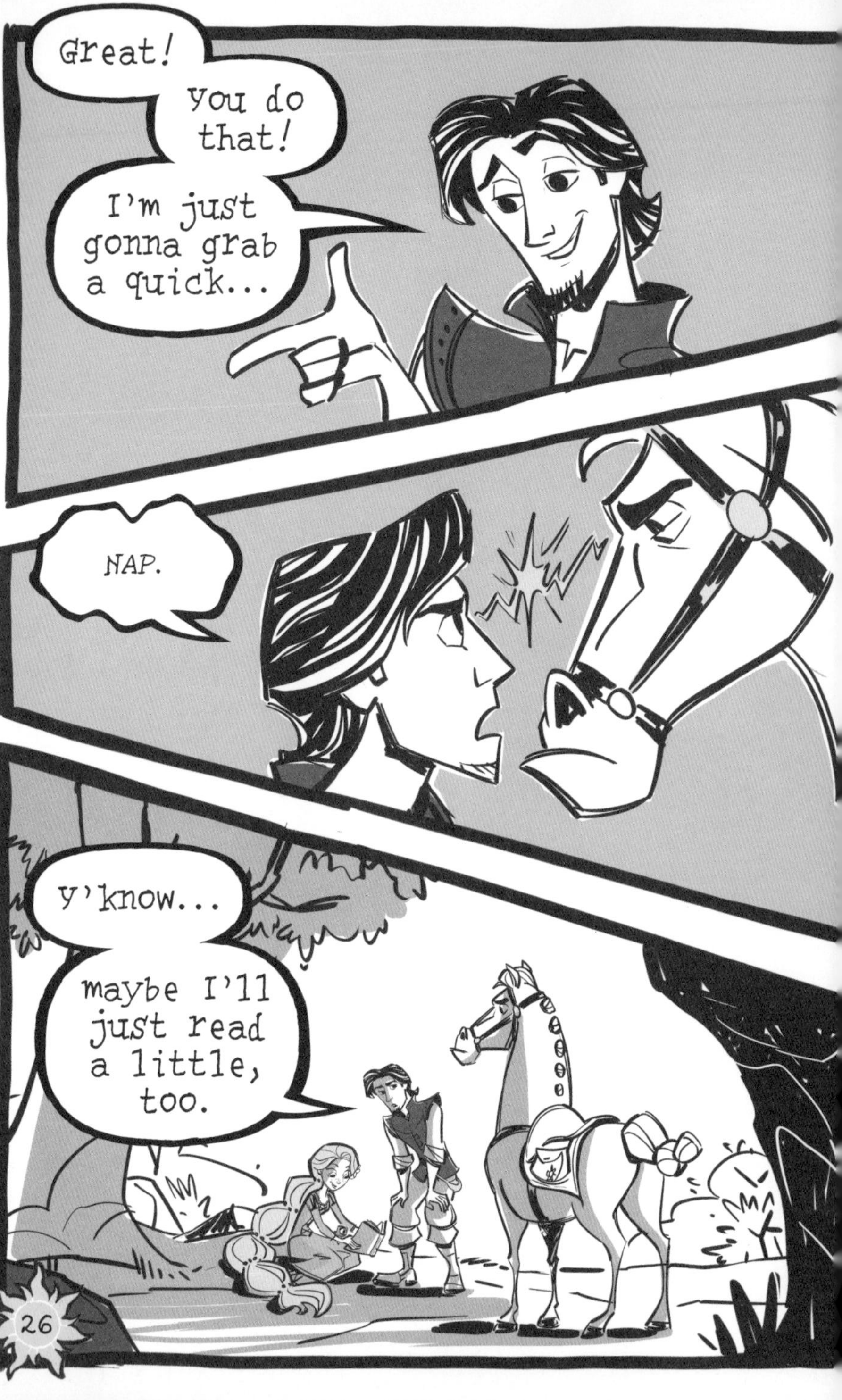
Great!
you do that!
I'm just gonna grab a quick...
NAP.
y'know...
maybe I'll just read a little, too.

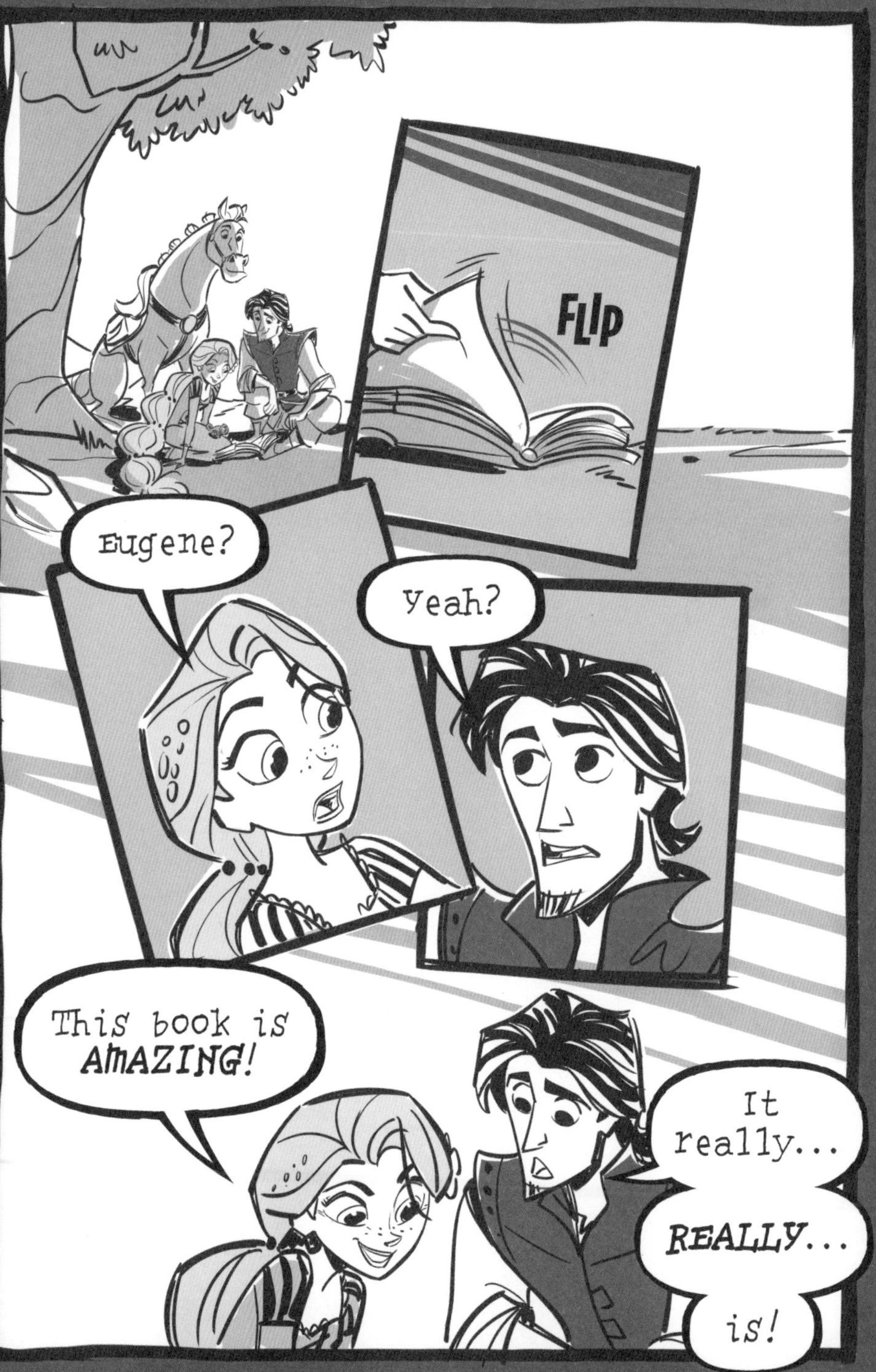
FLIP
Eugene?
Yeah?
This book is AMAZING!
It really...
REALLY...
is!

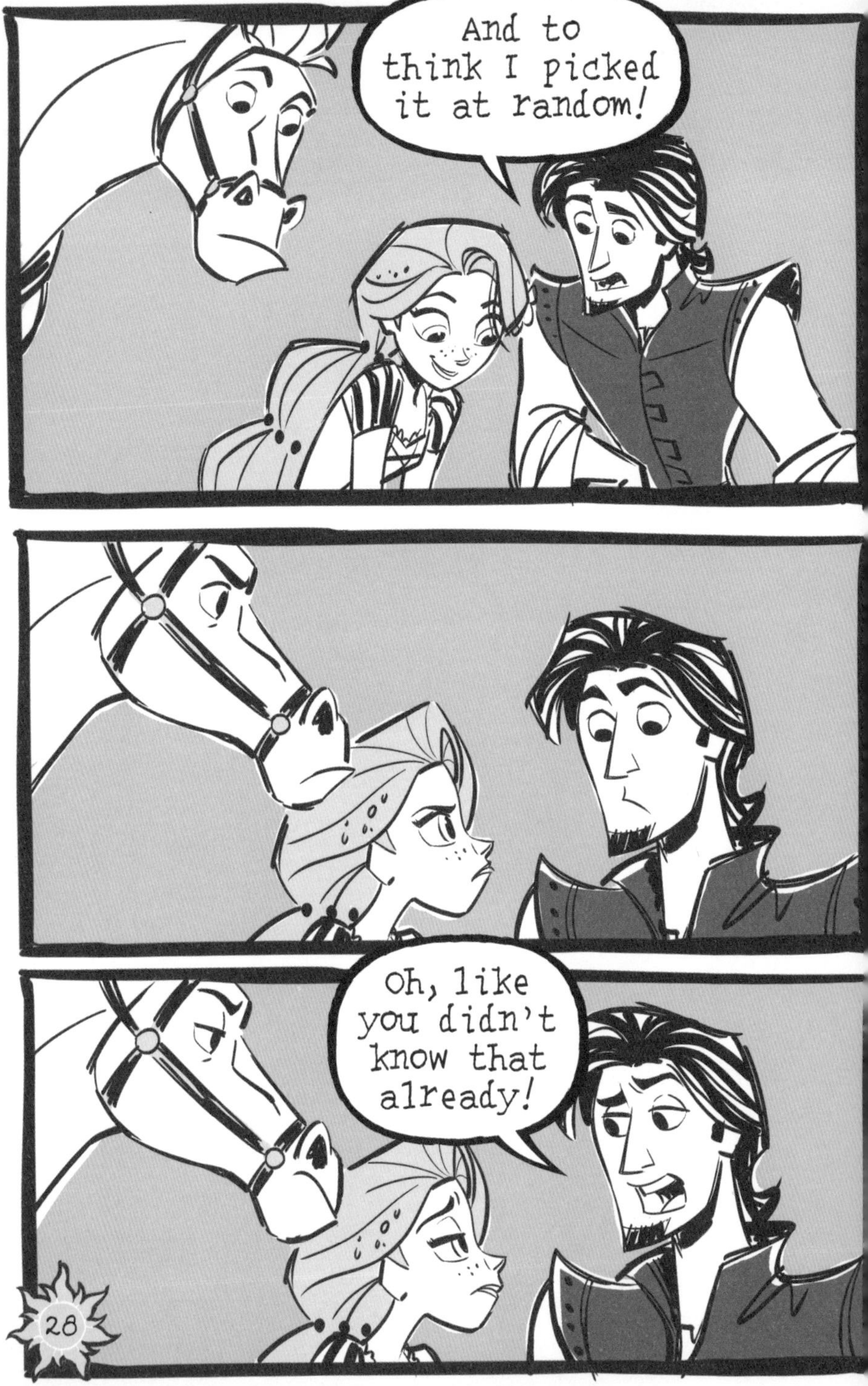
And to think I picked it at random!
Oh, like you didn't know that already!

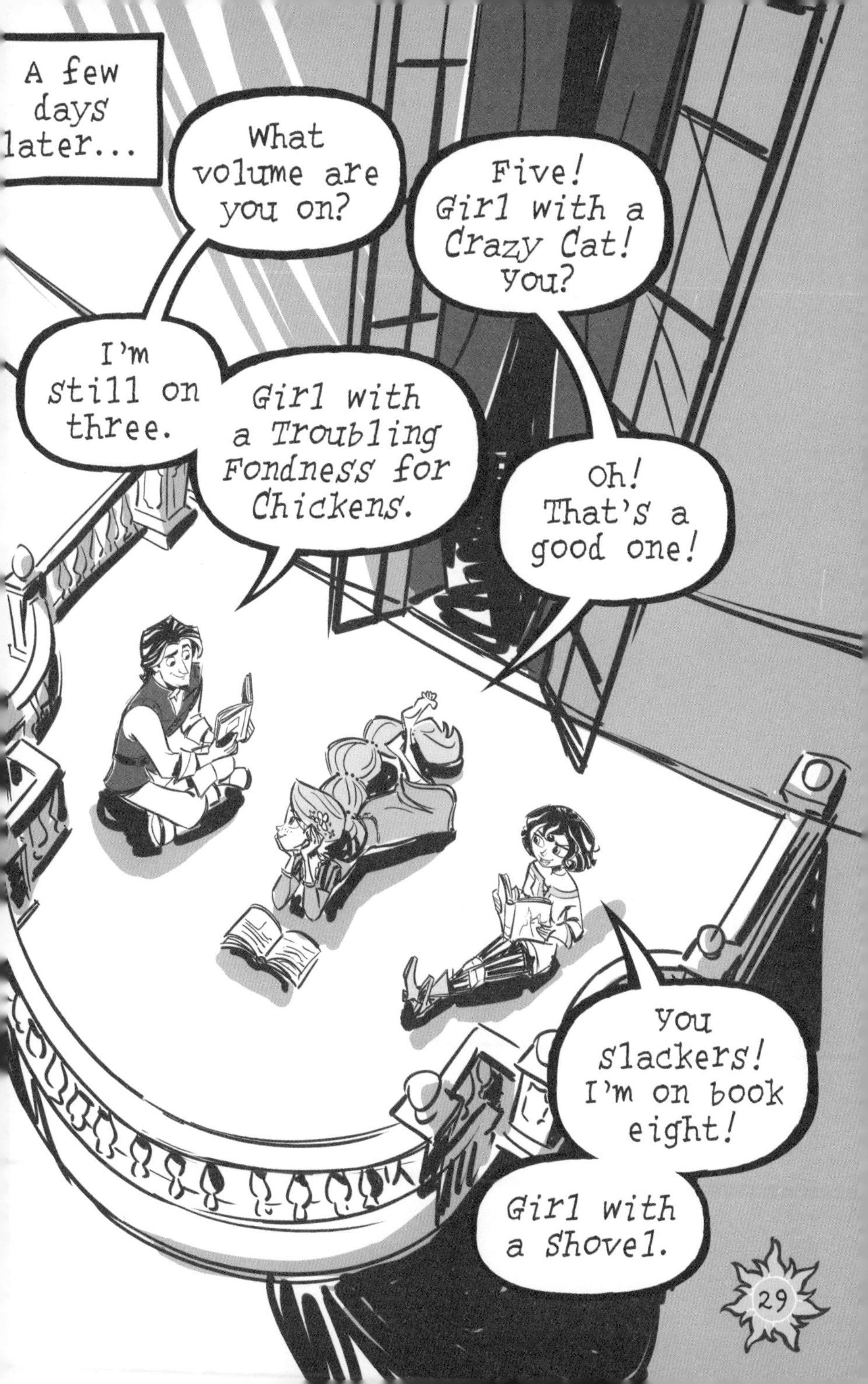
A few days later...
What volume are you on?
Five! *Girl with a Crazy Cat!* You?
I'm still on three.
Girl with a Troubling Fondness for Chickens.
Oh! That's a good one!
You slackers! I'm on book eight!
Girl with a Shovel.

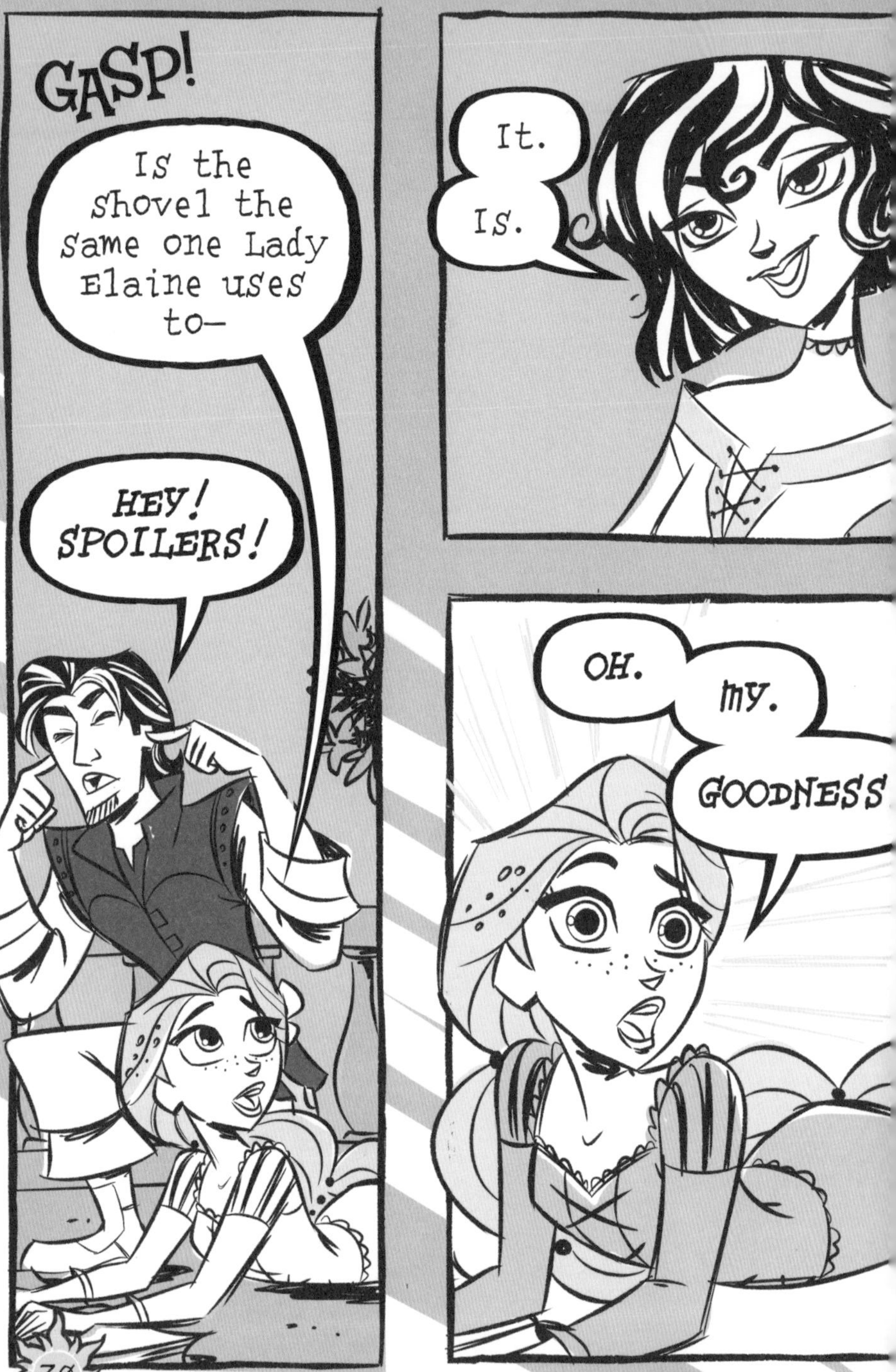
GASP!
Is the shovel the same one Lady Elaine uses to—
HEY! SPOILERS!
It.
Is.
OH.
my.
GOODNESS

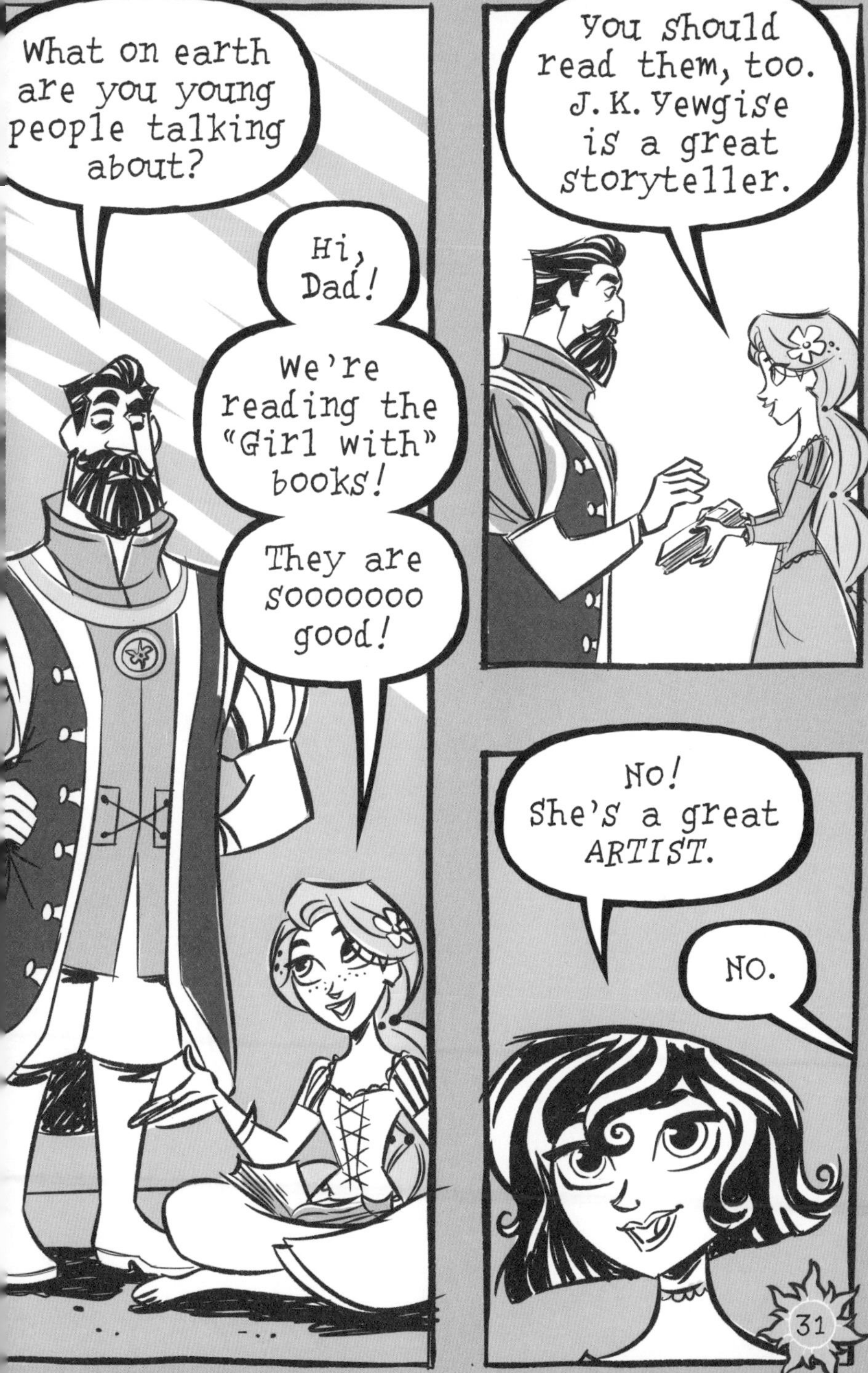
What on earth are you young people talking about?
Hi, Dad!
We're reading the "Girl with" books!
They are sooooooo good!
You should read them, too. J. K. Yewgise is a great storyteller.
No! She's a great ARTIST.
NO.

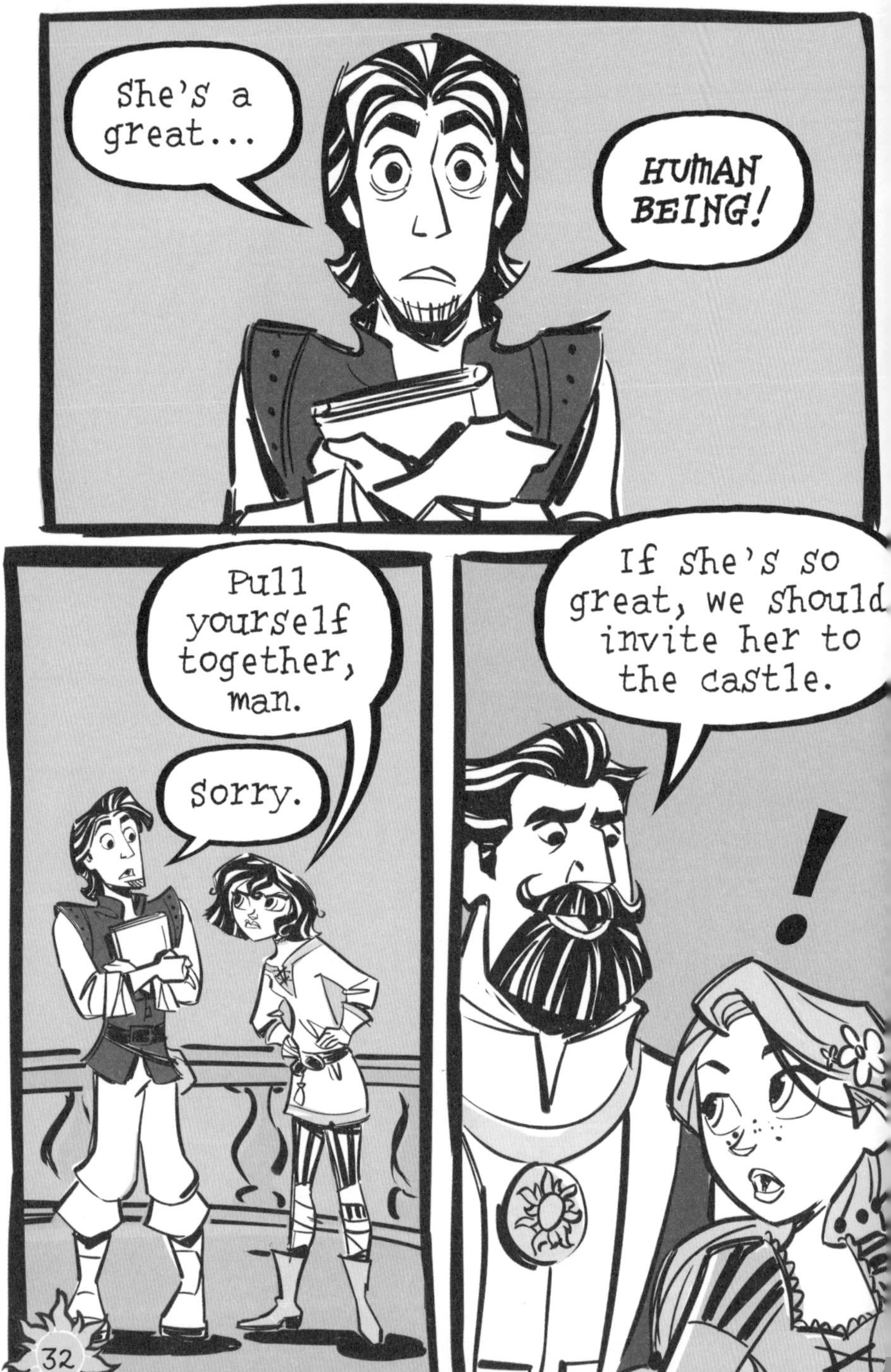
She's a great...
HUMAN BEING!
Pull yourself together, man.
Sorry.
If she's so great, we should invite her to the castle.
!

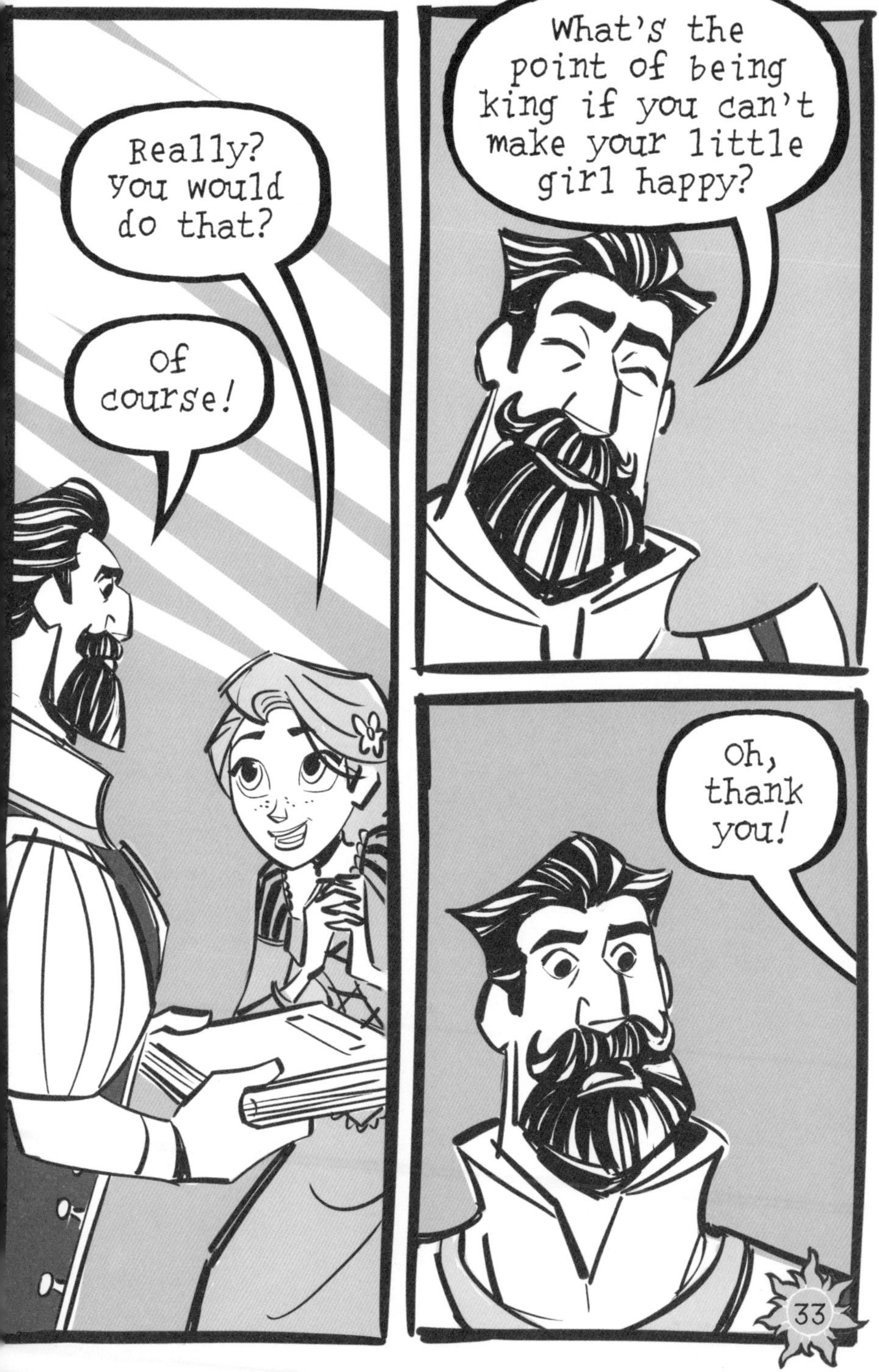
Really? you would do that?
Of course!
What's the point of being king if you can't make your little girl happy?
Oh, thank you!

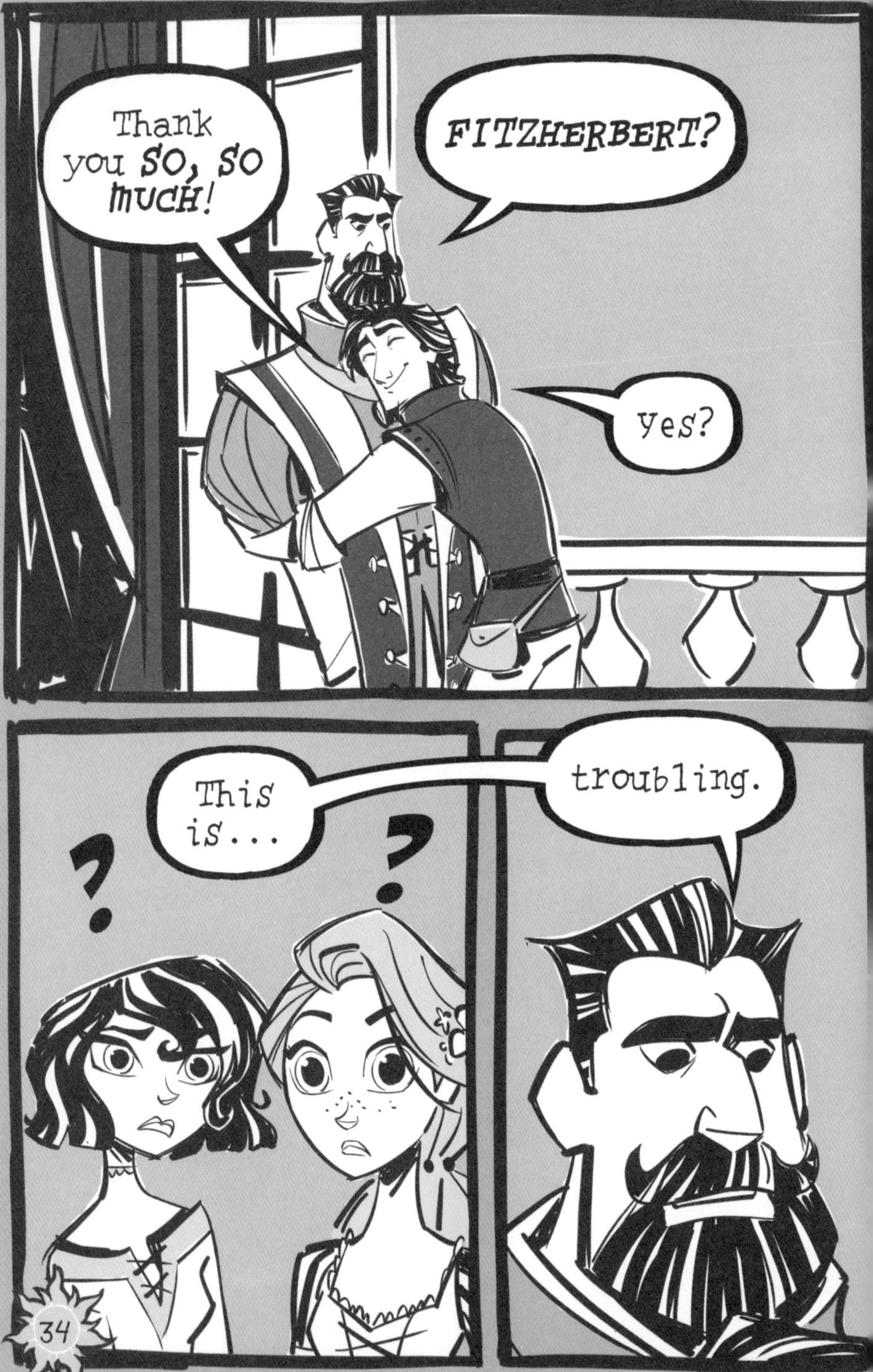
Thank you SO, SO MUCH!
FITZHERBERT?
yes?
This is...
troubling.

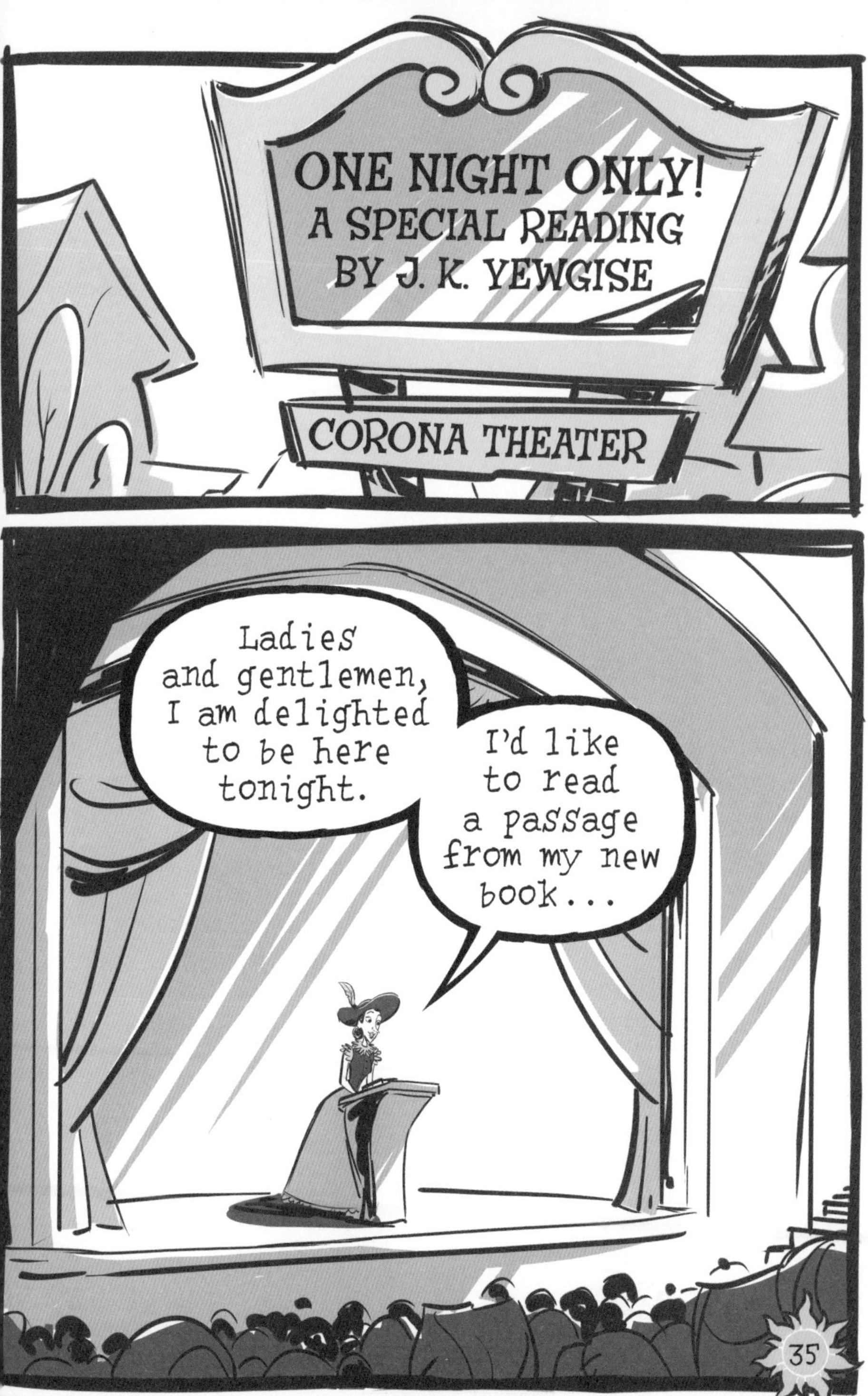
ONE NIGHT ONLY!
A SPECIAL READING
BY J. K. YEWGISE
CORONA THEATER
Ladies and gentlemen, I am delighted to be here tonight.
I'd like to read a passage from my new book...

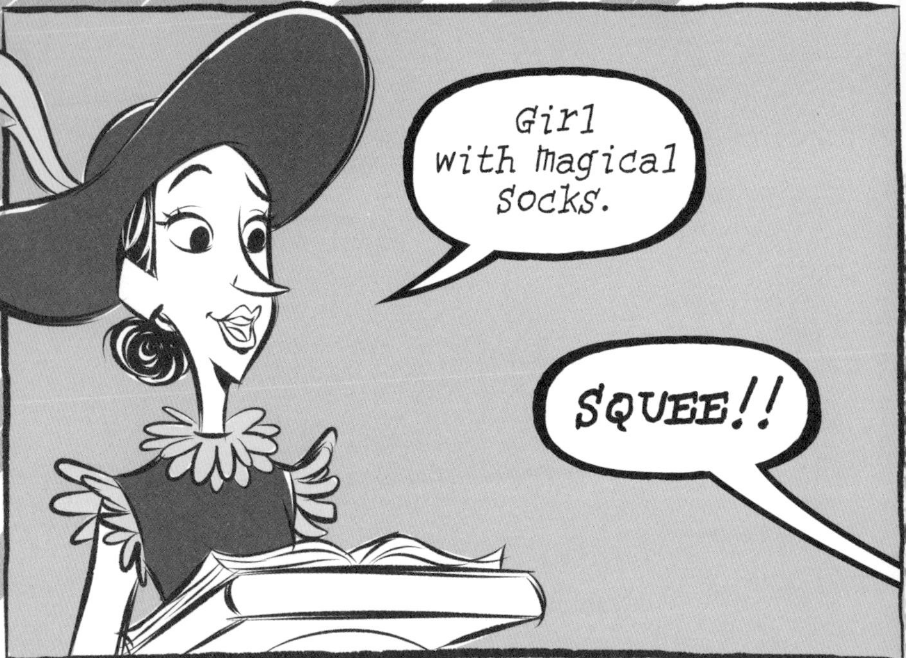
Girl with magical socks.
SQUEE!!
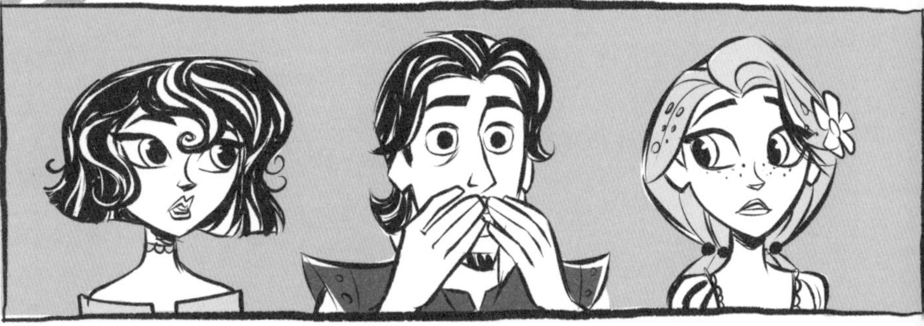
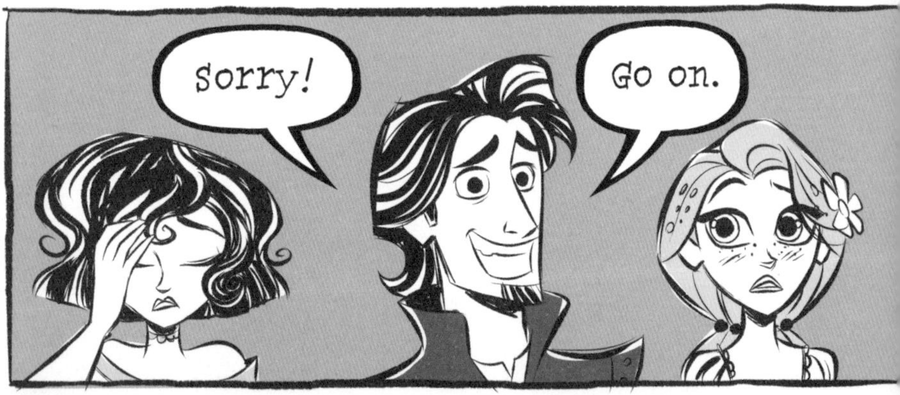
Sorry!
Go on.

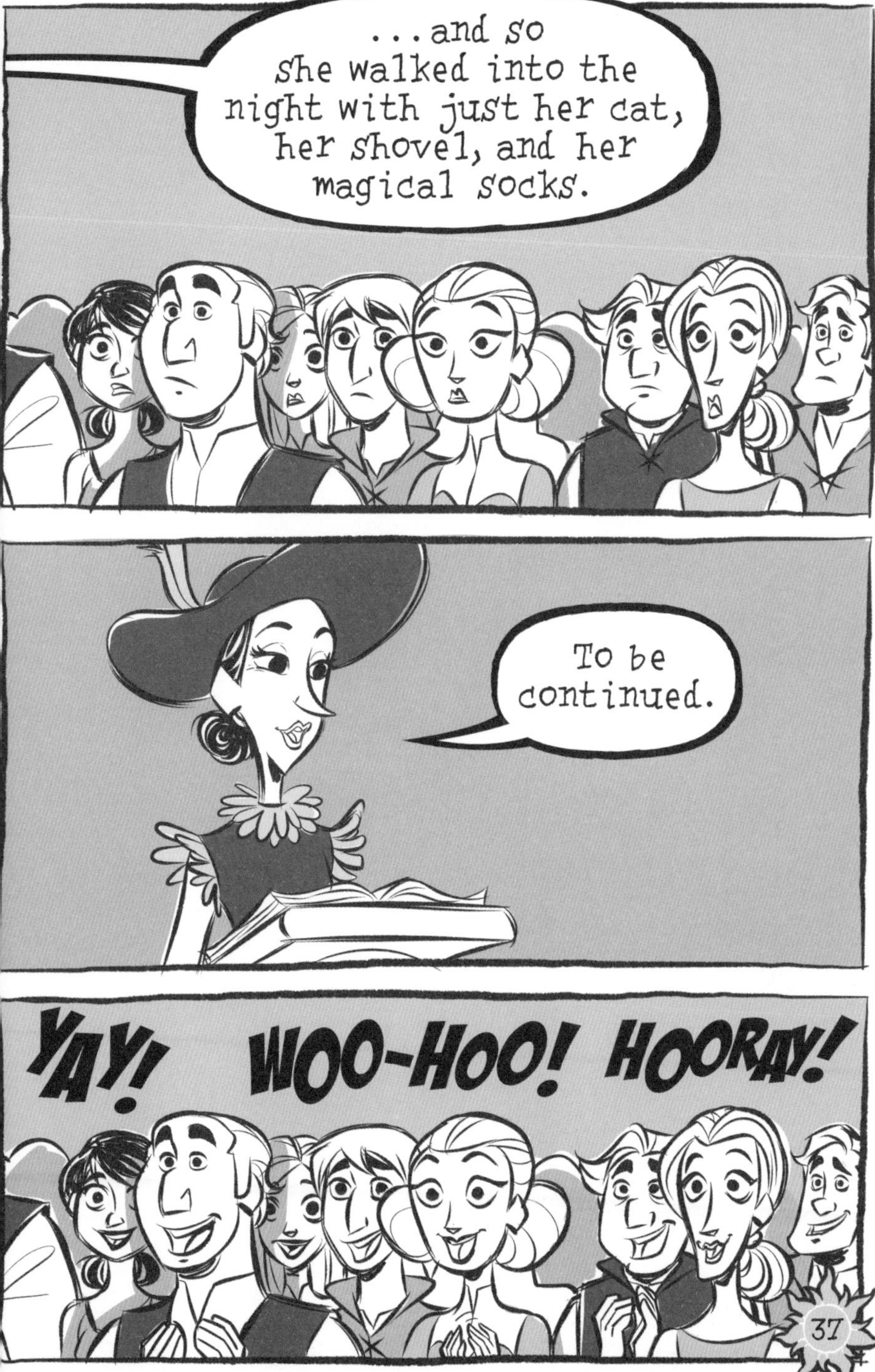

...and so she walked into the night with just her cat, her shovel, and her magical socks.
To be continued.
YAY!
WOO-HOO!
HOORAY!

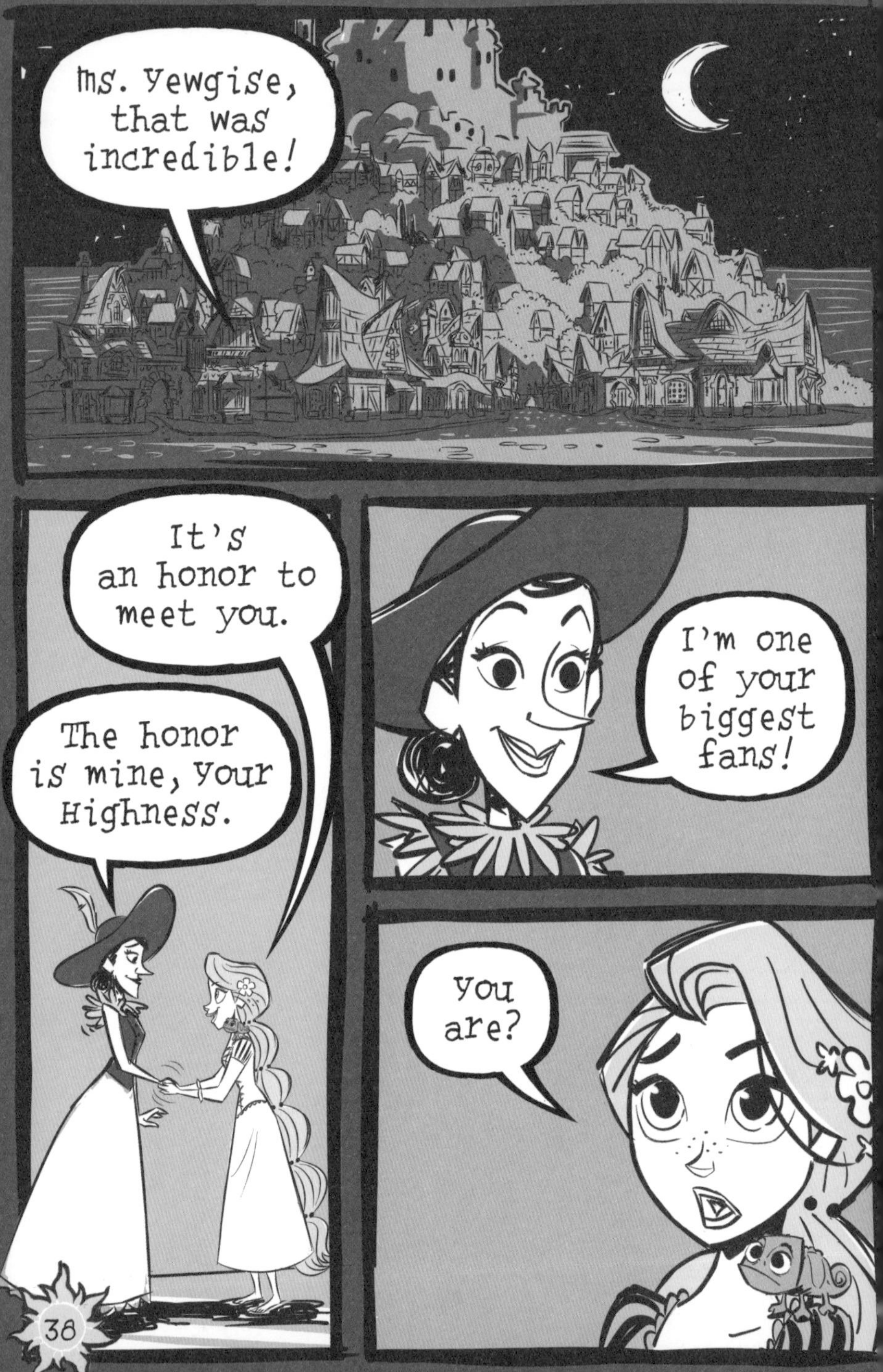
Ms. Yewgise, that was incredible!
It's an honor to meet you.
The honor is mine, your Highness.
I'm one of your biggest fans!
You are?

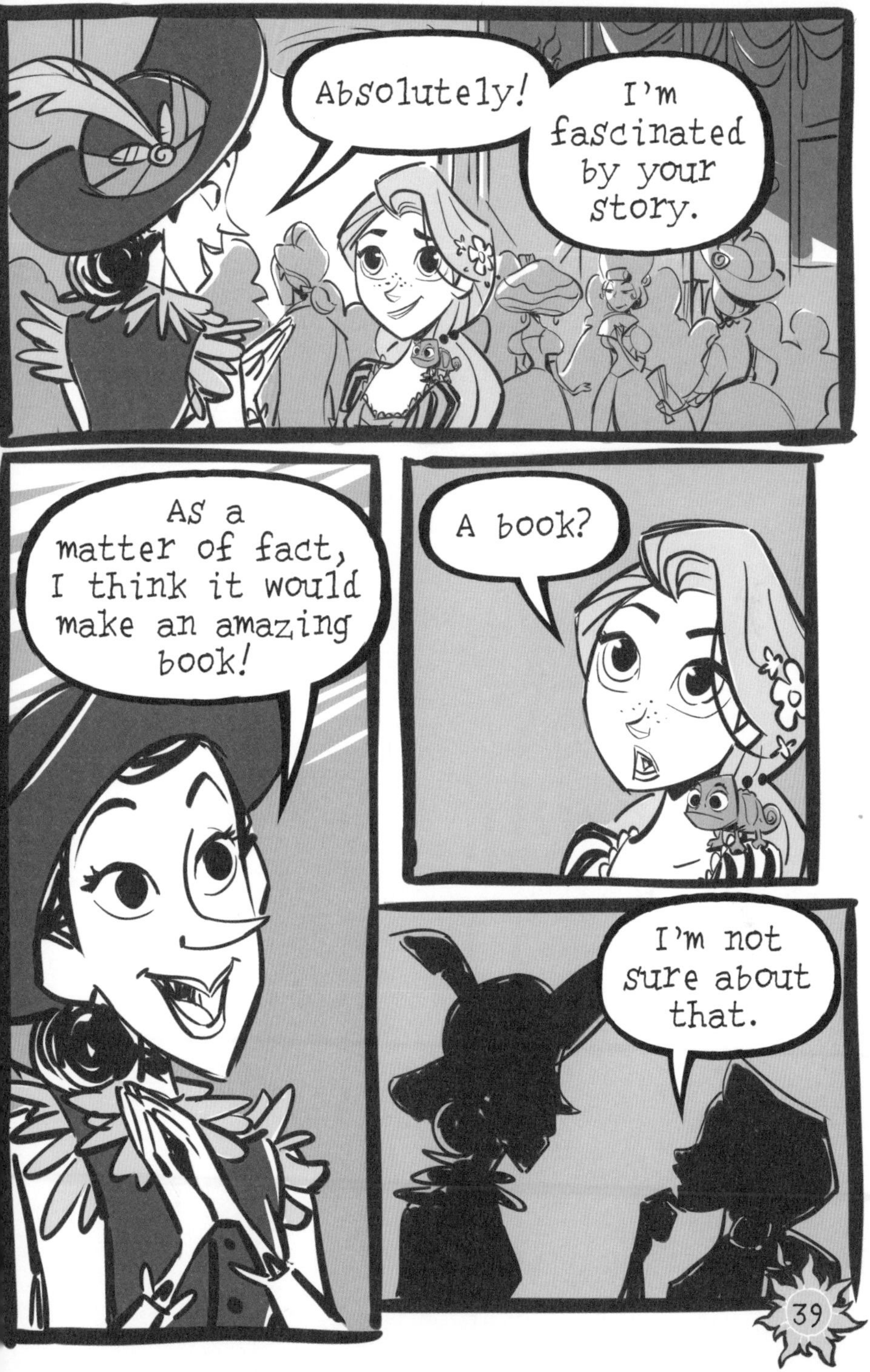
Absolutely!
I'm fascinated by your story.
As a matter of fact, I think it would make an amazing book!
A book?
I'm not sure about that.

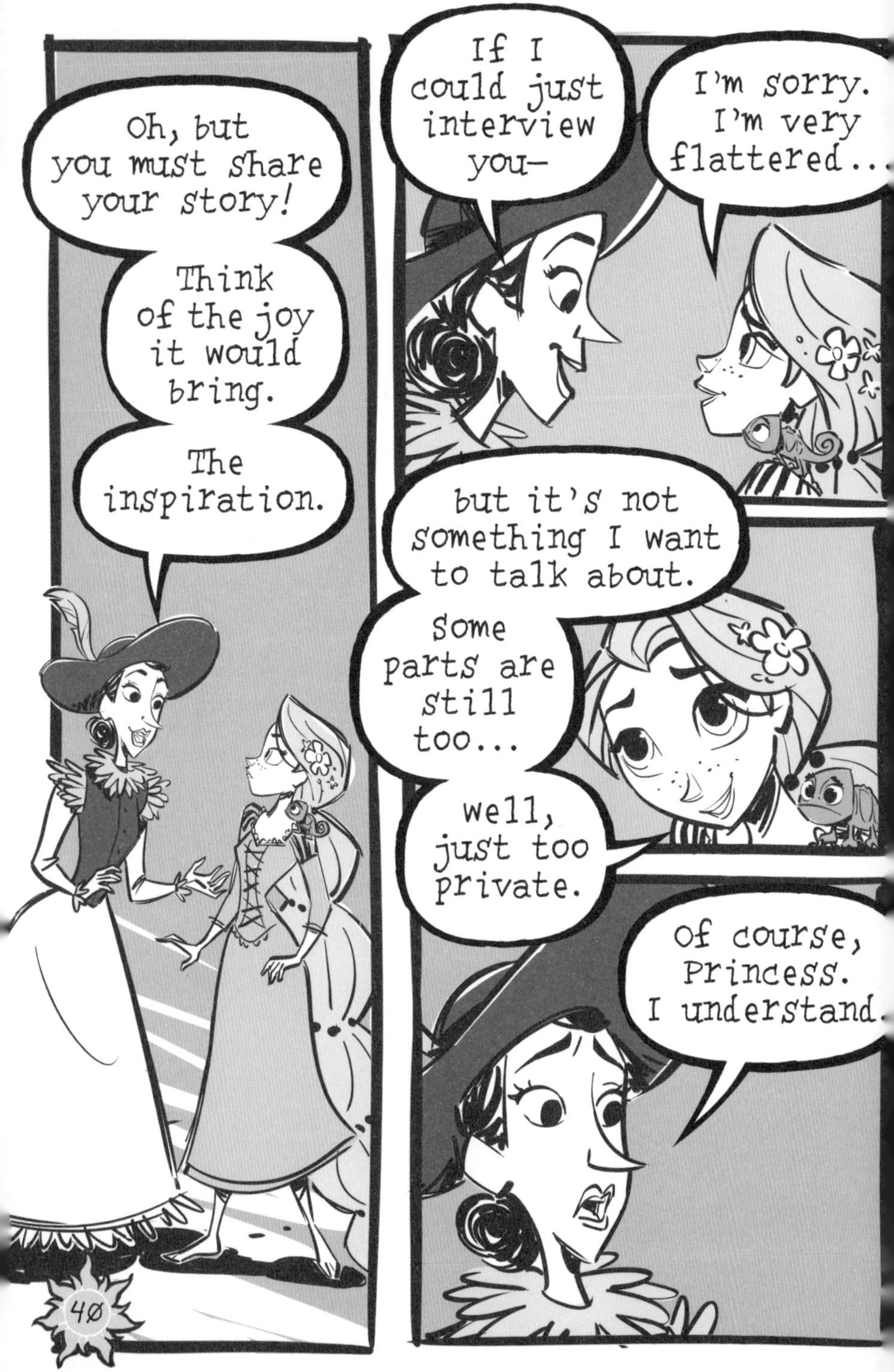
Oh, but you must share your story!
Think of the joy it would bring.
The inspiration.
If I could just interview you—
I'm sorry. I'm very flattered...
but it's not something I want to talk about.
Some parts are still too...
well, just too private.
Of course, Princess. I understand.

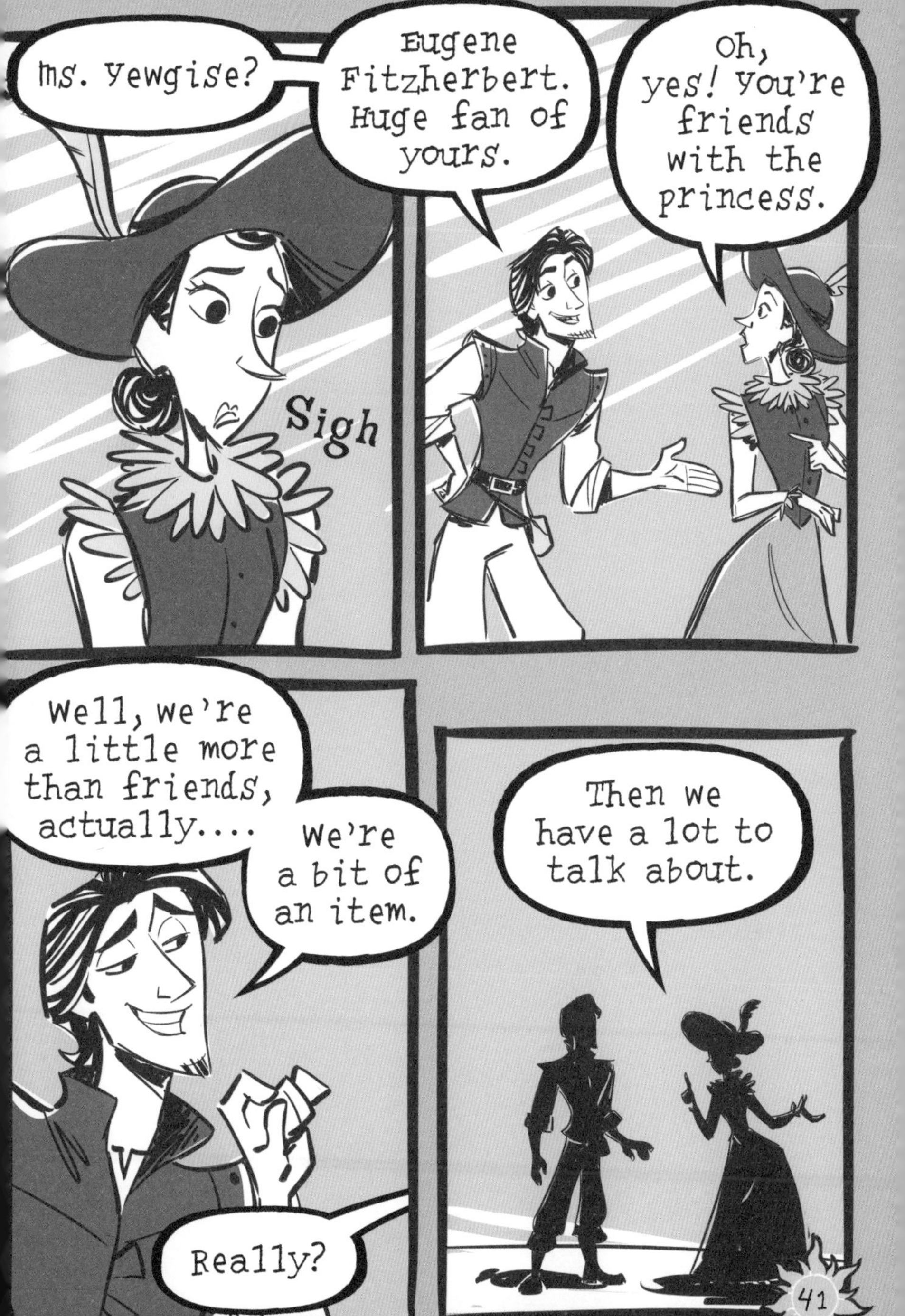

Ms. Yewgise?
Eugene Fitzherbert. Huge fan of yours.
Sigh
Oh, yes! You're friends with the princess.
Well, we're a little more than friends, actually....
We're a bit of an item.
Really?
Then we have a lot to talk about.

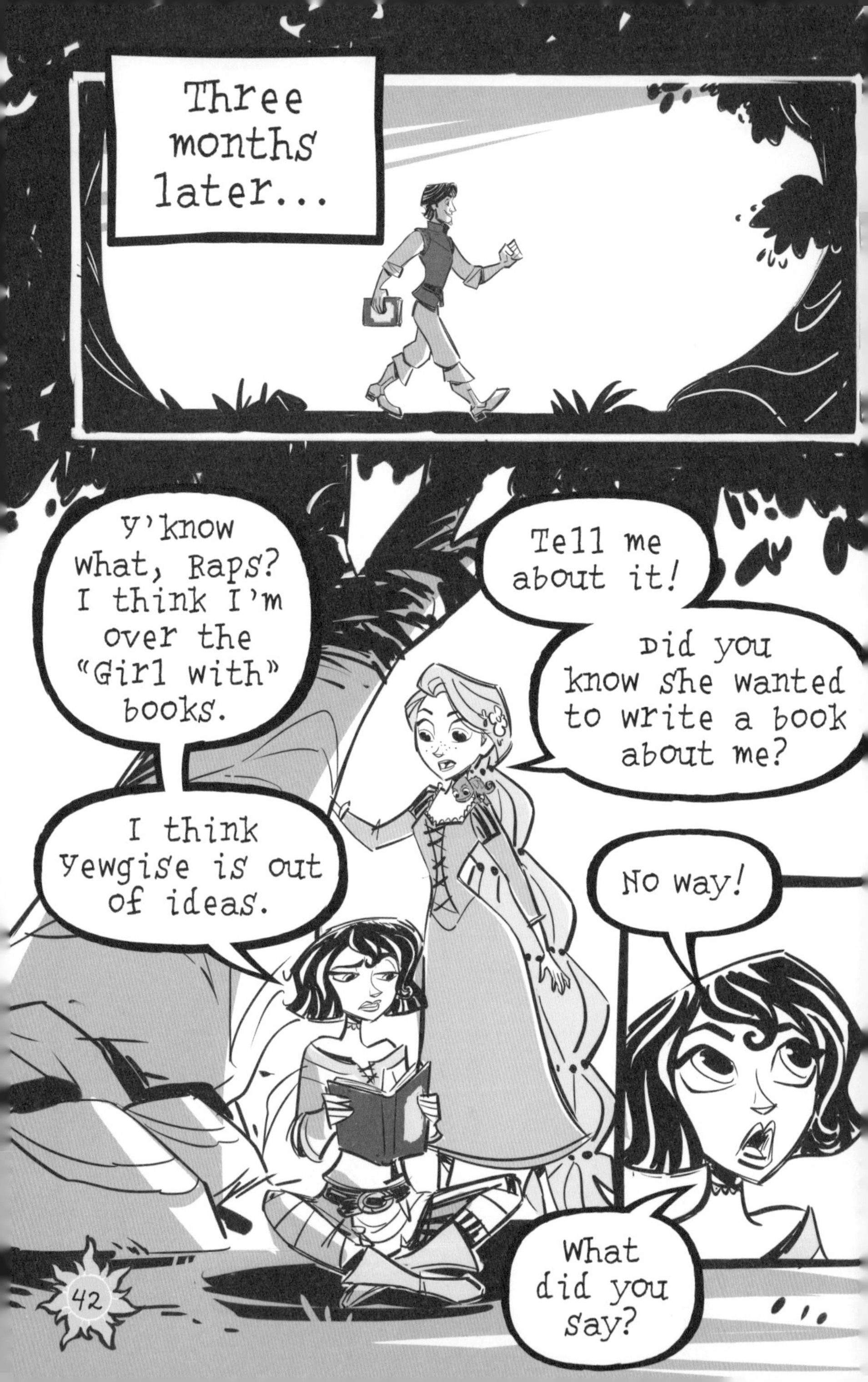
Three months later...
Y'know what, Raps? I think I'm over the "Girl with" books.
Tell me about it!
Did you know she wanted to write a book about me?
I think Yewgise is out of ideas.
No way!
What did you say?

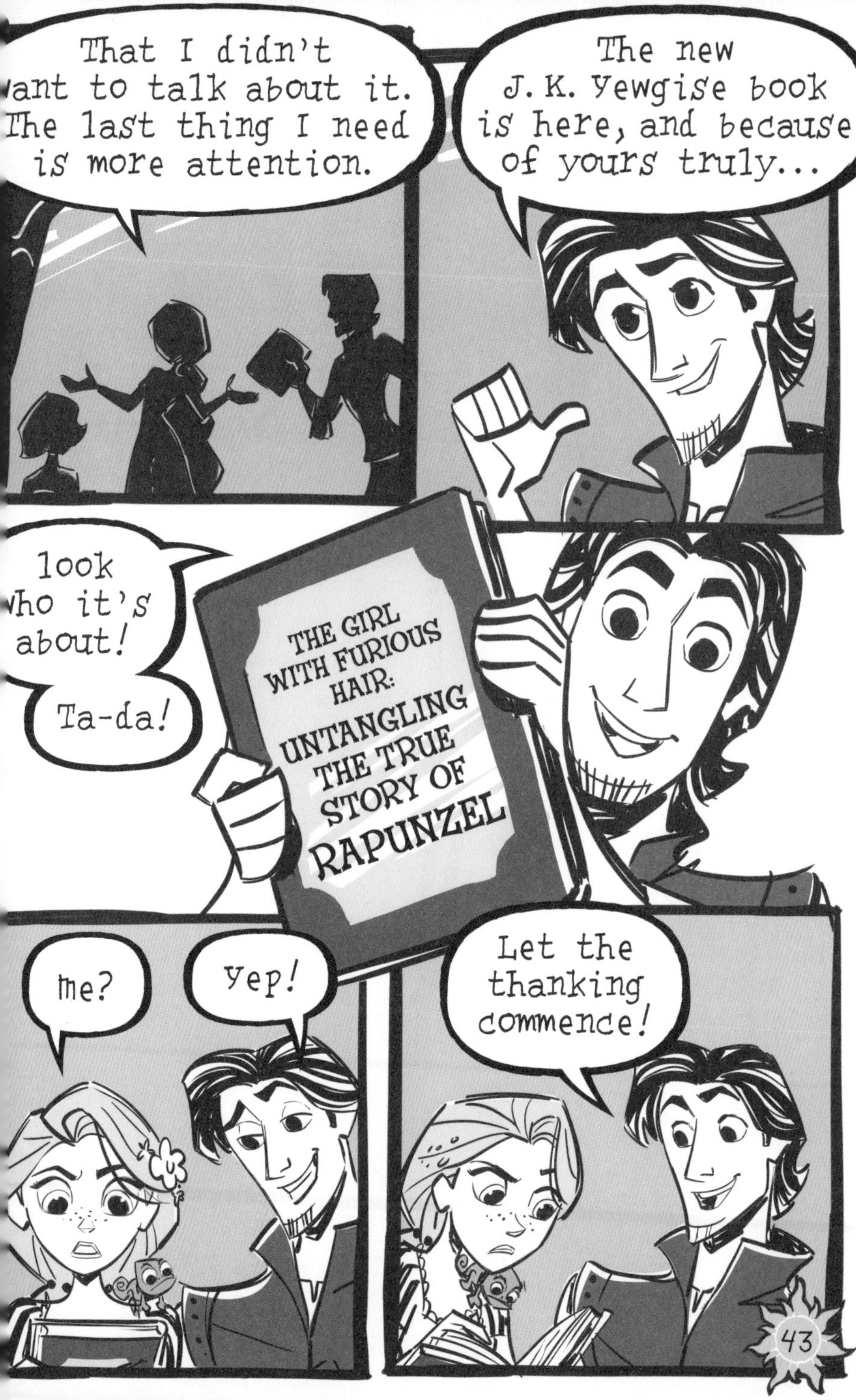

That I didn't want to talk about it. The last thing I need is more attention.
The new J. K. Yewgise book is here, and because of yours truly...
look who it's about!
Ta-da!
THE GIRL WITH FURIOUS HAIR: UNTANGLING THE TRUE STORY OF RAPUNZEL
me?
yep!
Let the thanking commence!

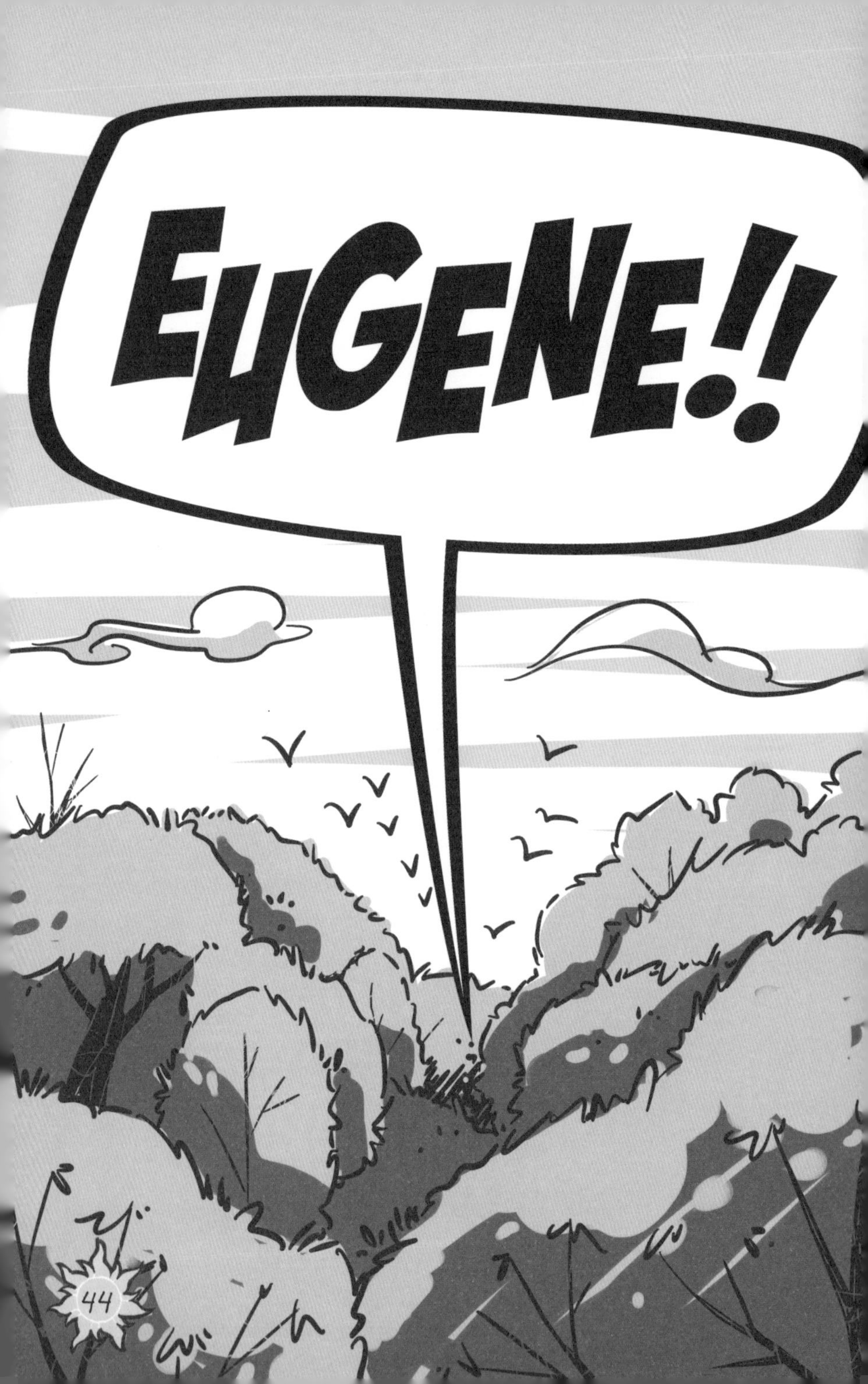
EUGENE!!

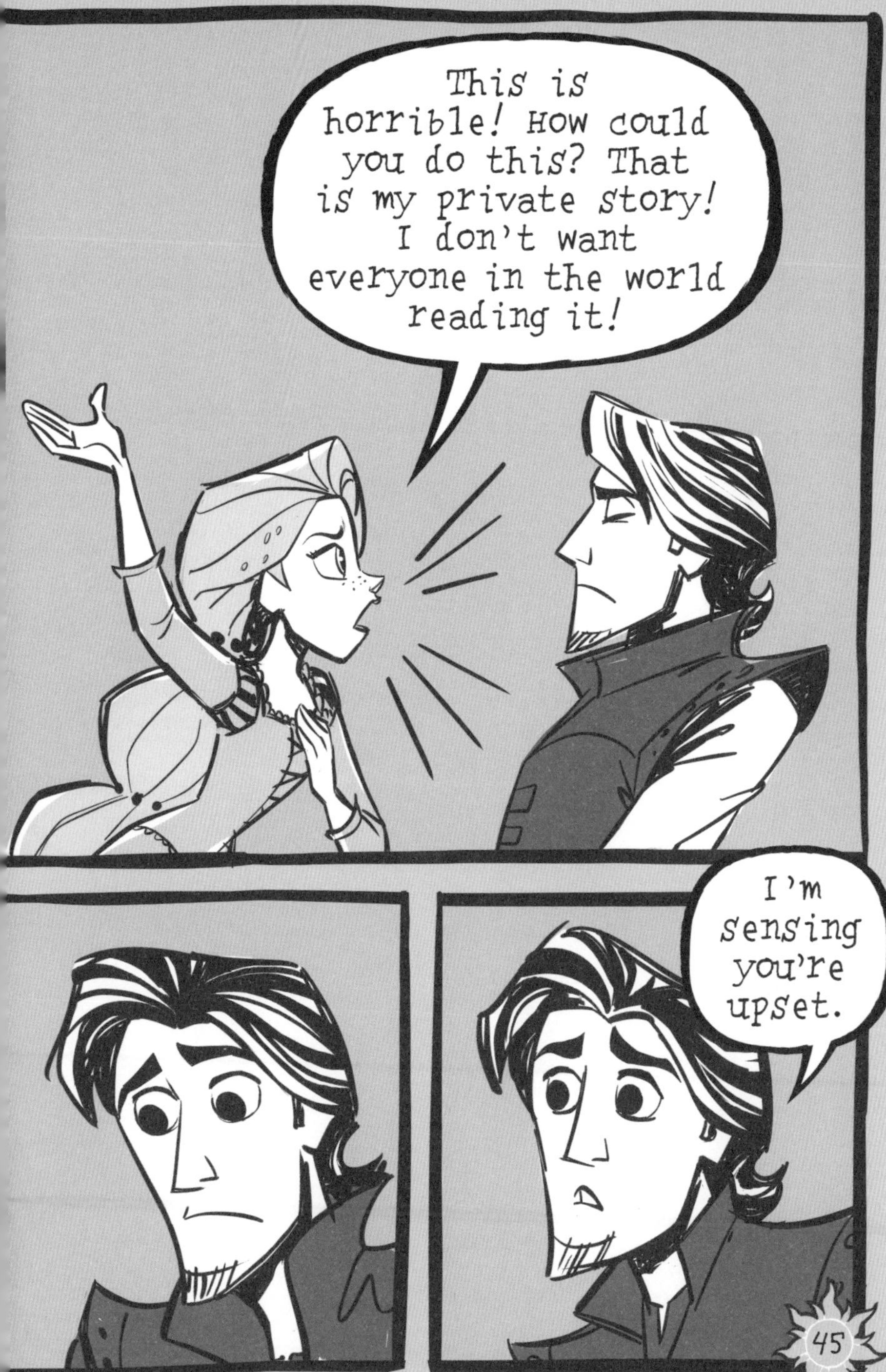
This is horrible! How could you do this? That is my private story! I don't want everyone in the world reading it!
I'm sensing you're upset.

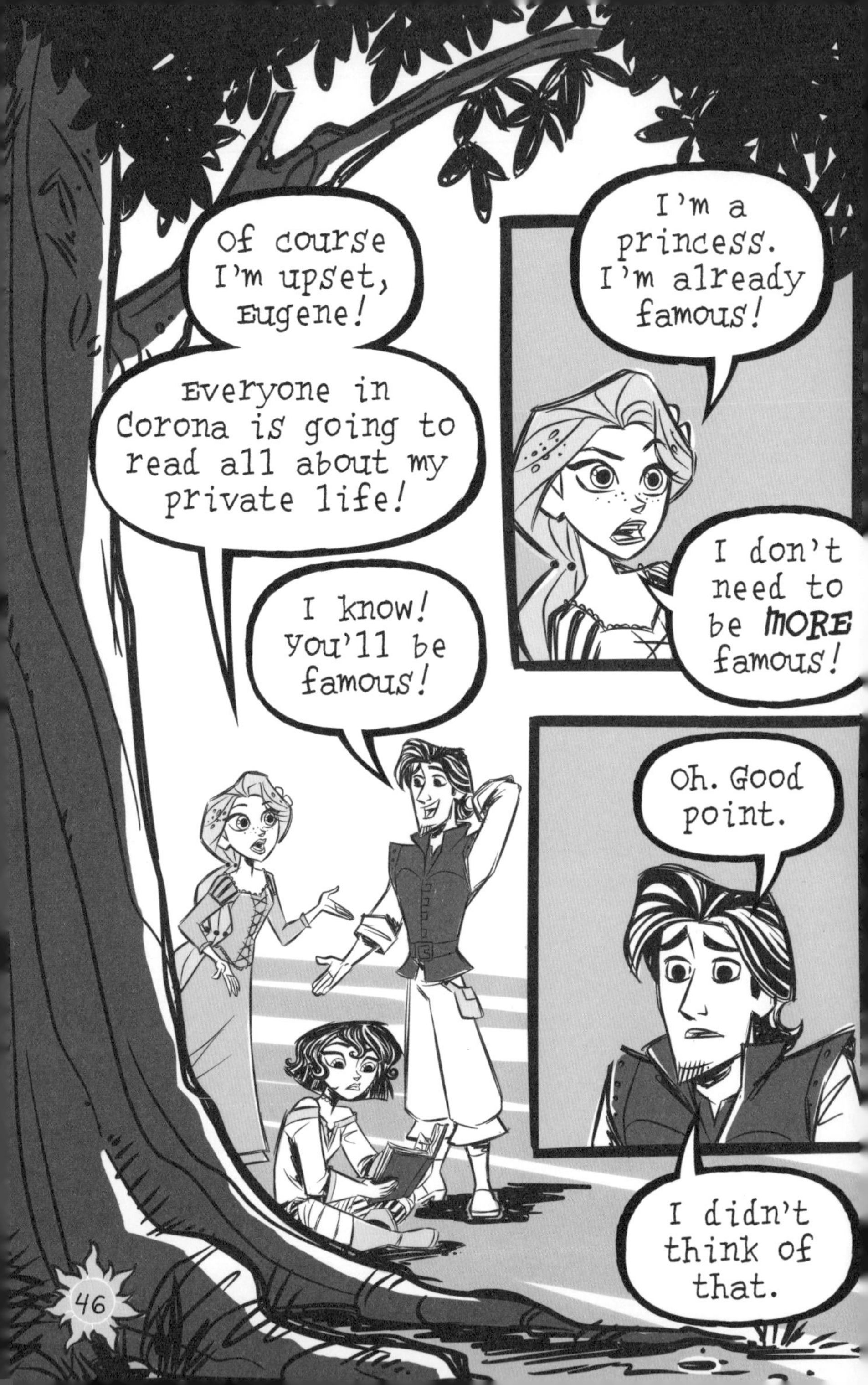
Of course I'm upset, Eugene!
Everyone in Corona is going to read all about my private life!
I know! You'll be famous!
I'm a princess. I'm already famous!
I don't need to be MORE famous!
Oh. Good point.
I didn't think of that.

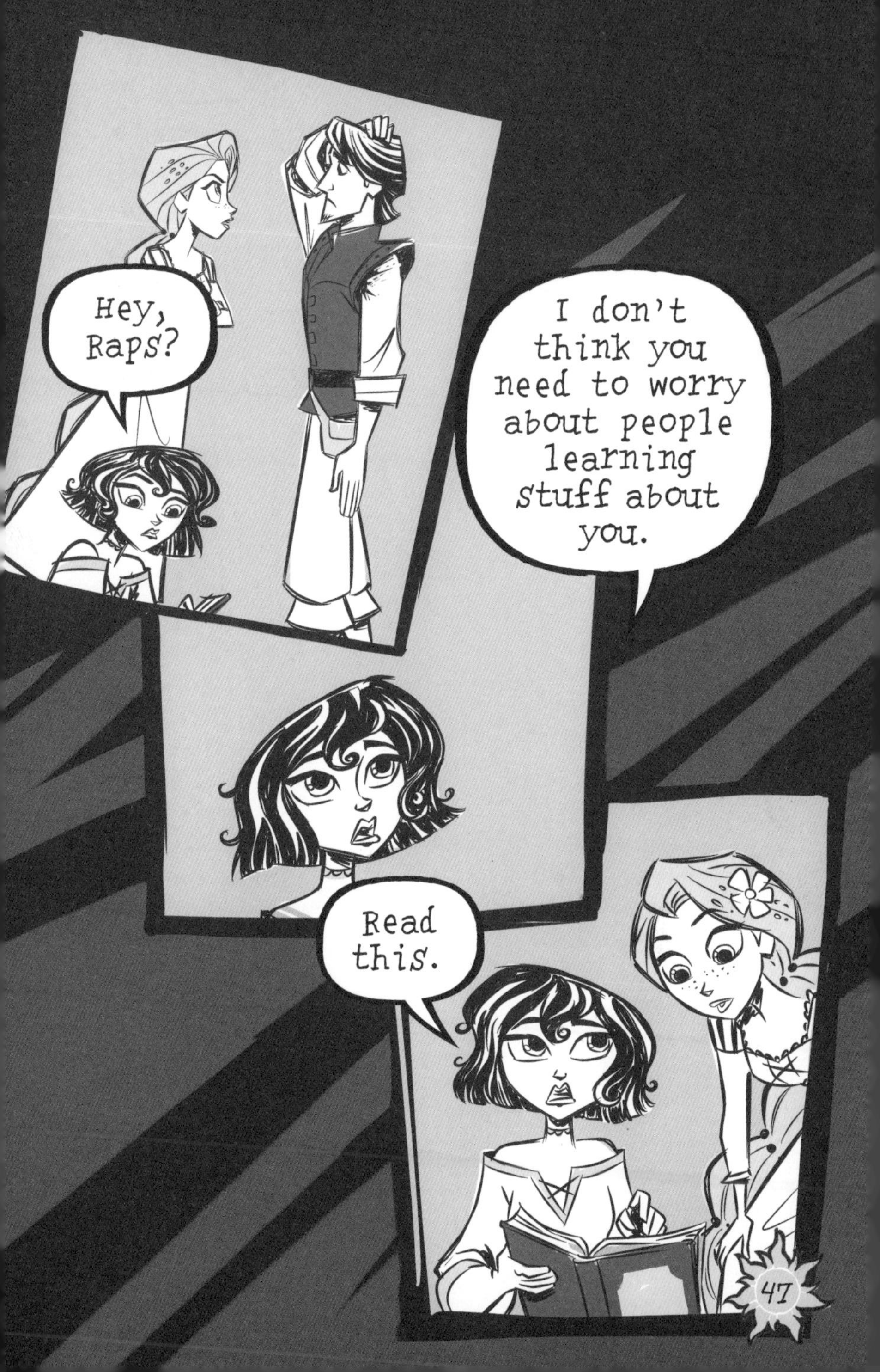
Hey, Raps?
I don't think you need to worry about people learning stuff about you.
Read this.

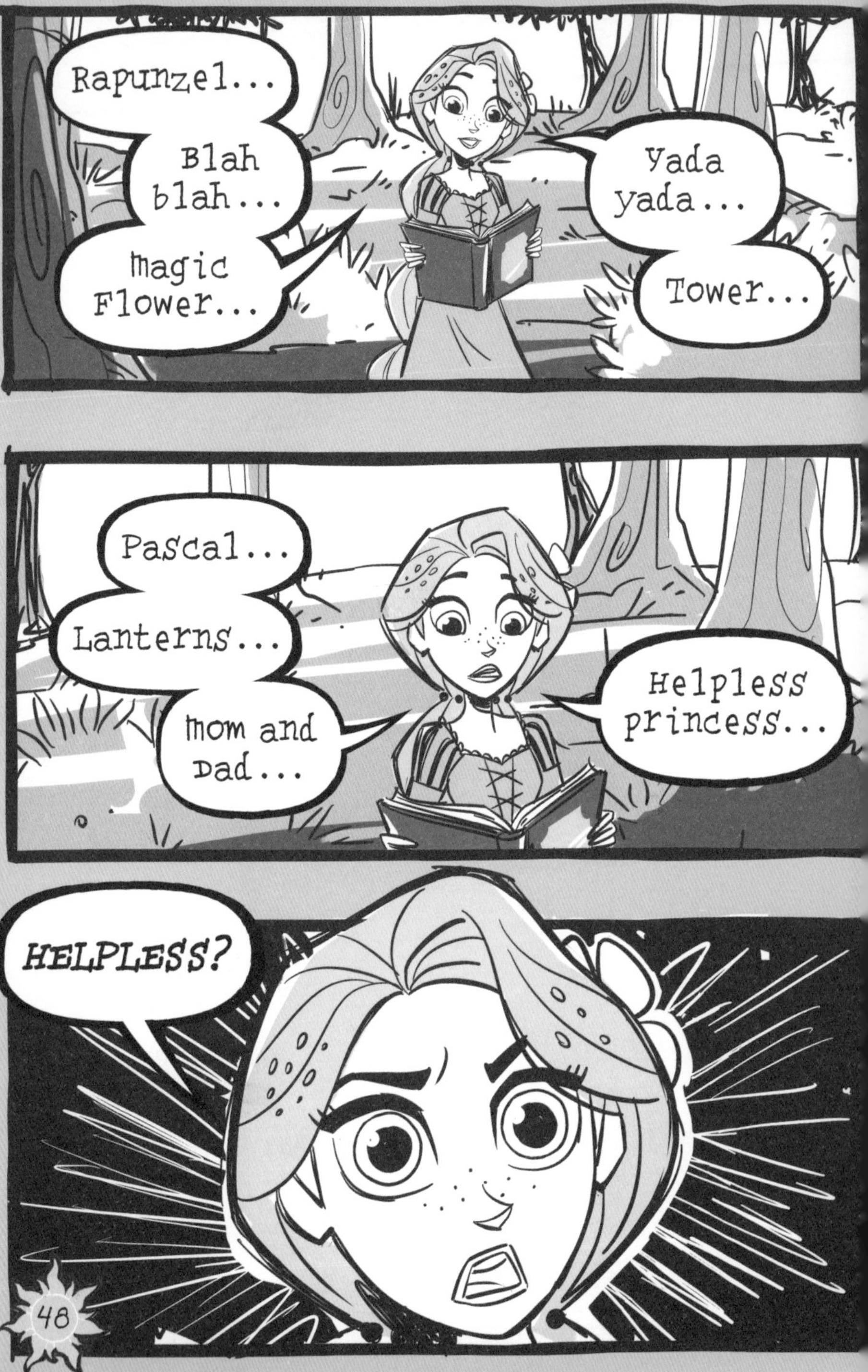

Rapunzel...
Blah blah...
Magic Flower...
Yada yada...
Tower...
Pascal...
Lanterns...
Mom and Dad...
Helpless princess...
HELPLESS?

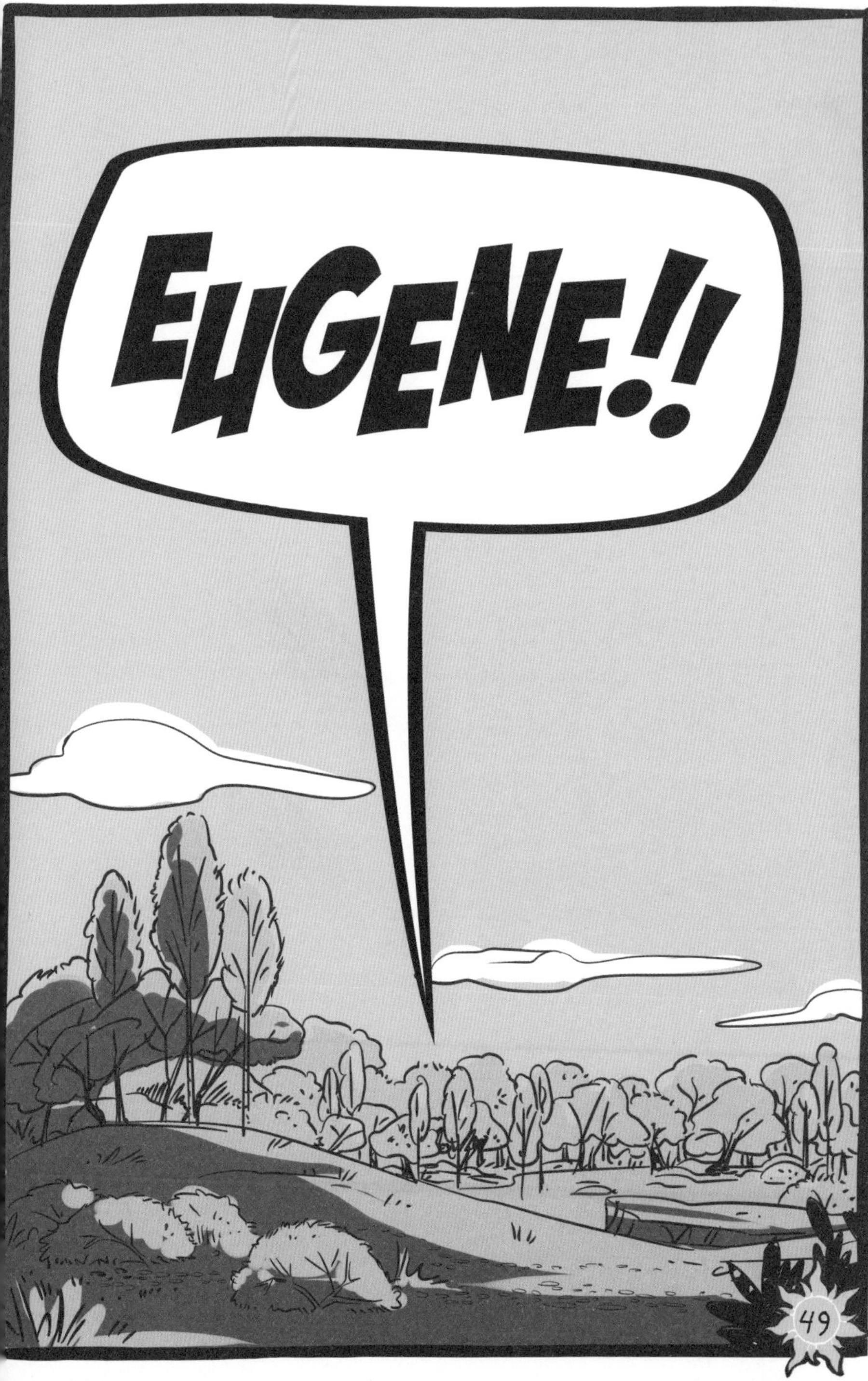
EUGENE!!

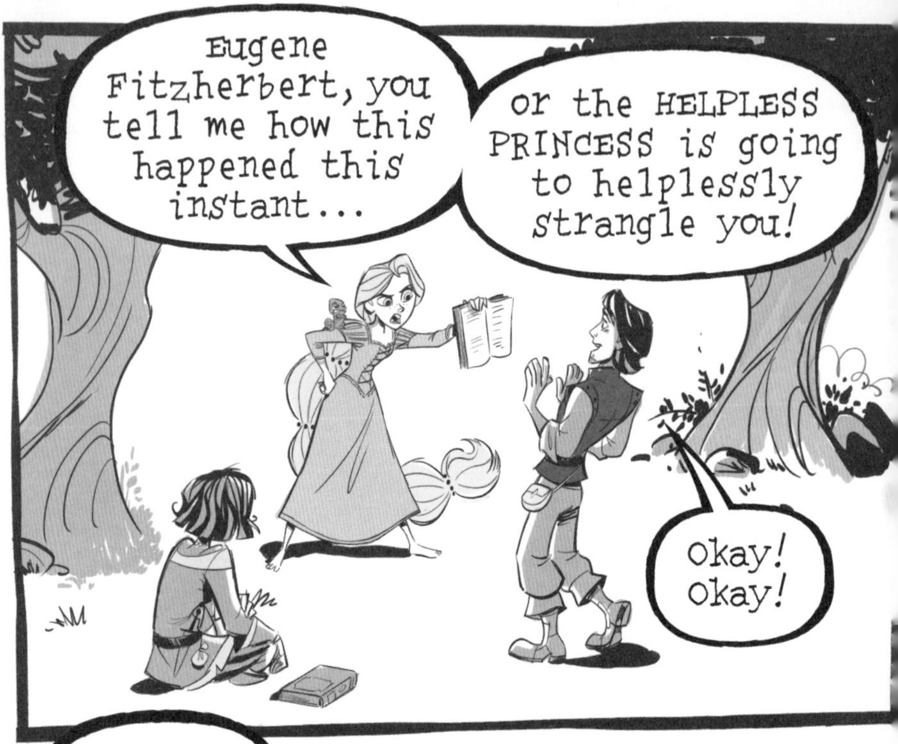
Eugene Fitzherbert, you tell me how this happened this instant...
Or the HELPLESS PRINCESS is going to helplessly strangle you!
Okay! Okay!

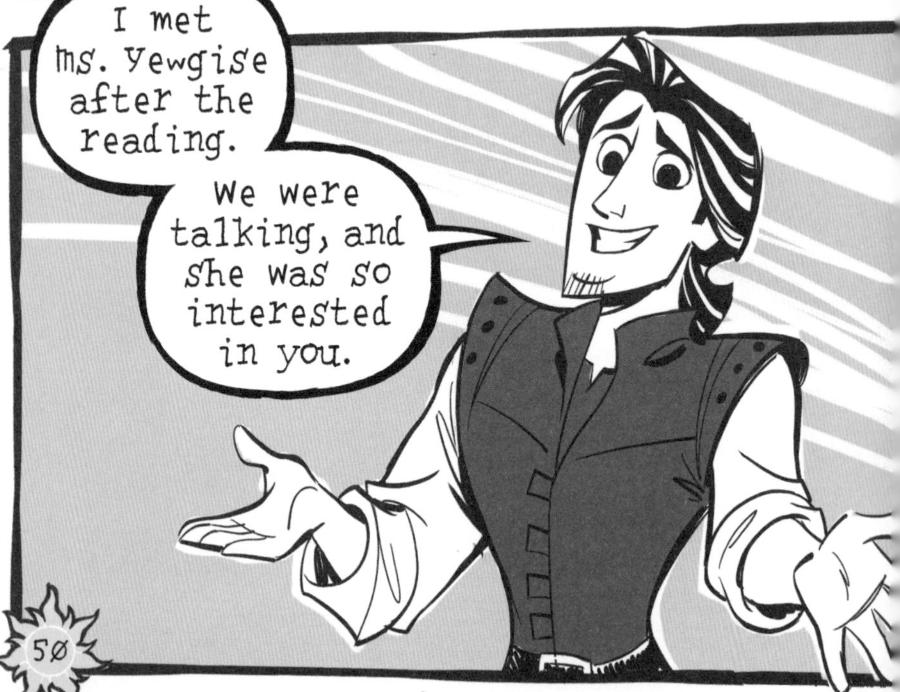
I met Ms. Yewgise after the reading.
We were talking, and she was so interested in you.

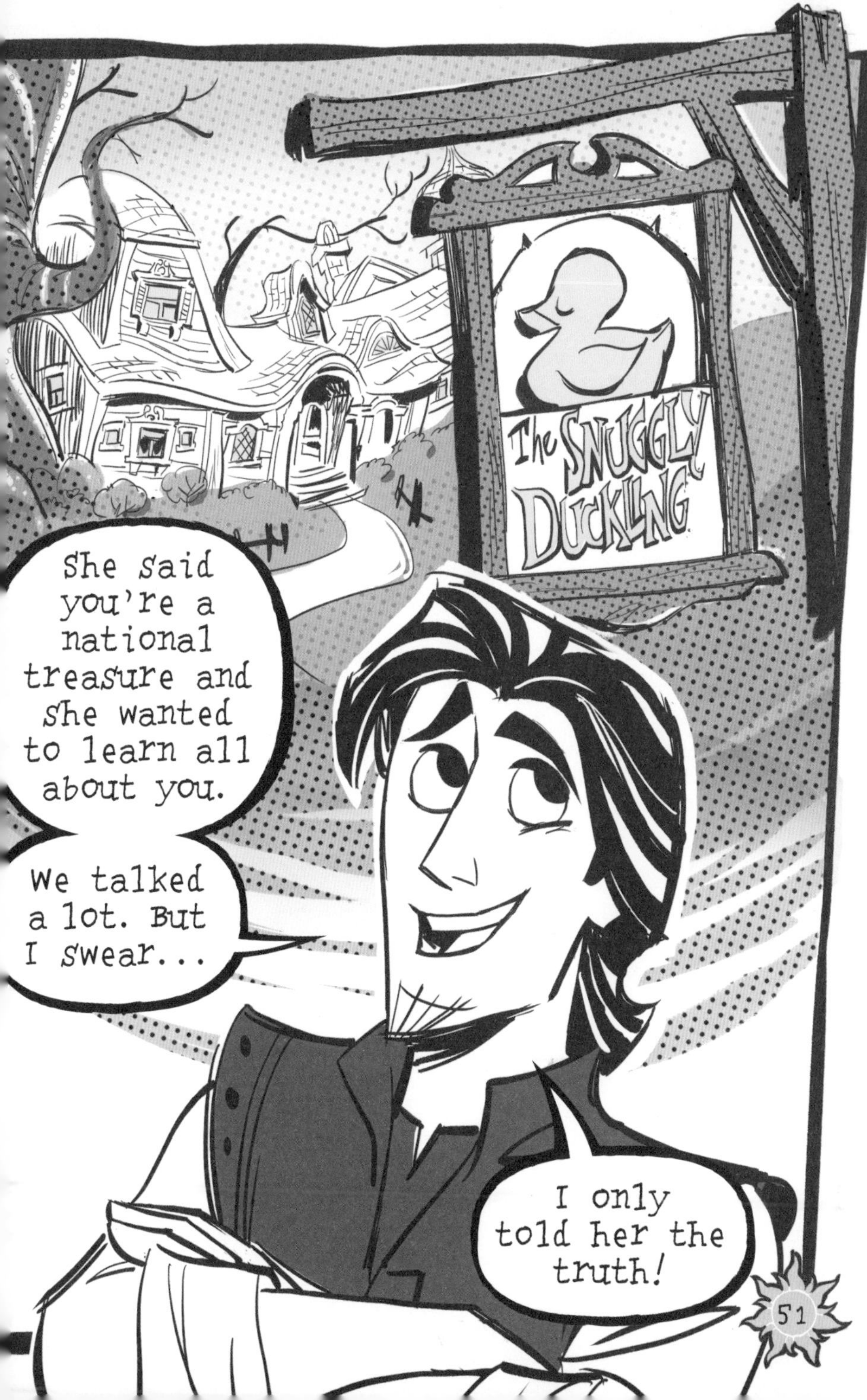
The Snuggly Duckling
She said you're a national treasure and she wanted to learn all about you.
We talked a lot. But I swear...
I only told her the truth!

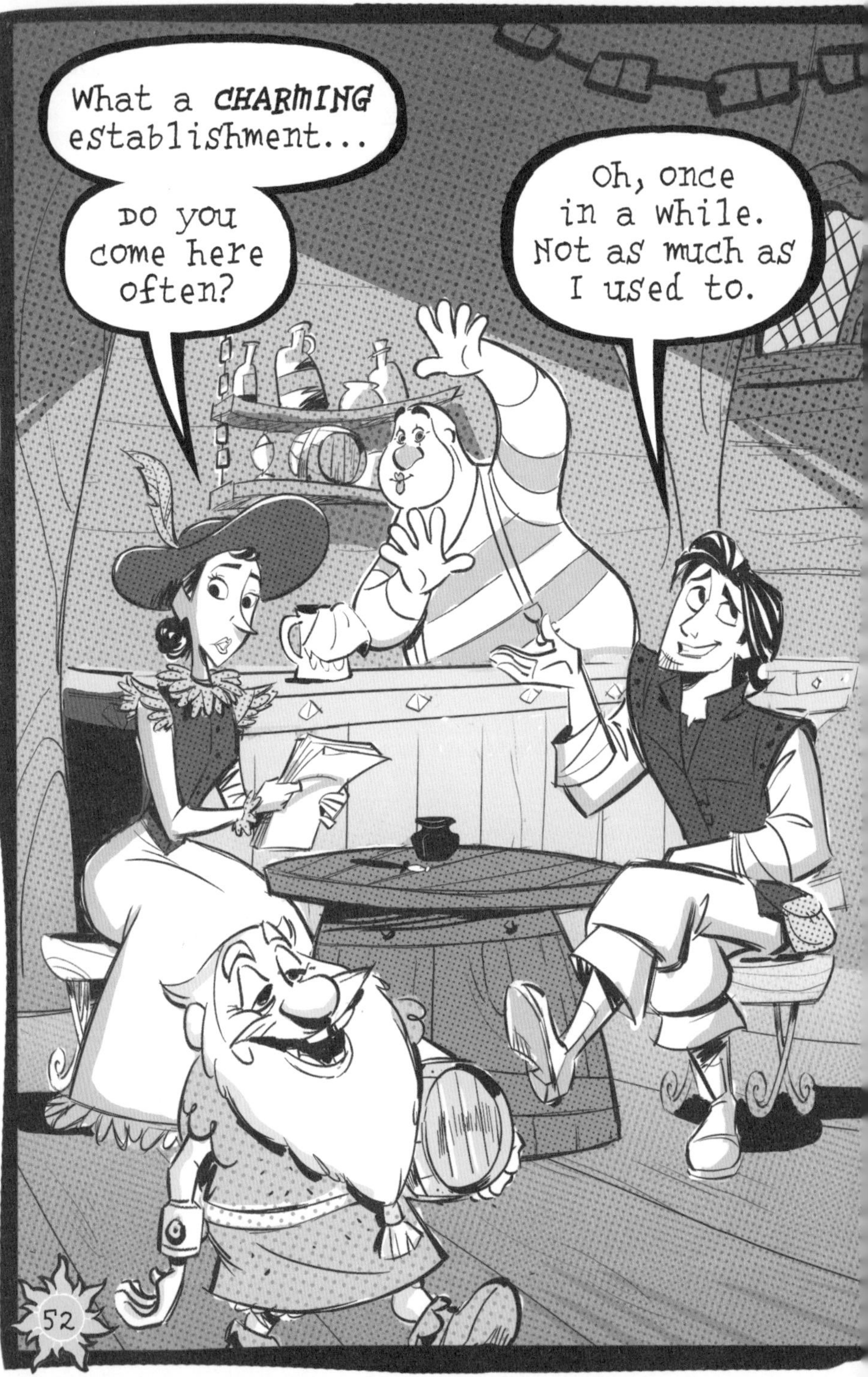
What a **CHARMING** establishment...
Do you come here often?
Oh, once in a while. Not as much as I used to.

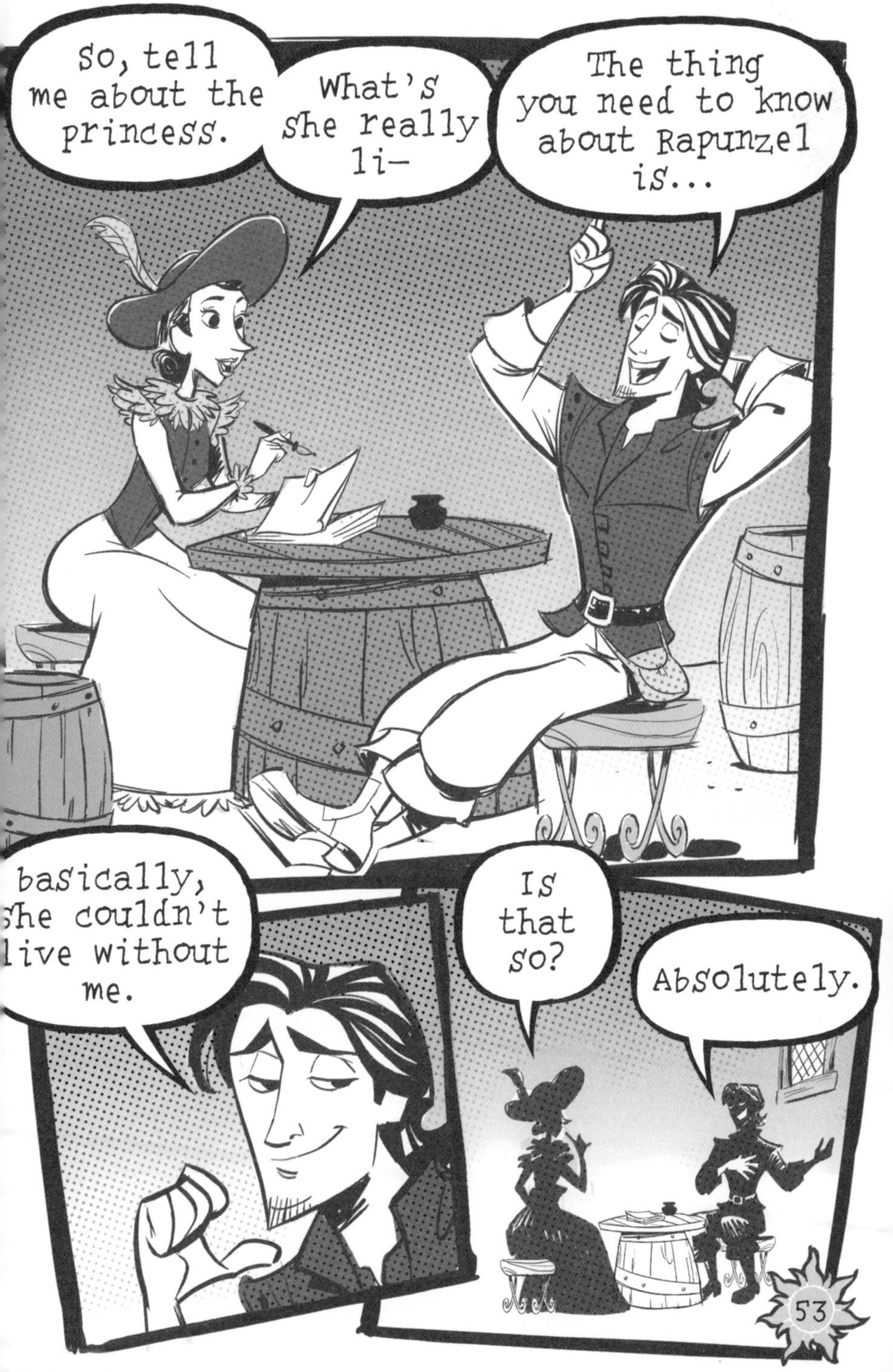

So, tell me about the princess.
What's she really li–
The thing you need to know about Rapunzel is...
basically, she couldn't live without me.
Is that so?
Absolutely.

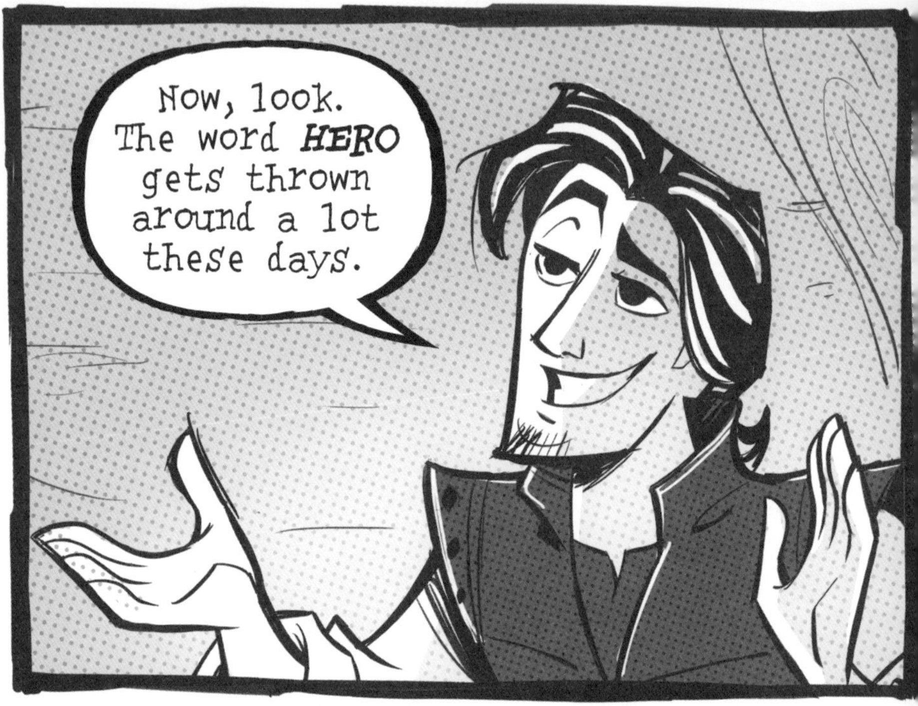
Now, look. The word **HERO** gets thrown around a lot these days.

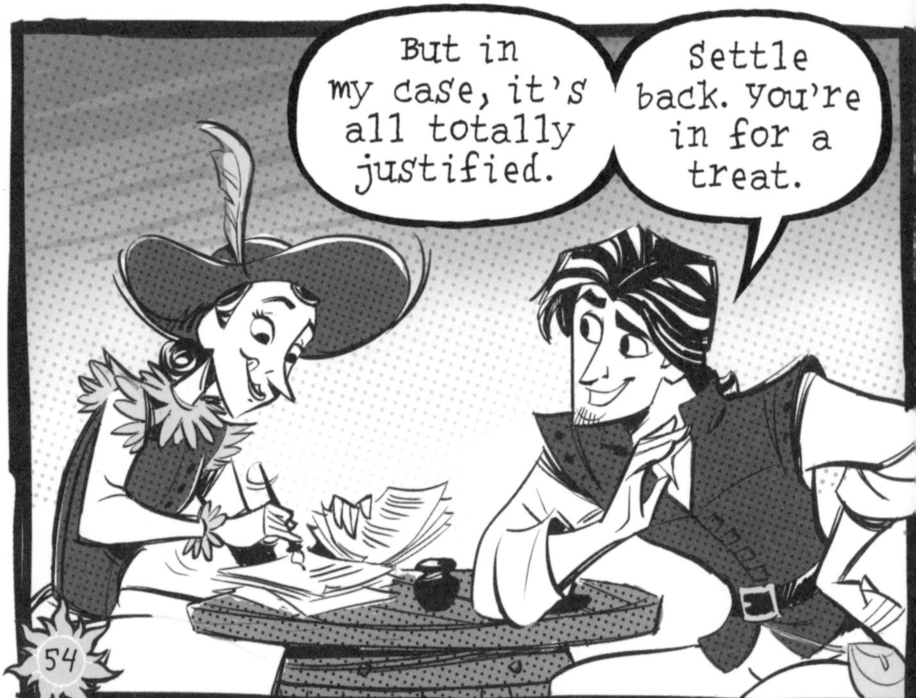
But in my case, it's all totally justified.
Settle back. You're in for a treat.

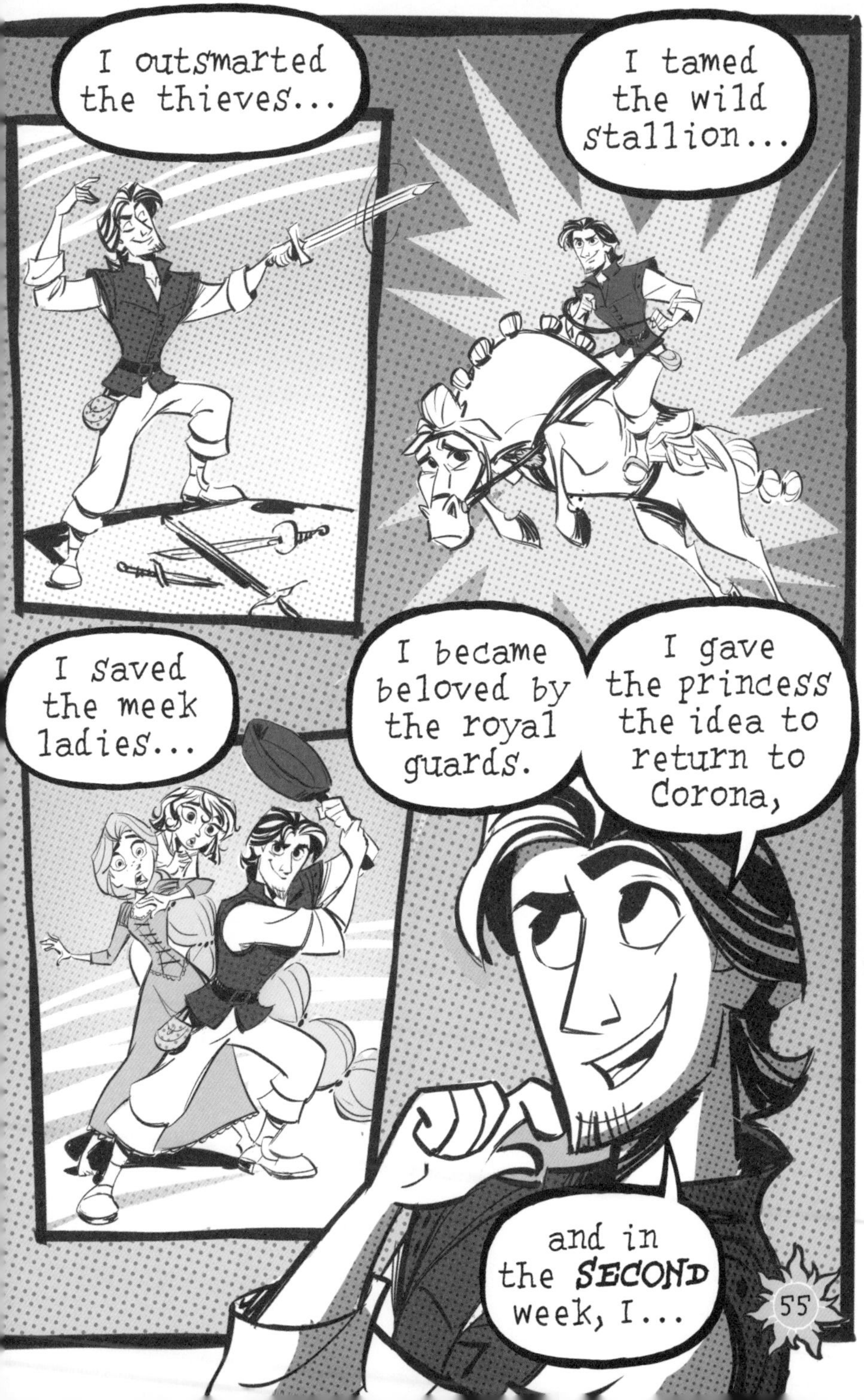
I outsmarted the thieves...
I tamed the wild stallion...
I saved the meek ladies...
I became beloved by the royal guards.
I gave the princess the idea to return to Corona,
and in the SECOND week, I...

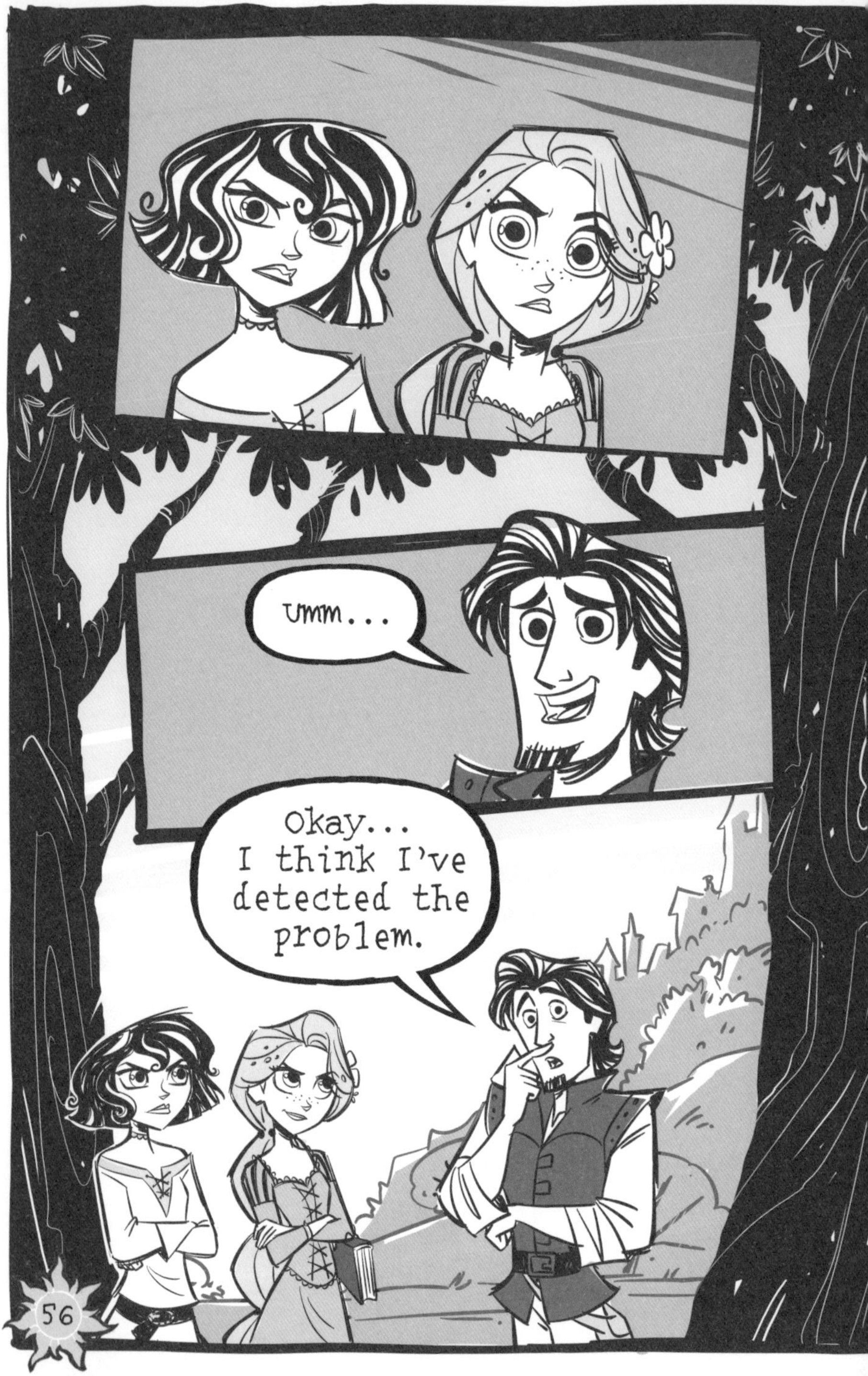
Umm...
Okay... I think I've detected the problem.

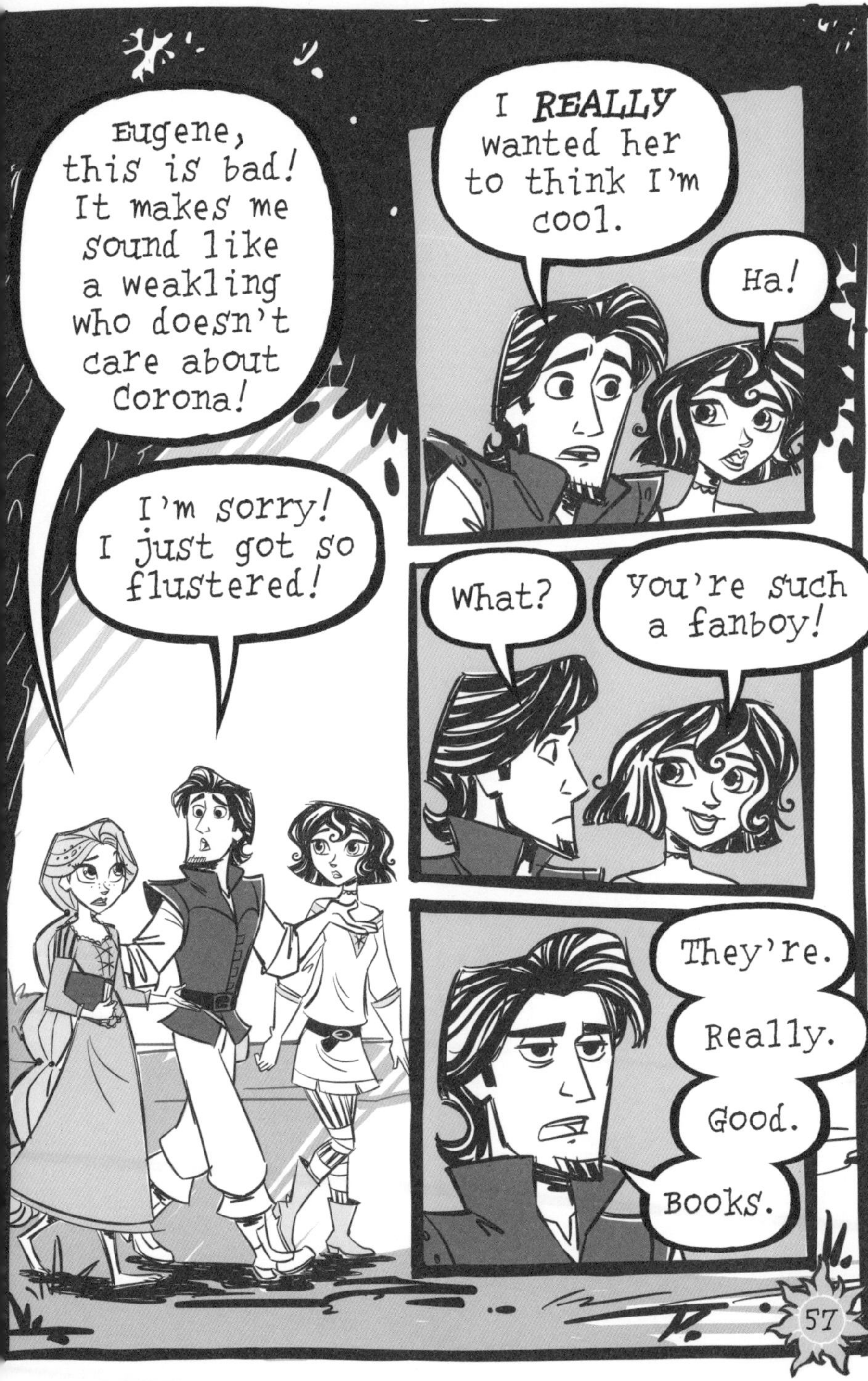

Eugene, this is bad! It makes me sound like a weakling who doesn't care about Corona!
I **REALLY** wanted her to think I'm cool.
Ha!
I'm sorry! I just got so flustered!
What?
You're such a fanboy!
They're.
Really.
Good.
Books.

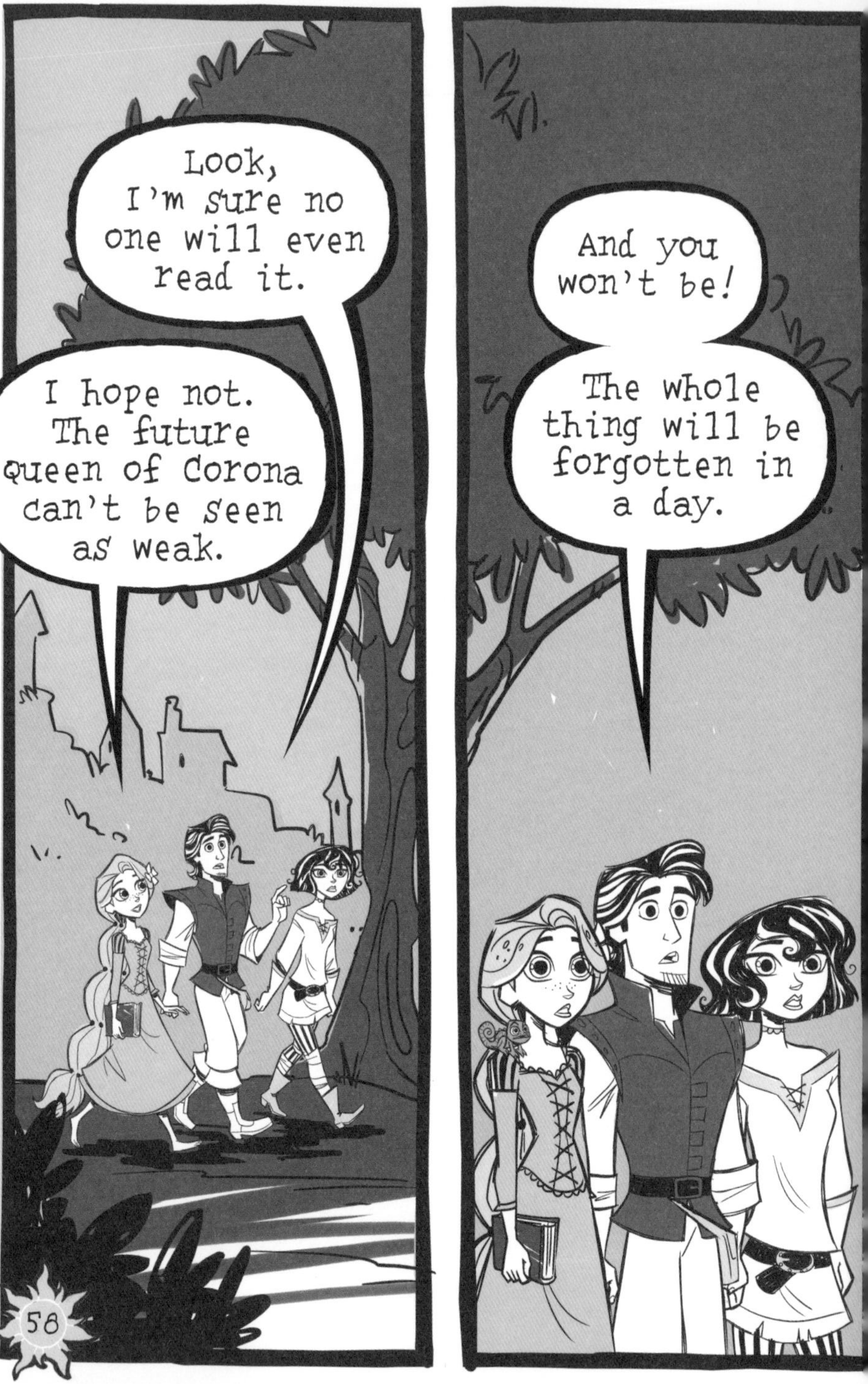
Look, I'm sure no one will even read it.
I hope not. The future queen of Corona can't be seen as weak.
And you won't be!
The whole thing will be forgotten in a day.

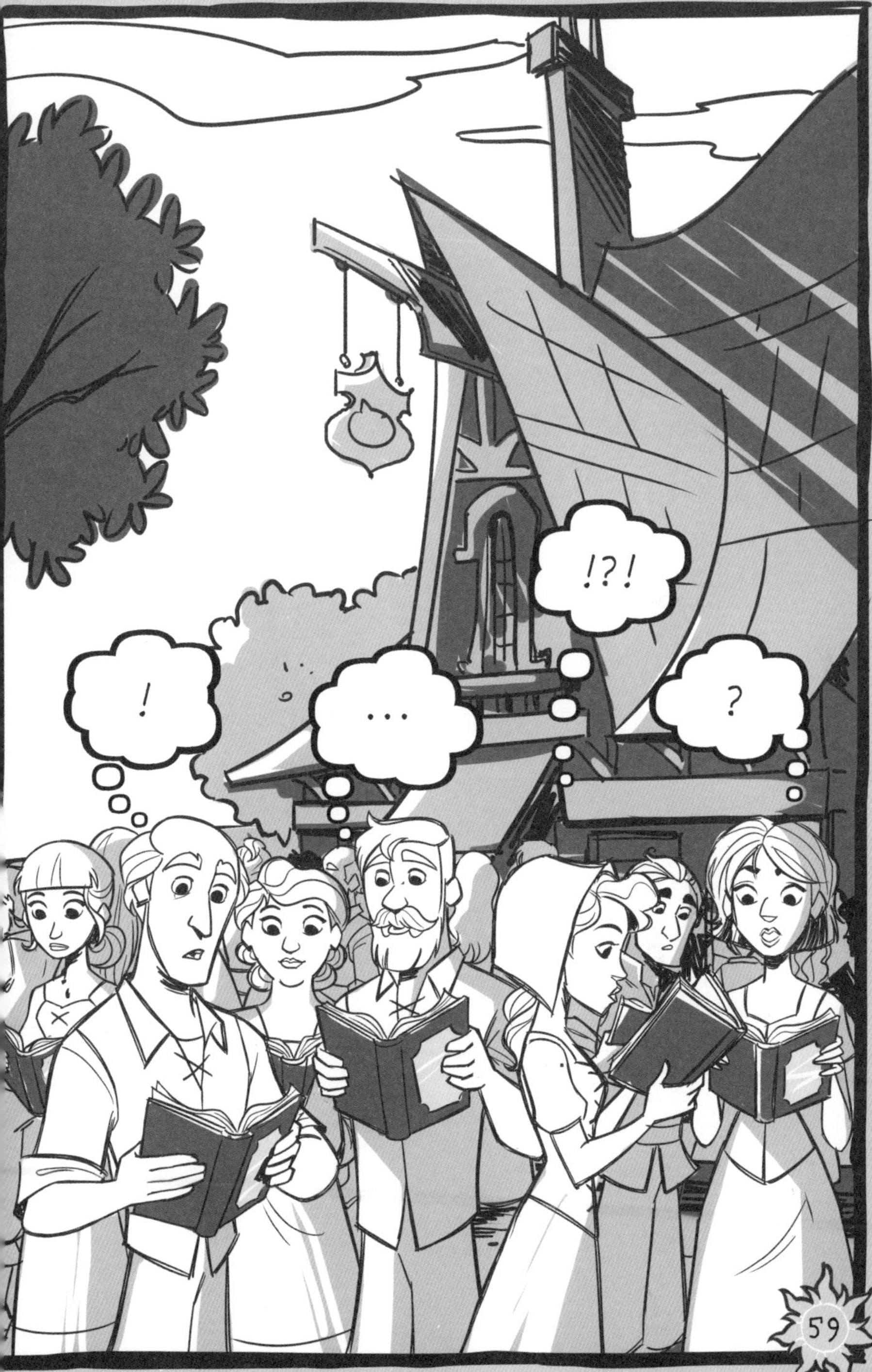
!?!
!
...
?

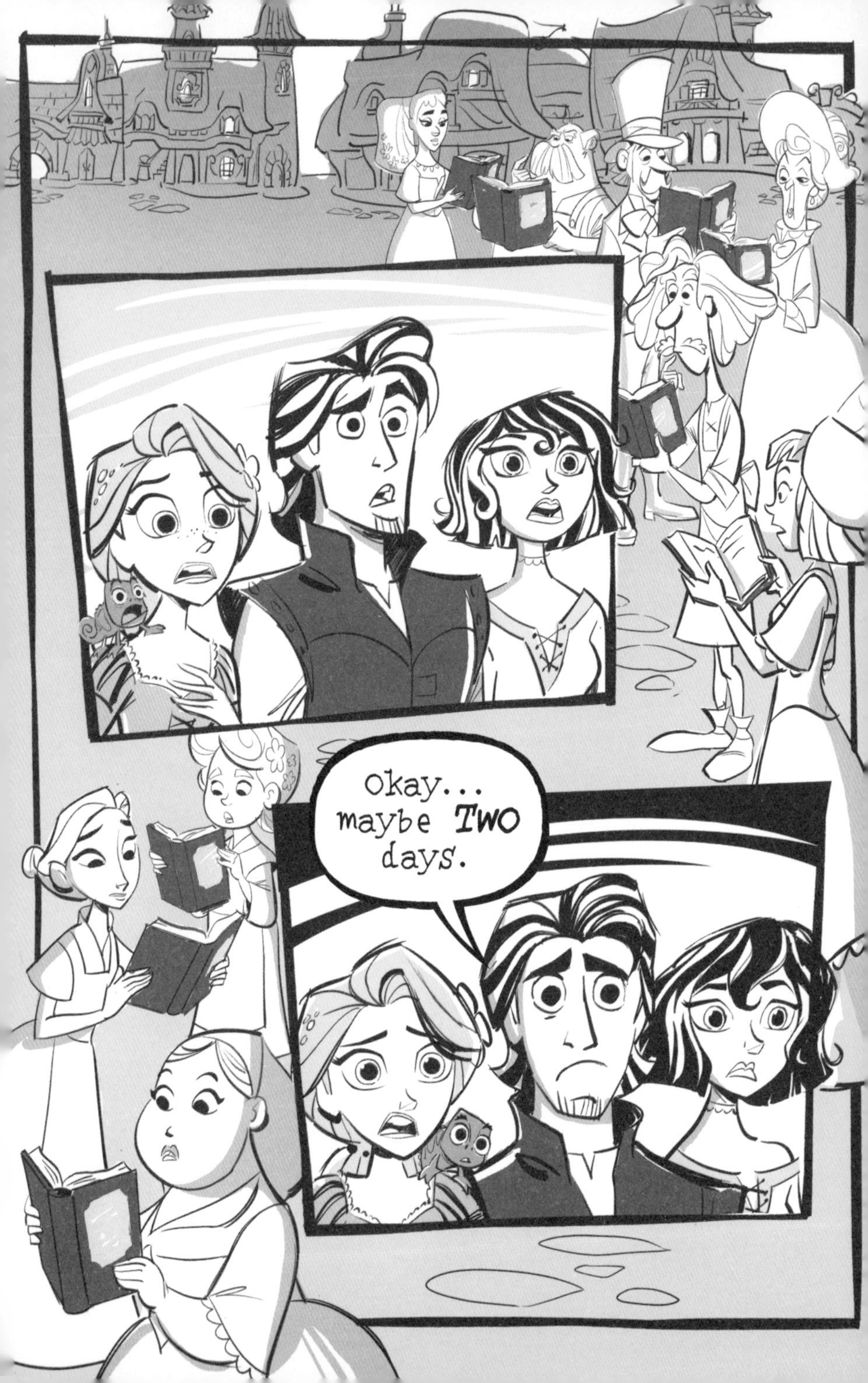
Okay... maybe TWO days.

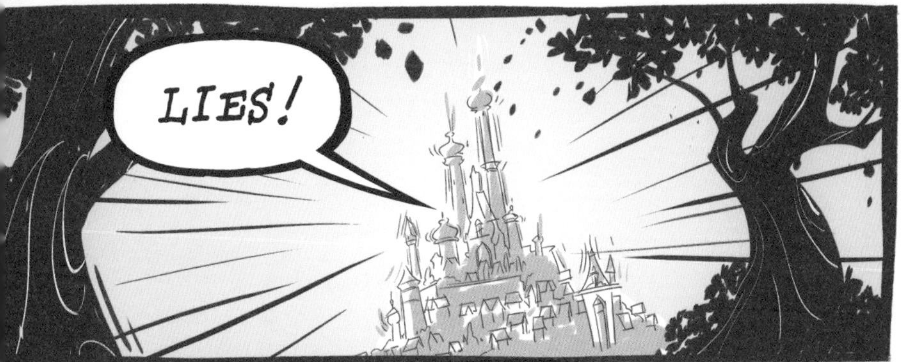
LIES!

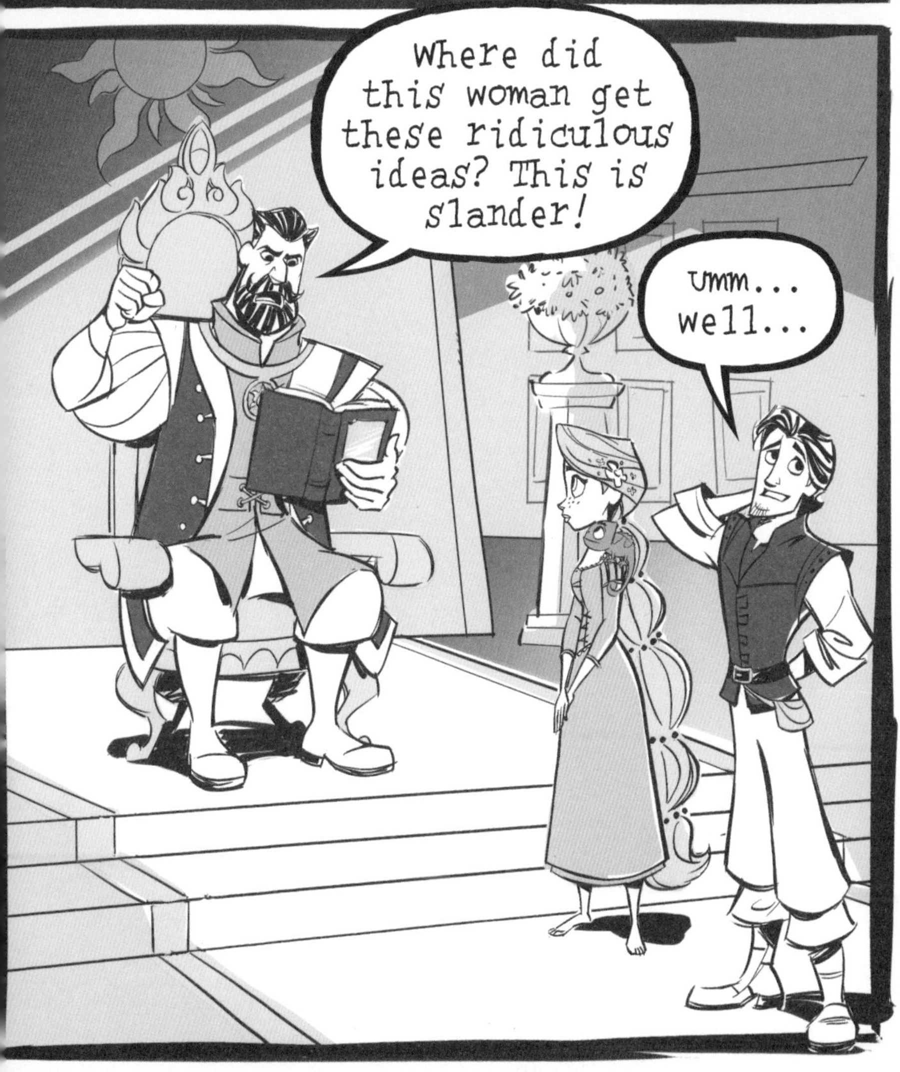
Where did this woman get these ridiculous ideas? This is slander!
Umm... well...

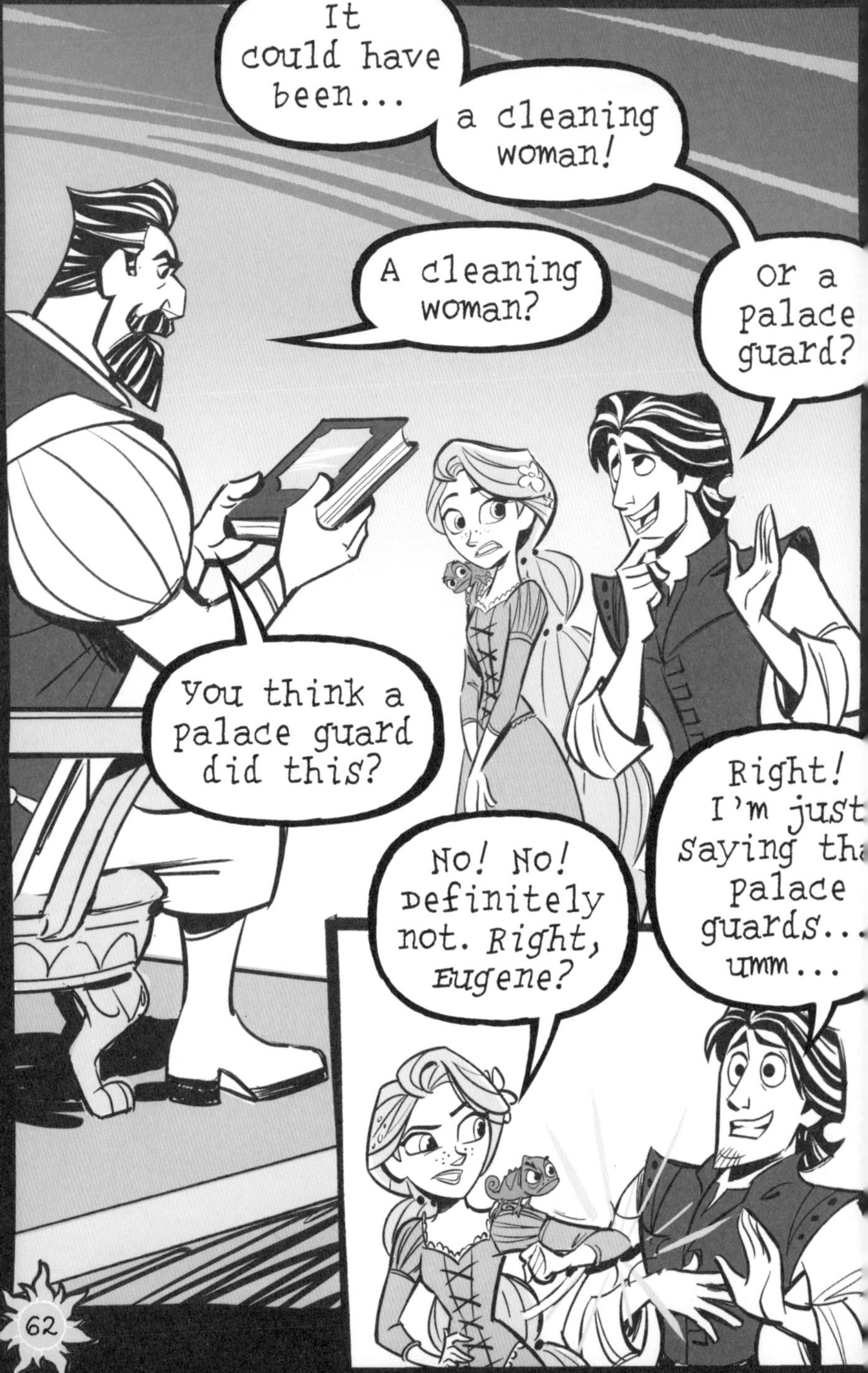
It could have been...
a cleaning woman!
A cleaning woman?
Or a palace guard?
You think a palace guard did this?
No! No! Definitely not. *Right*, Eugene?
Right! I'm just saying th
palace guards... umm...

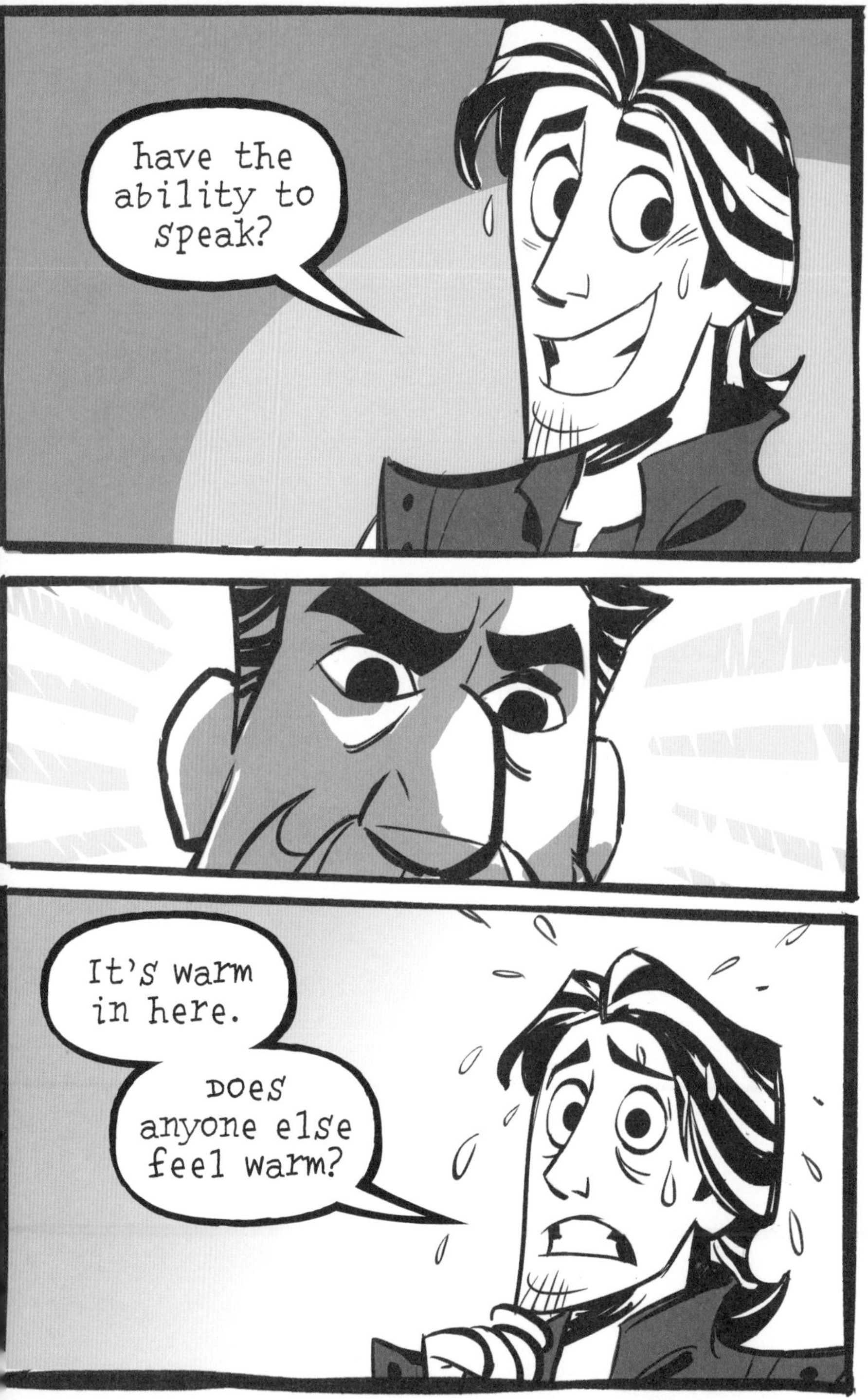
have the ability to speak?
It's warm in here.
Does anyone else feel warm?

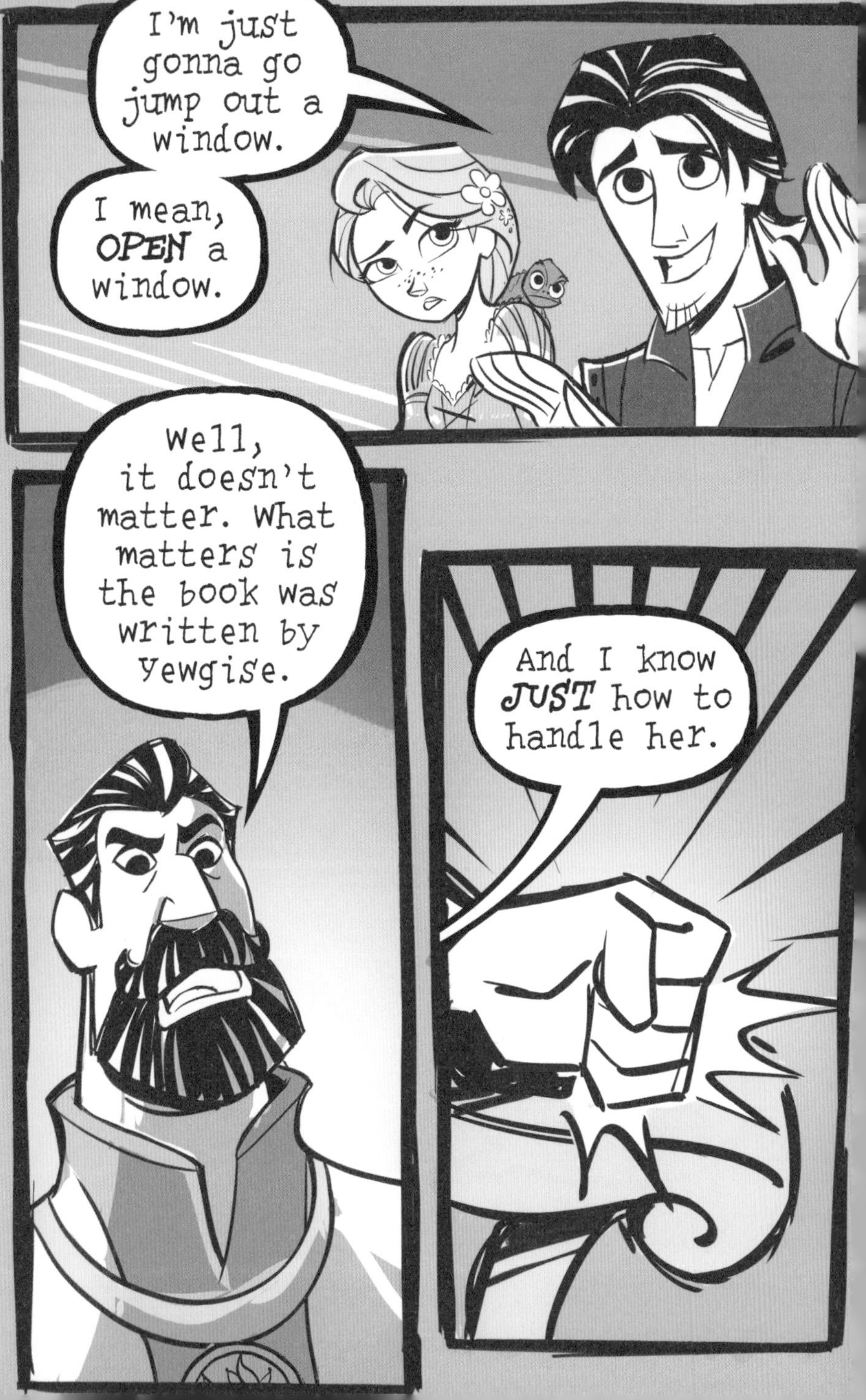
I'm just gonna go jump out a window.
I mean, OPEN a window.
Well, it doesn't matter. What matters is the book was written by Yewgise.
And I know JUST how to handle her.

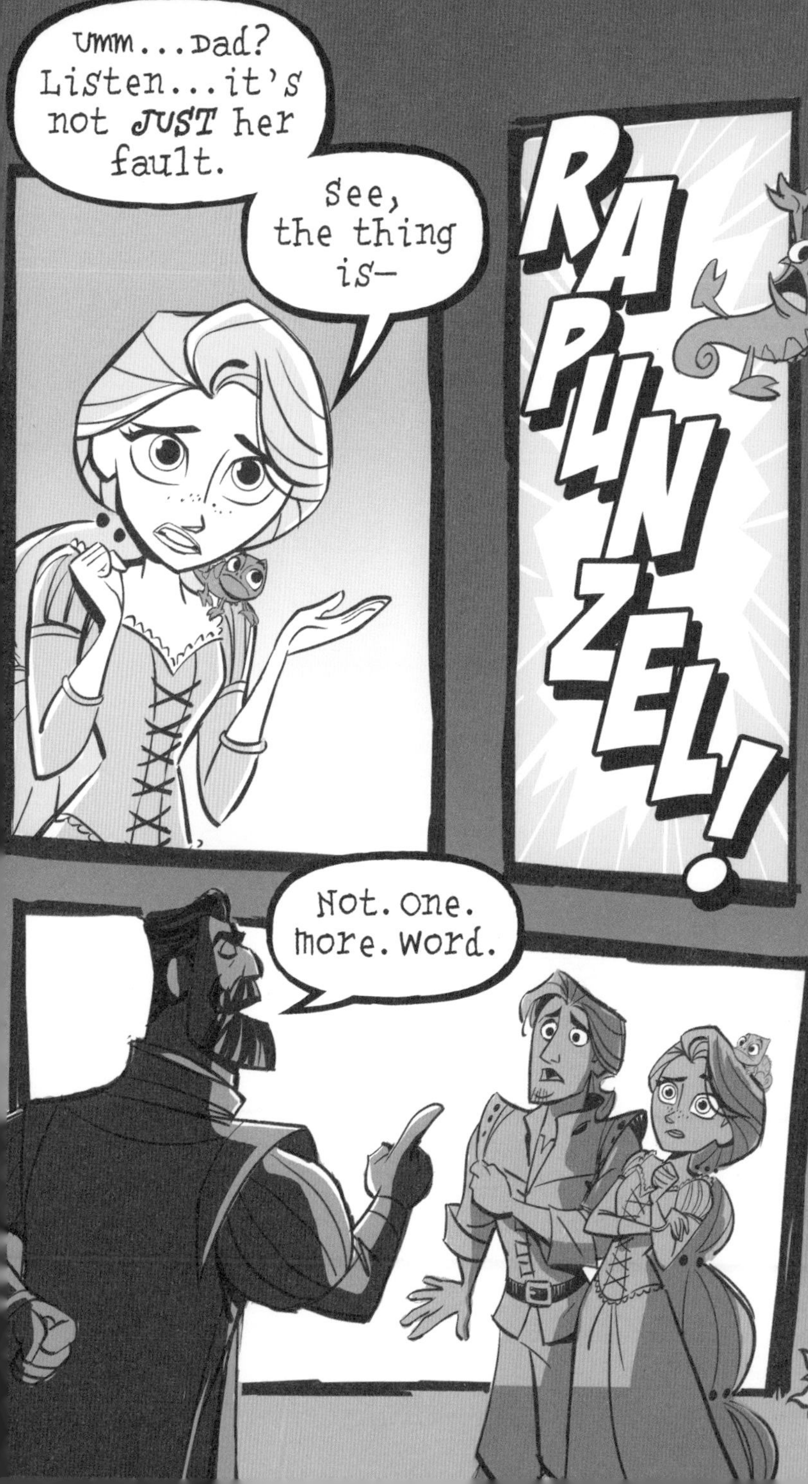
Umm...Dad? Listen...it's not JUST her fault.
See, the thing is—
RAPUNZEL!
Not. One. more. Word.

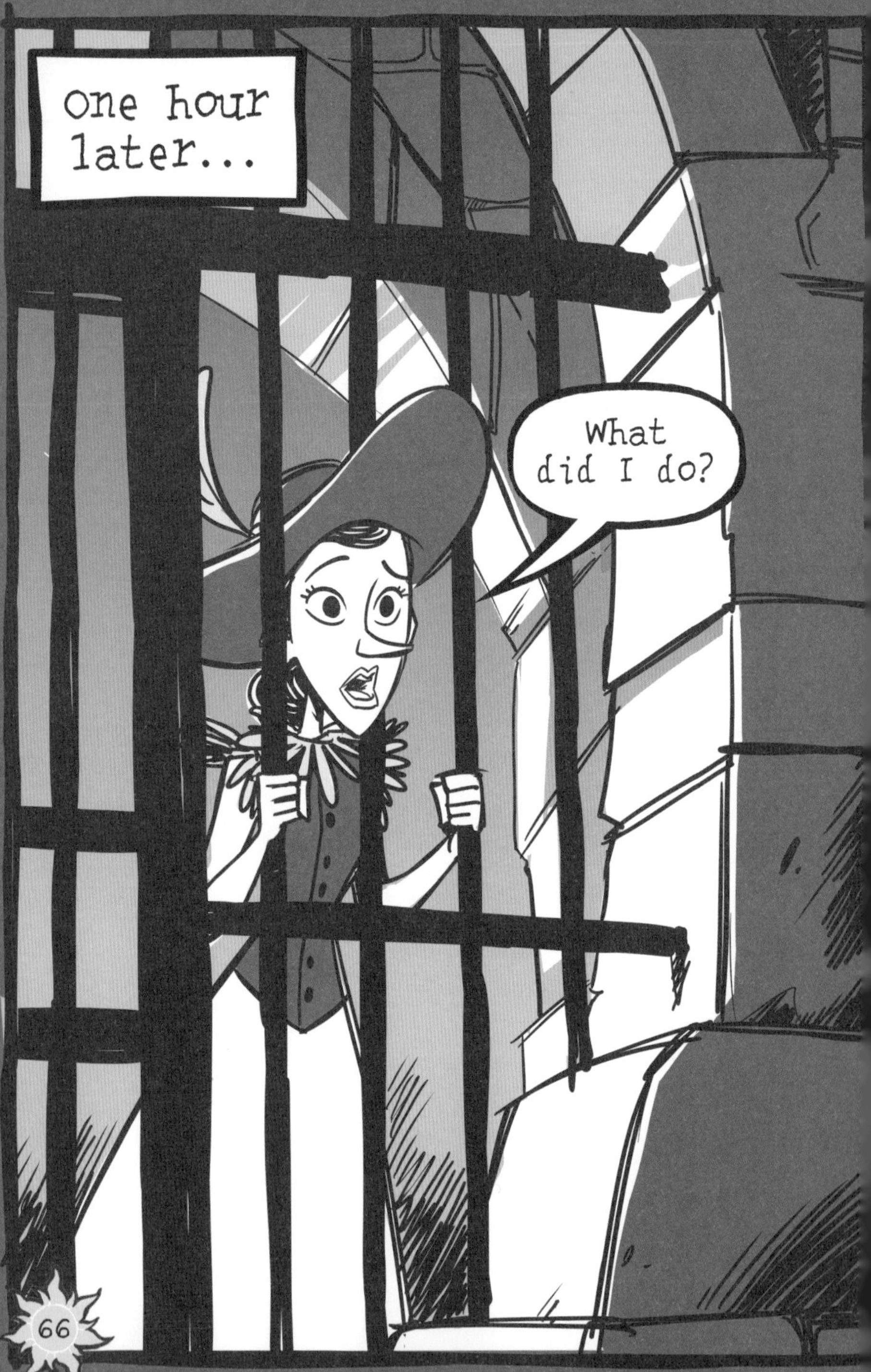
One hour later...
What did I do?

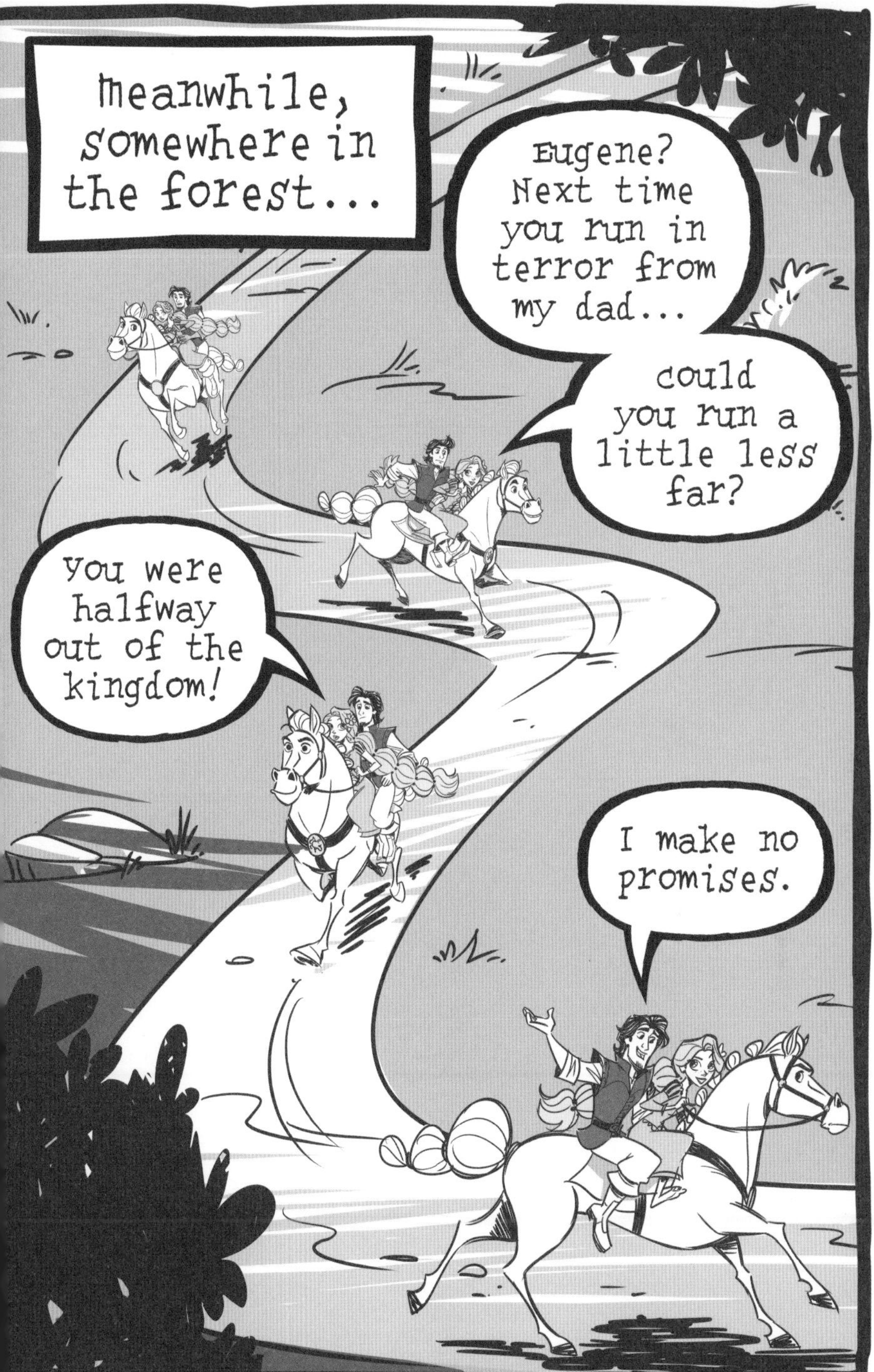
Meanwhile, somewhere in the forest...
Eugene? Next time you run in terror from my dad...
could you run a little less far?
You were halfway out of the kingdom!
I make no promises.

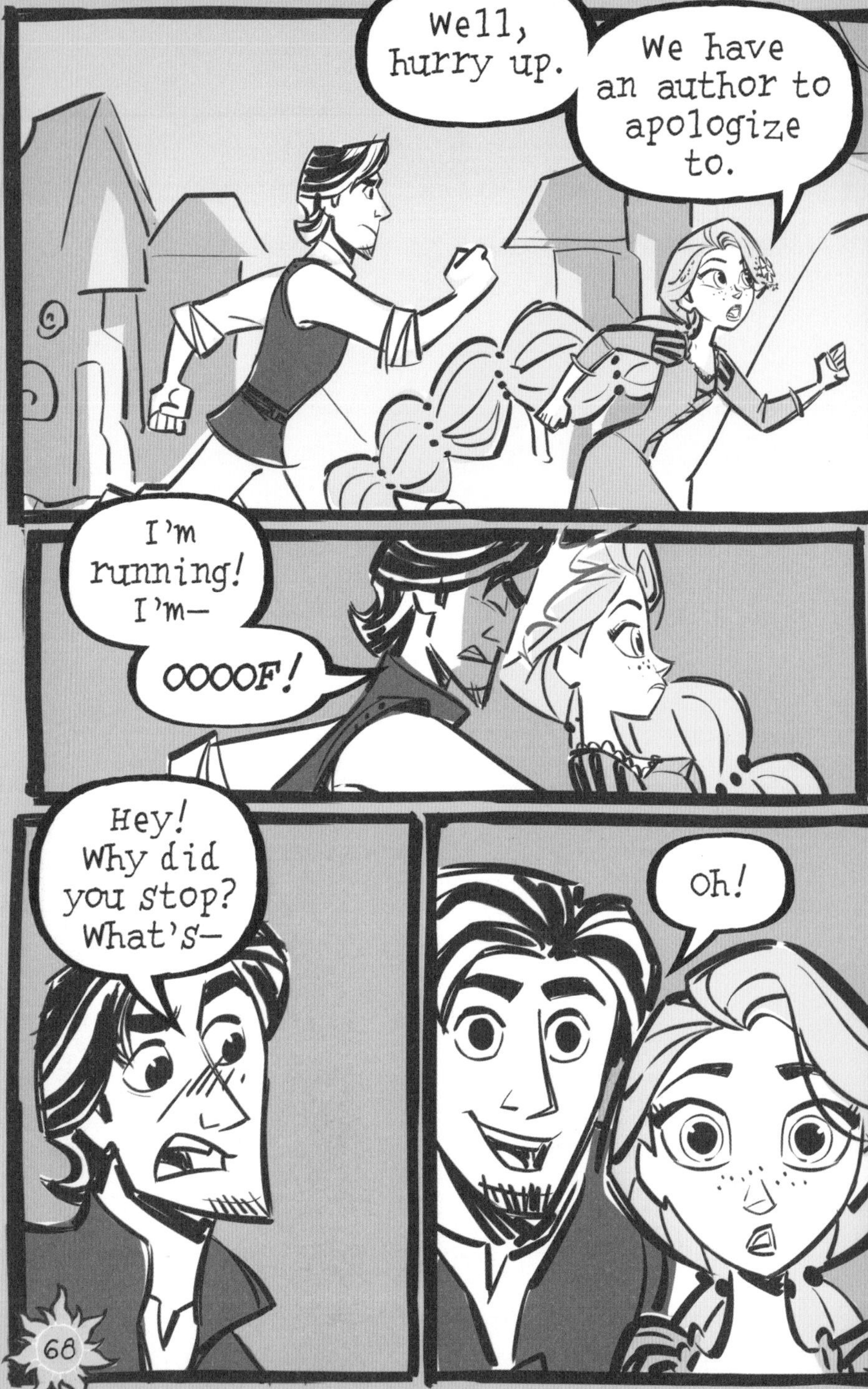
Well, hurry up.
We have an author to apologize to.
I'm running! I'm—
OOOOF!
Hey! Why did you stop? What's—
Oh!

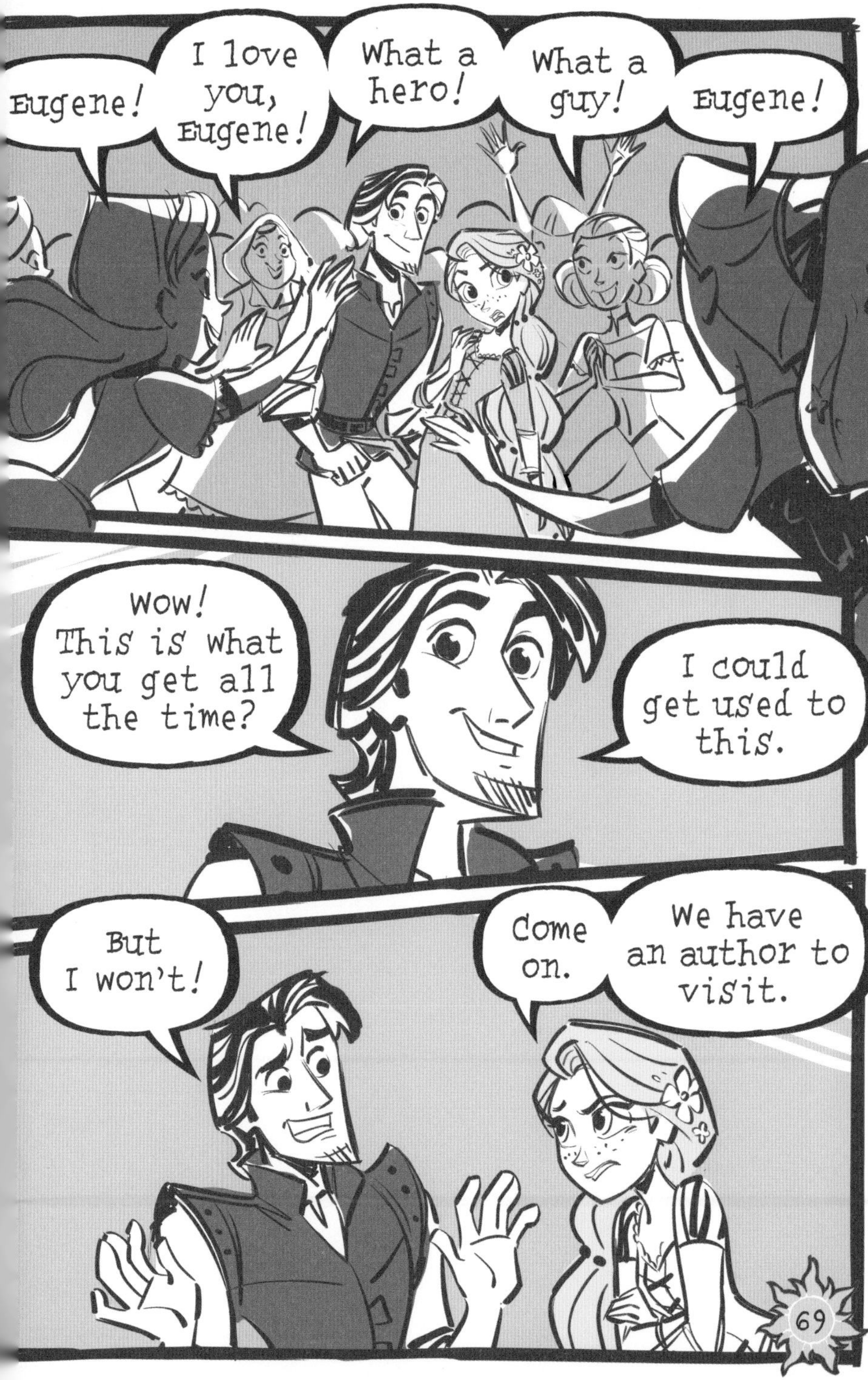
Eugene!
I love you, Eugene!
What a hero!
What a guy!
Eugene!
Wow! This is what you get all the time?
I could get used to this.
But I won't!
Come on.
We have an author to visit.

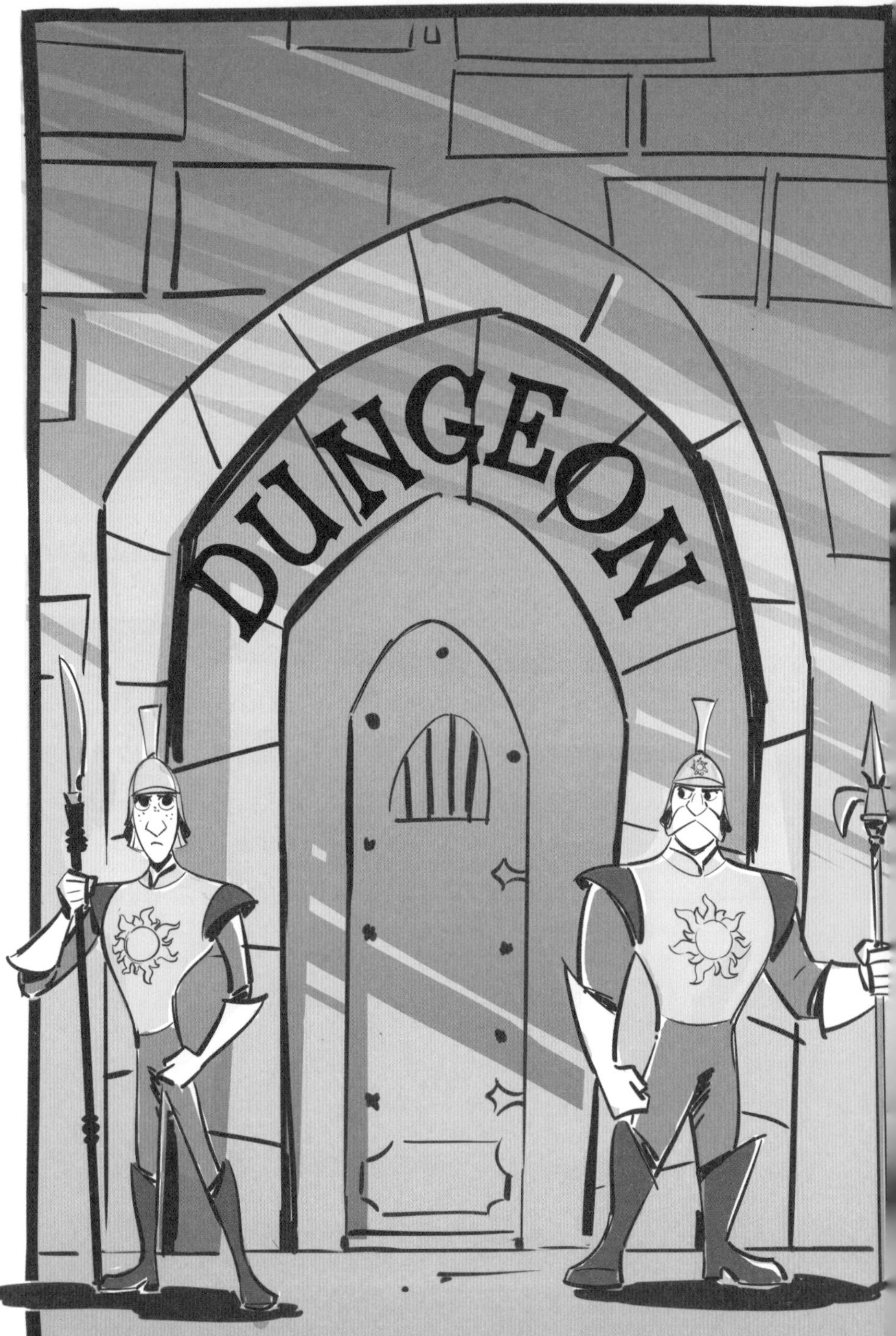
DUNGEON

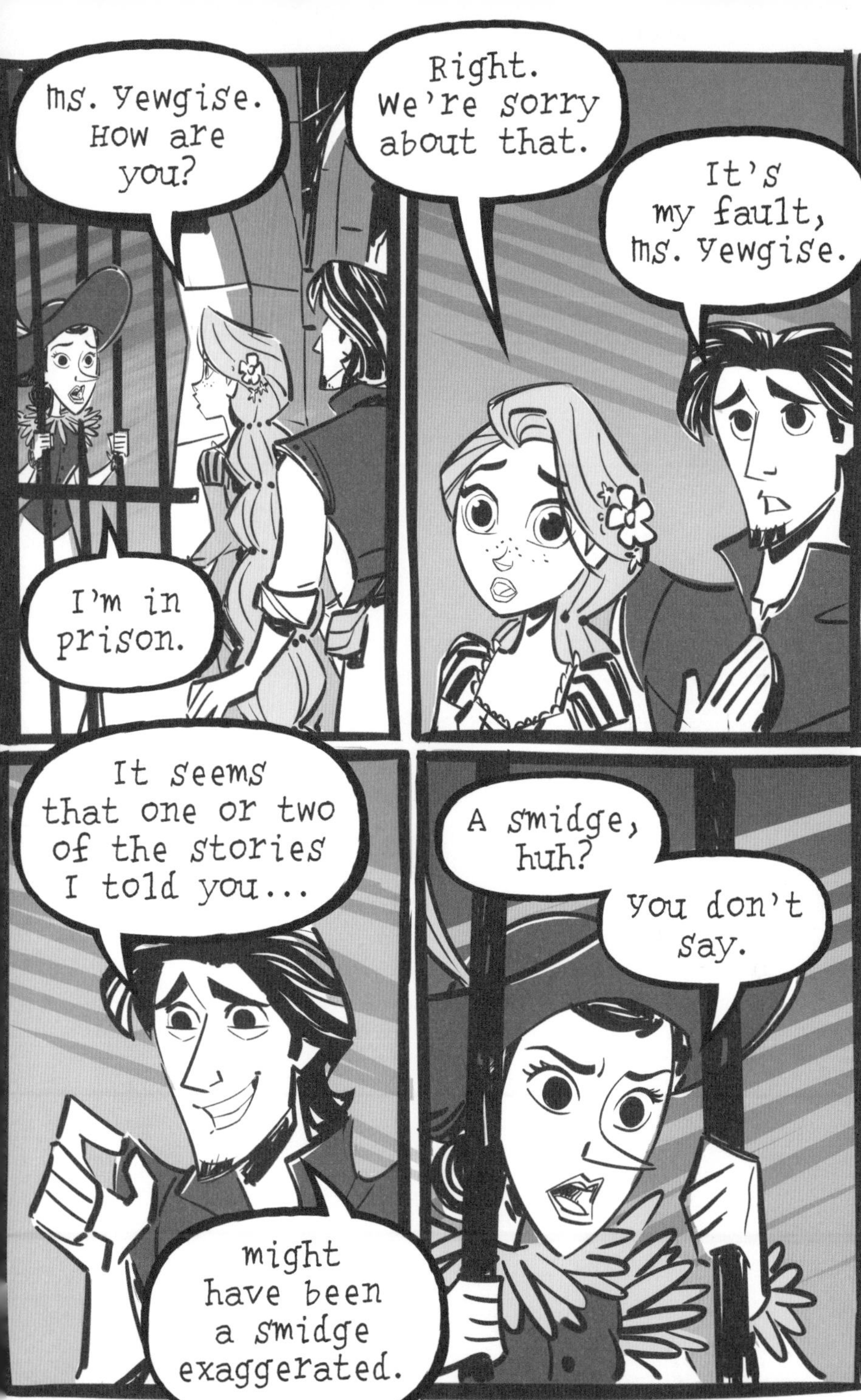
Ms. Yewgise. How are you?
I'm in prison.
Right. We're sorry about that.
It's my fault, Ms. Yewgise.
It seems that one or two of the stories I told you...
might have been a smidge exaggerated.
A smidge, huh?
You don't say.

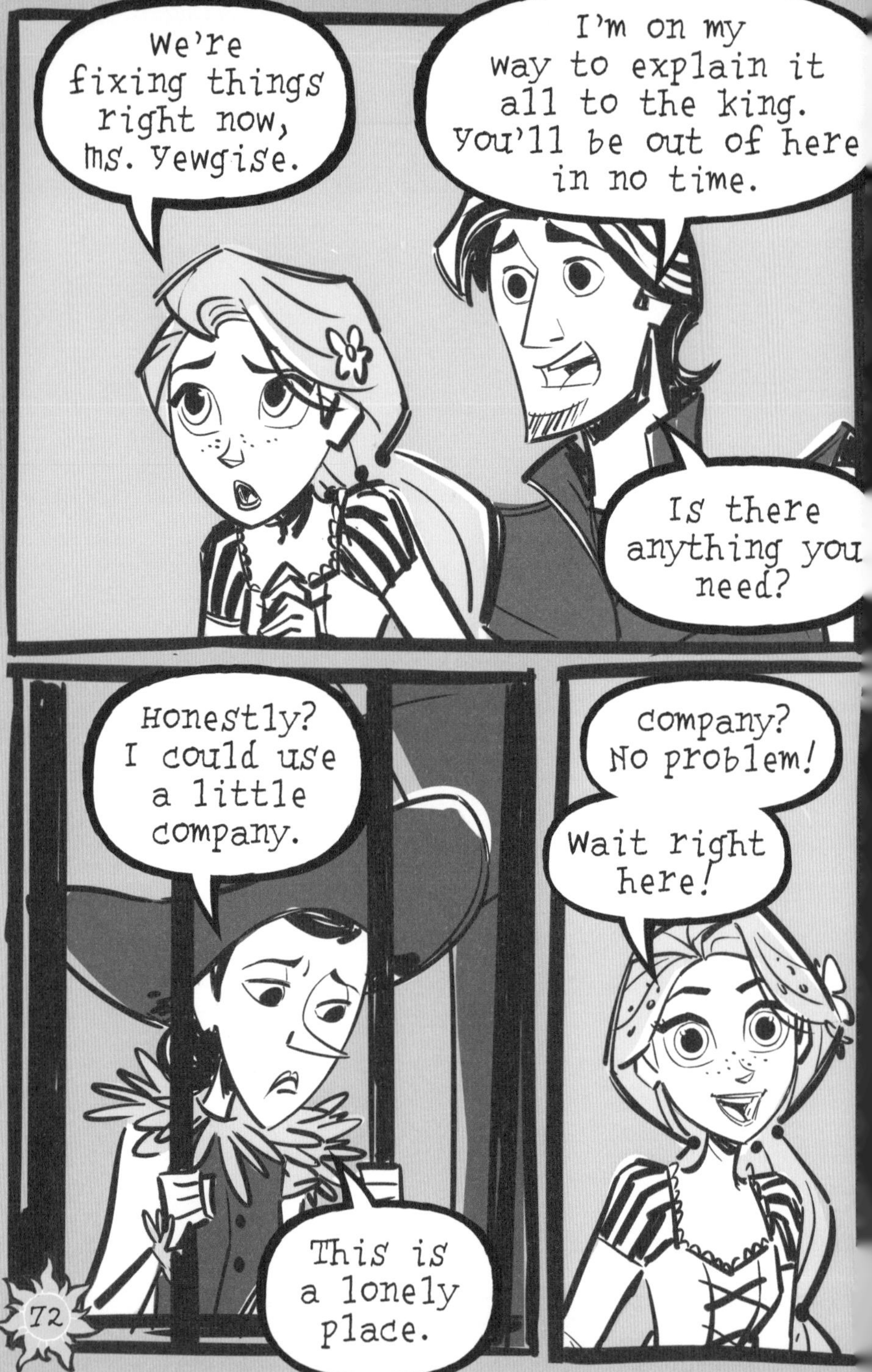

We're fixing things right now, Ms. Yewgise.
I'm on my way to explain it all to the king. You'll be out of here in no time.
Is there anything you need?
Honestly? I could use a little company.
This is a lonely place.
Company? No problem!
Wait right here!

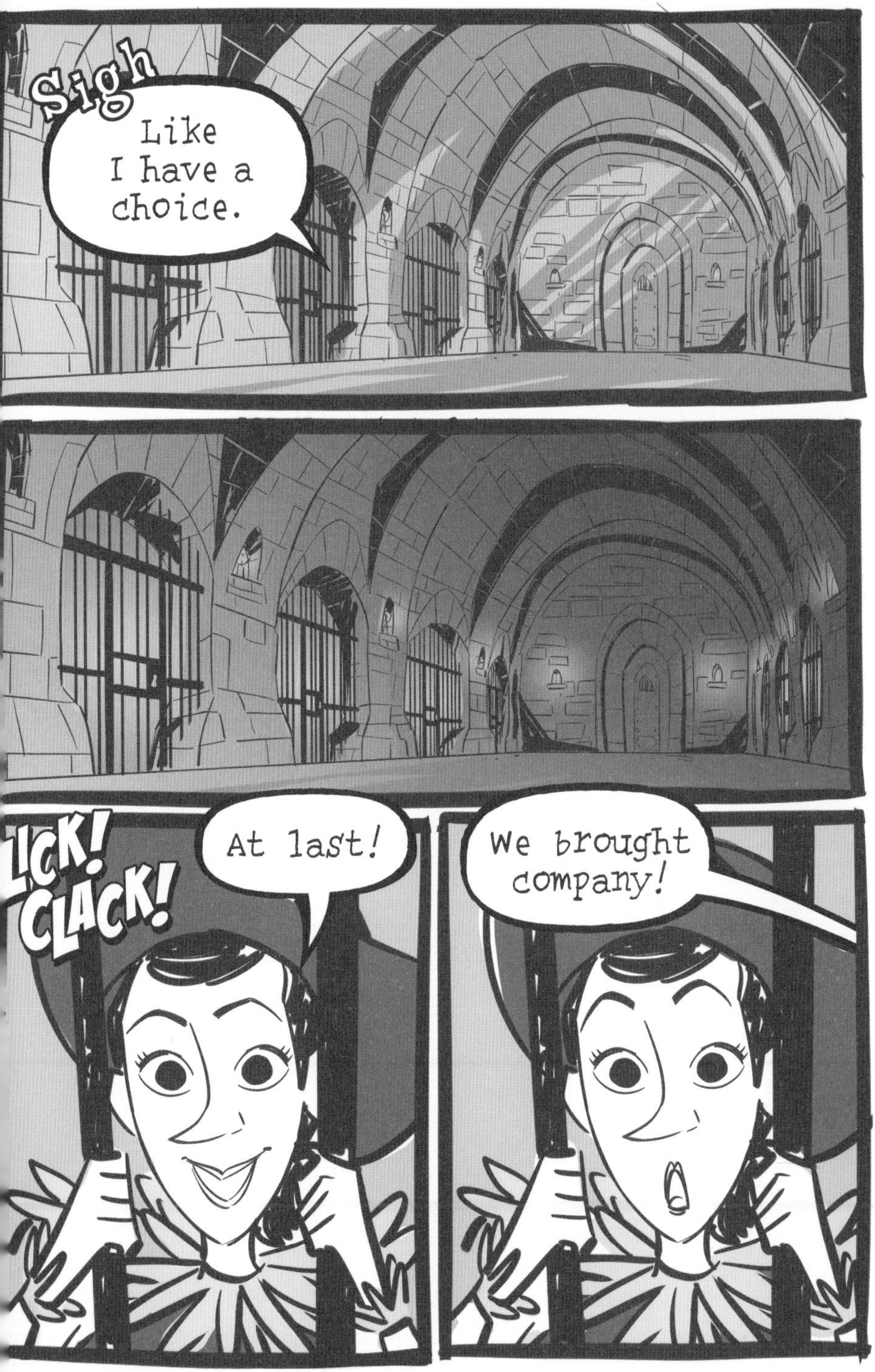
Sigh
Like I have a choice.
CLACK!
At last!
We brought company!

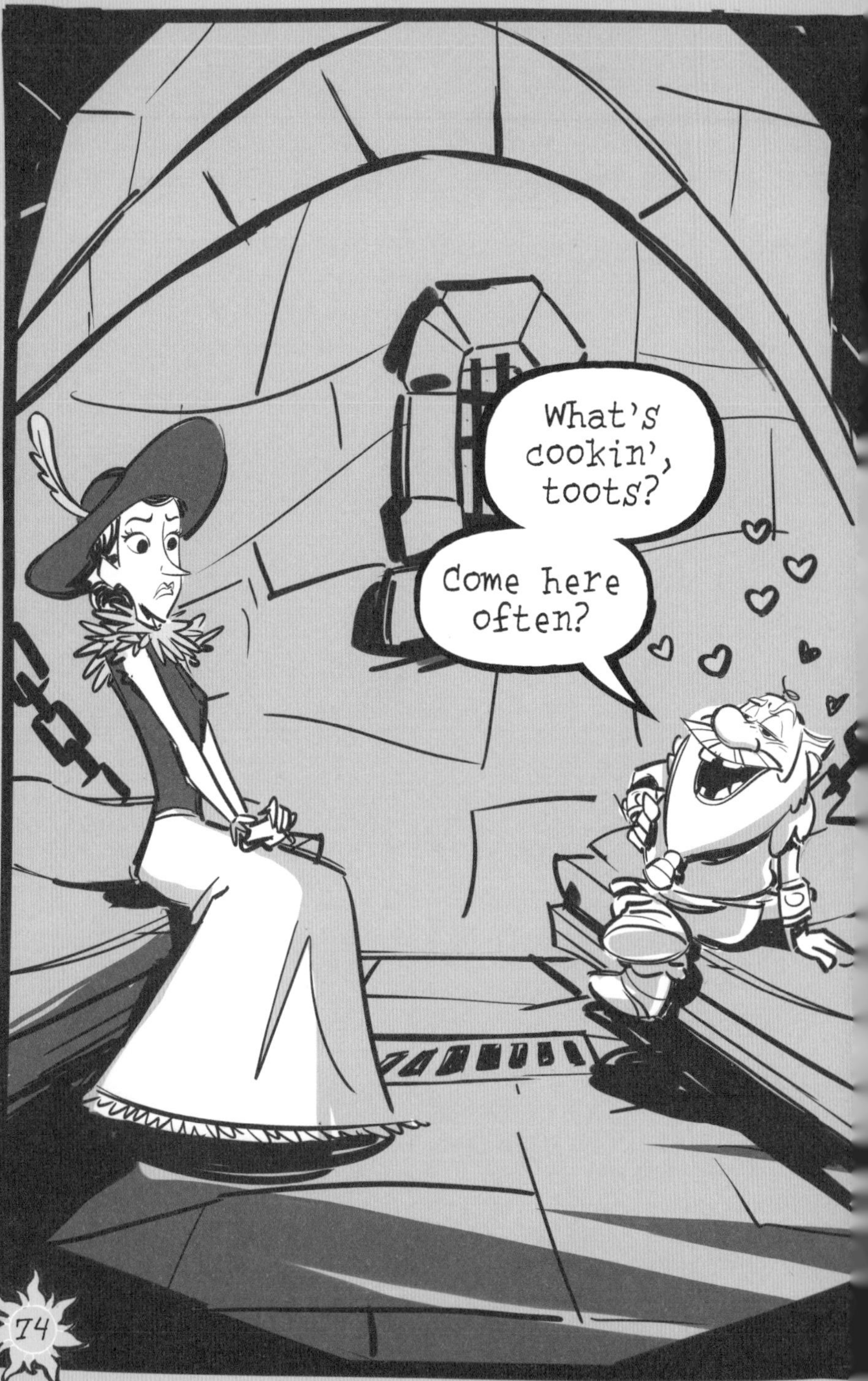
What's cookin', toots?
Come here often?

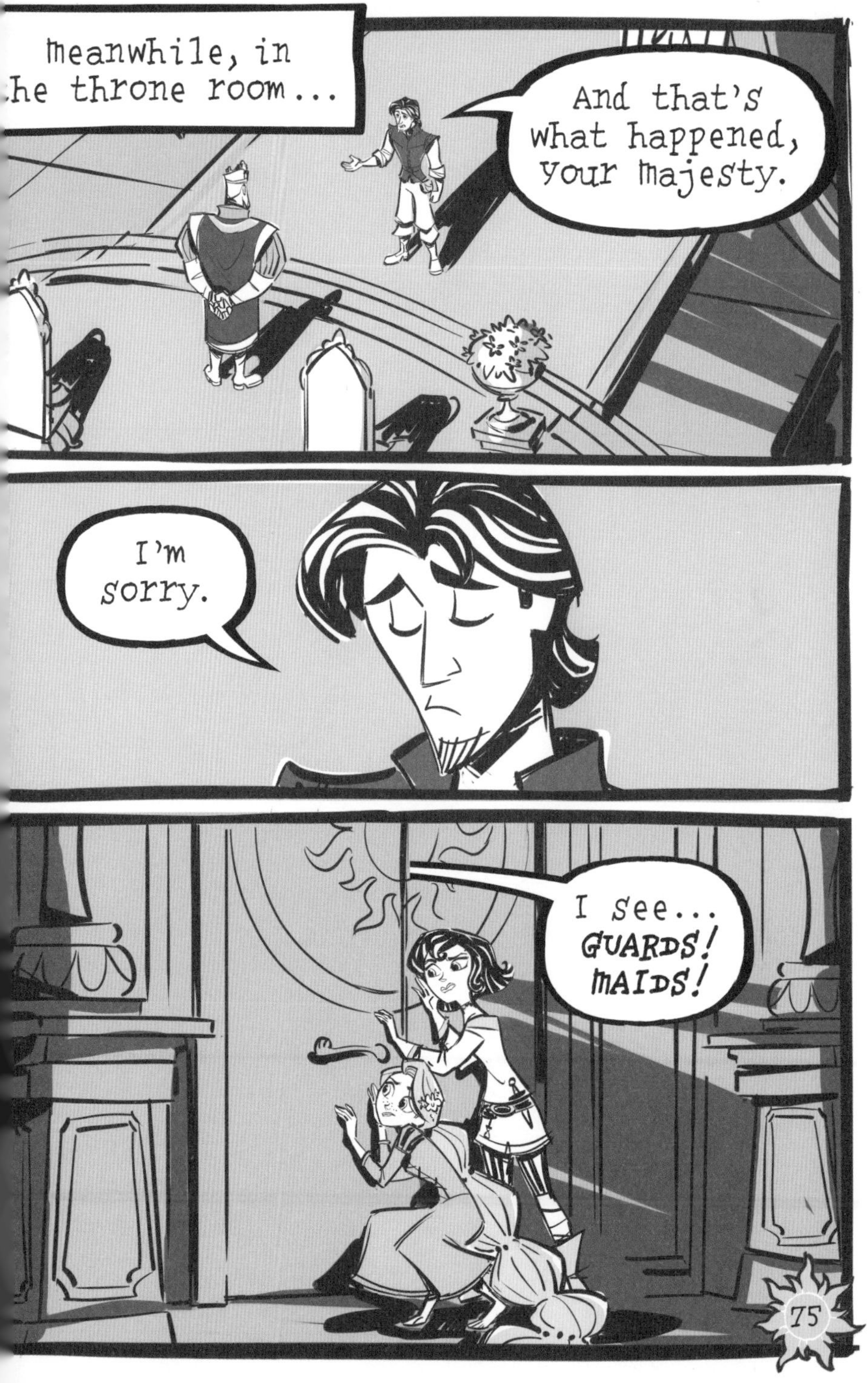
Meanwhile, in the throne room...
And that's what happened, your majesty.
I'm sorry.
I see... GUARDS! MAIDS!

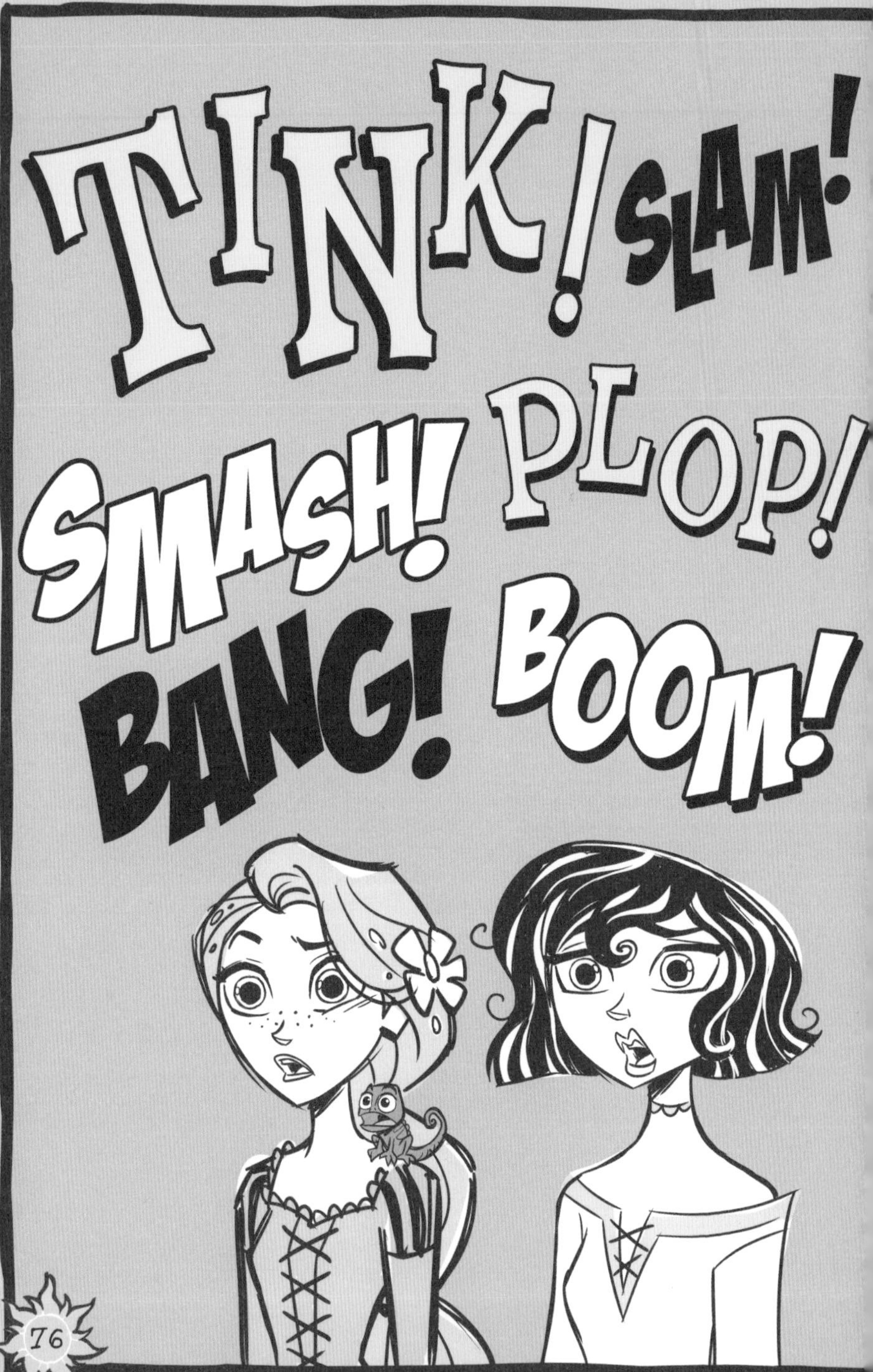
TINK!
SLAM!
SMASH!
PLOP!
BANG!
BOOM!

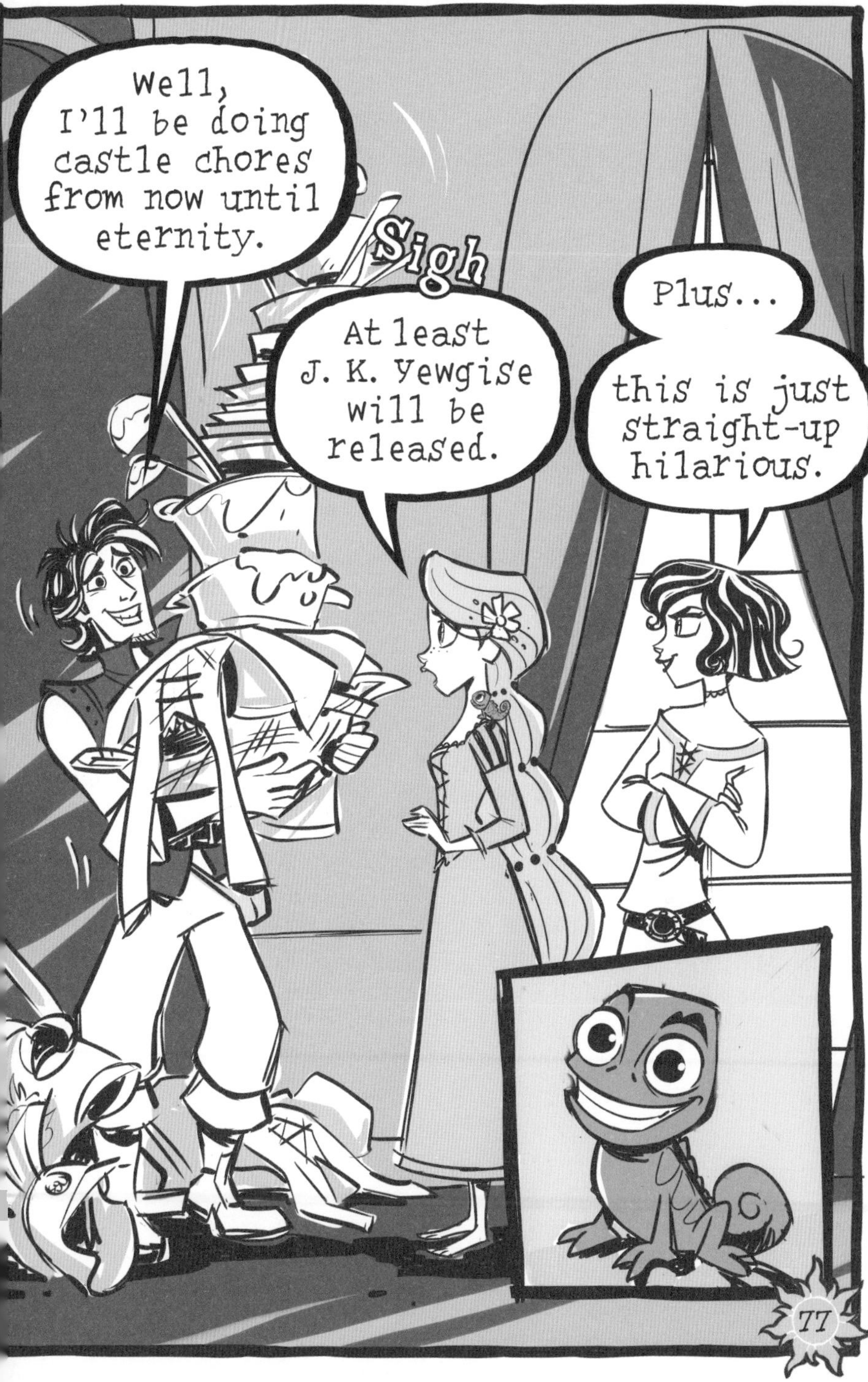
Well, I'll be doing castle chores from now until eternity.
Sigh
At least J. K. Yewgise will be released.
Plus...
this is just straight-up hilarious.

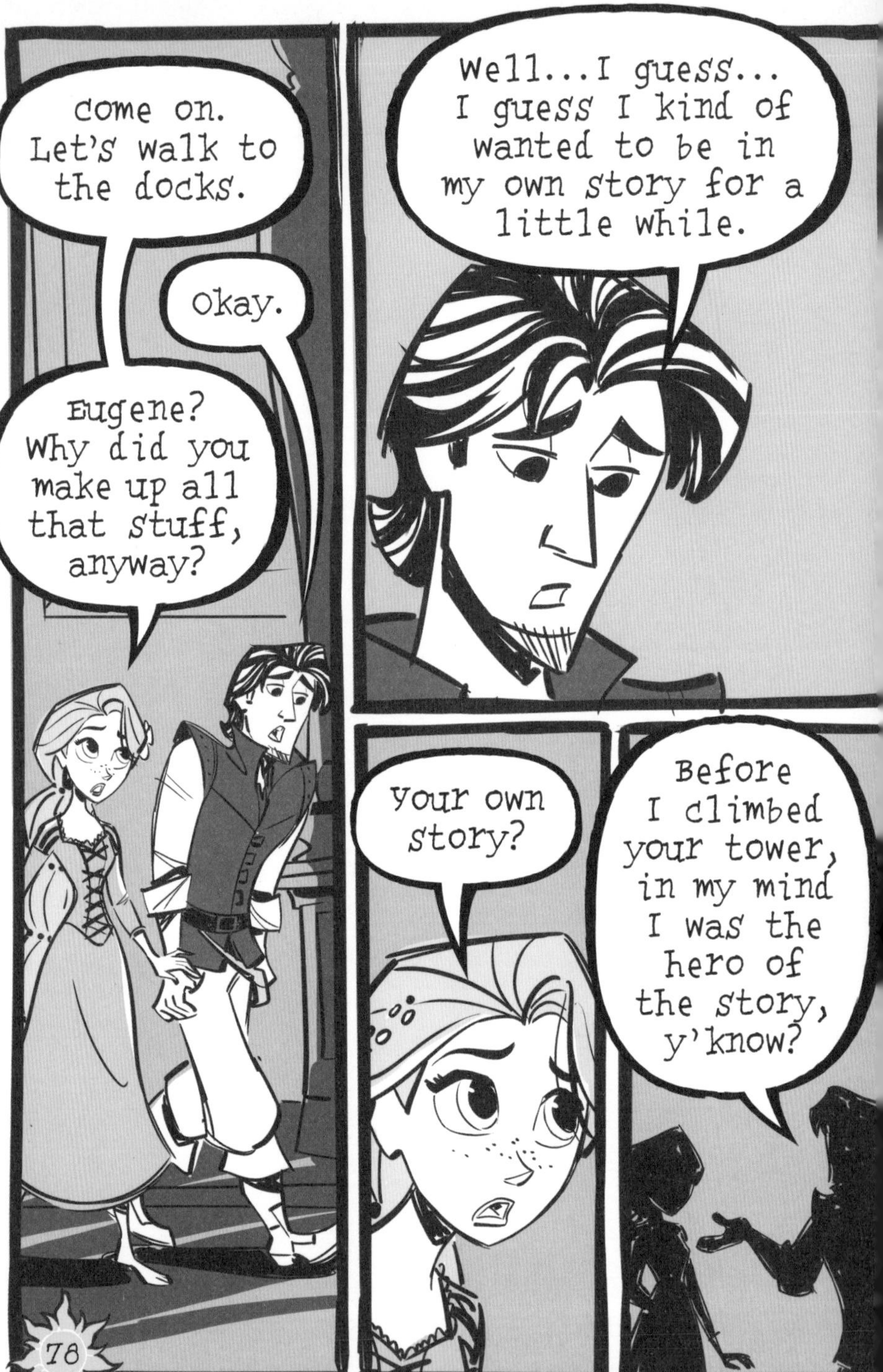
Come on. Let's walk to the docks.
Okay.
Eugene? Why did you make up all that stuff, anyway?
Well...I guess... I guess I kind of wanted to be in my own story for a little while.
Your own story?
Before I climbed your tower, in my mind I was the hero of the story, y'know?

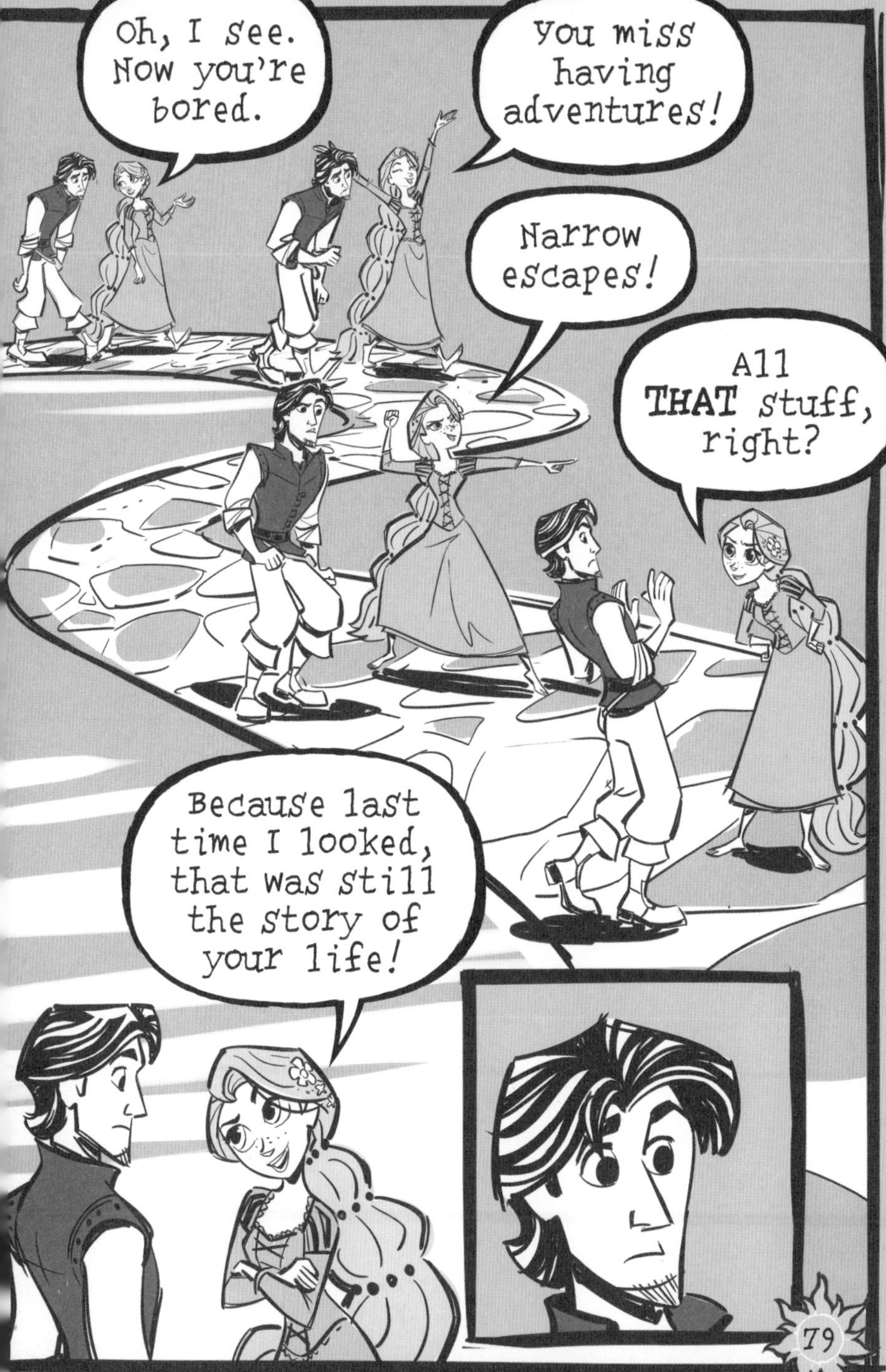
Oh, I see. Now you're bored.
You miss having adventures!
Narrow escapes!
All THAT stuff, right?
Because last time I looked, that was still the story of your life!

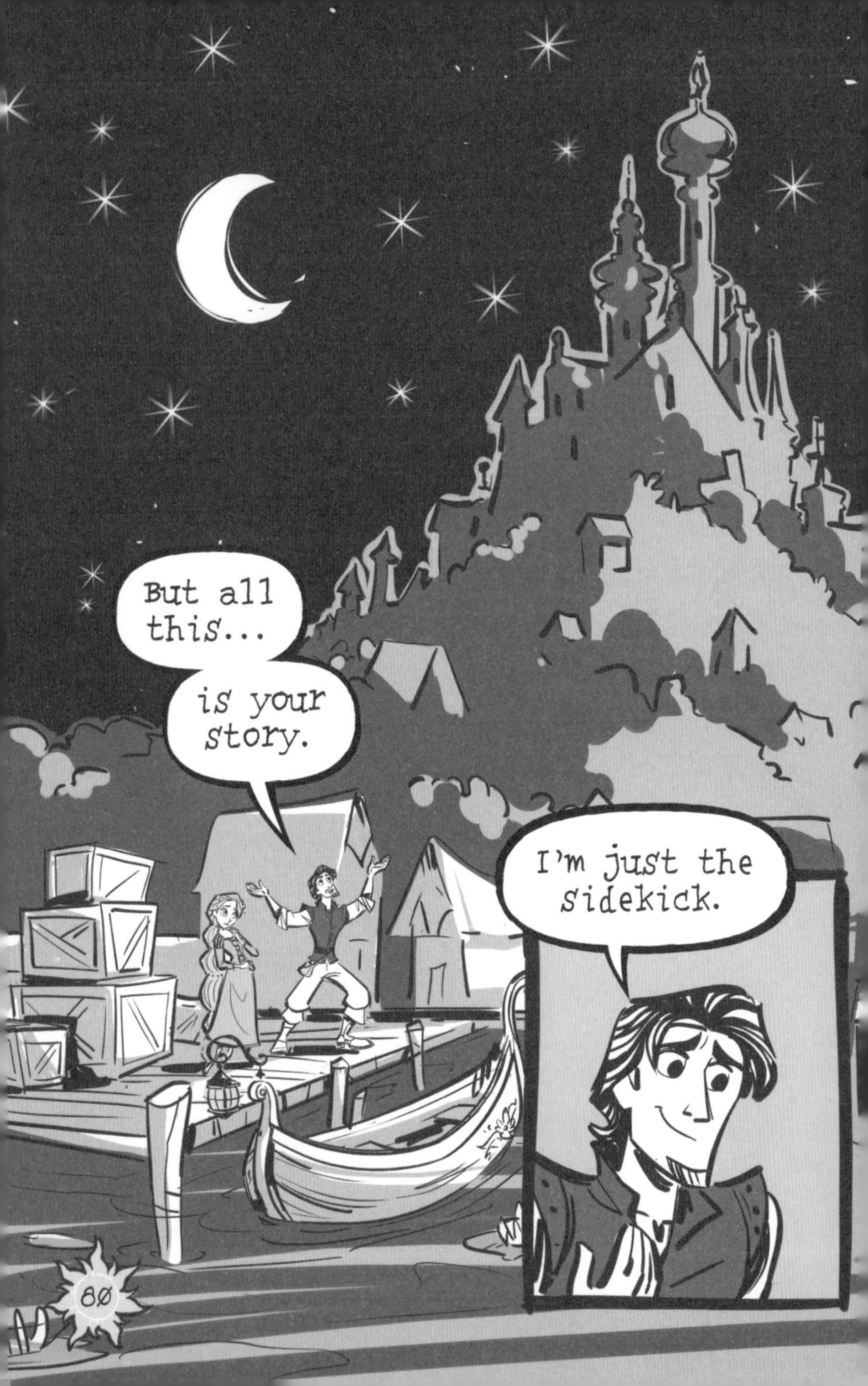
But all this...
is your story.
I'm just the sidekick.

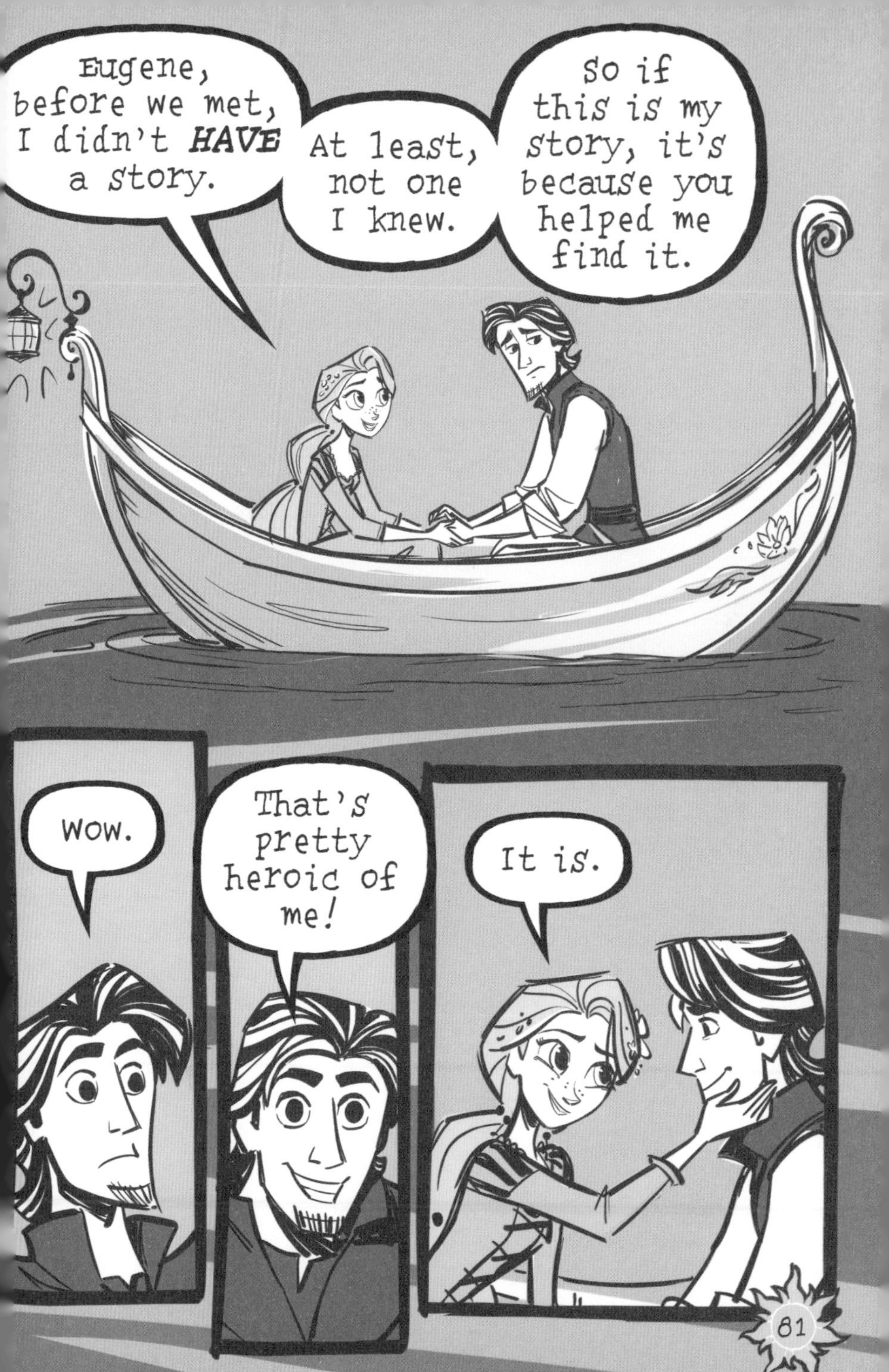
Eugene, before we met, I didn't ***HAVE*** a story.
At least, not one I knew.
So if *this is* my *story*, it's because you helped me find it.
WOW.
That's pretty heroic of me!
It *is*.

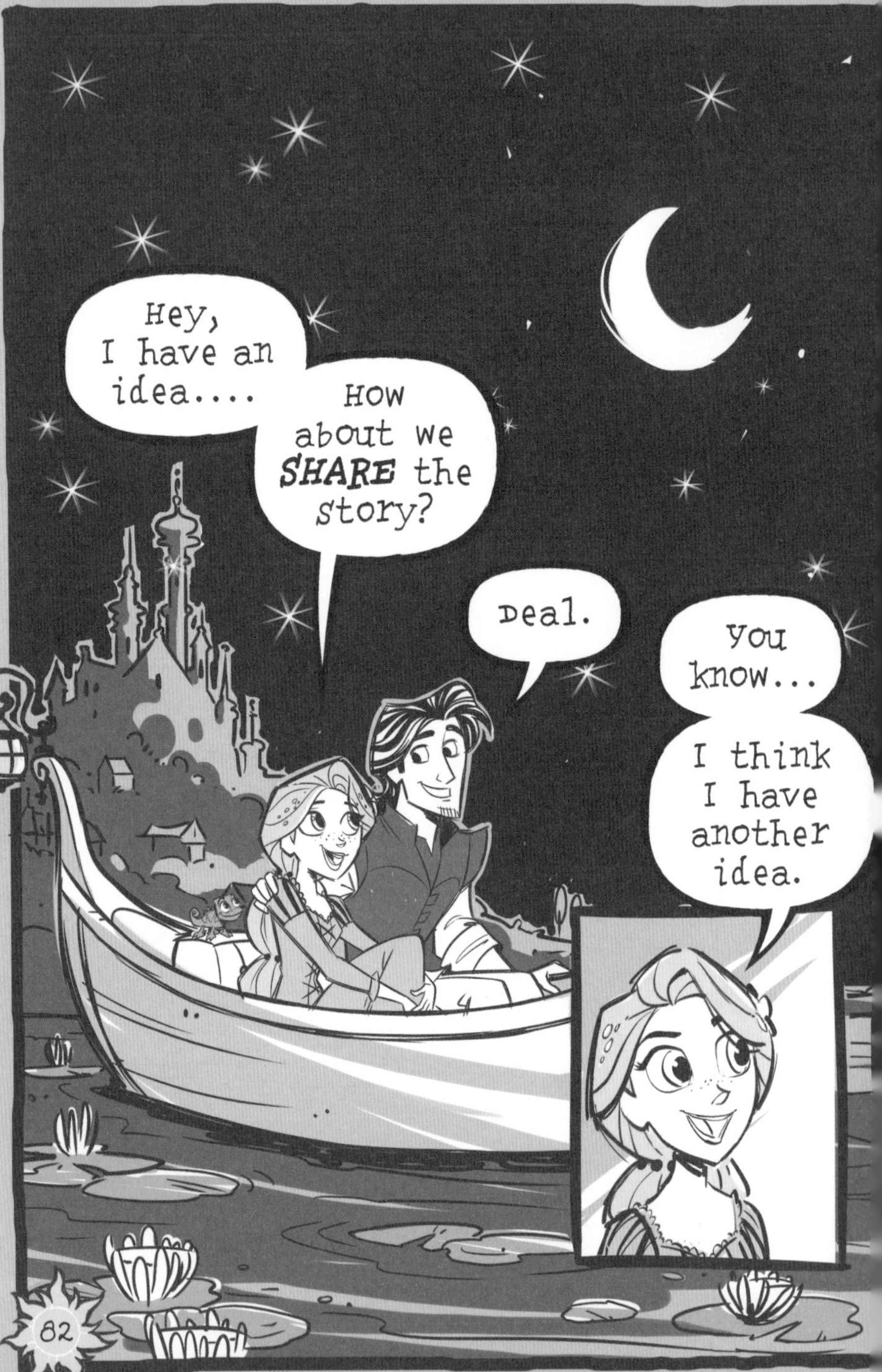
Hey, I have an idea....
How about we SHARE the story?
Deal.
You know...
I think I have another idea.

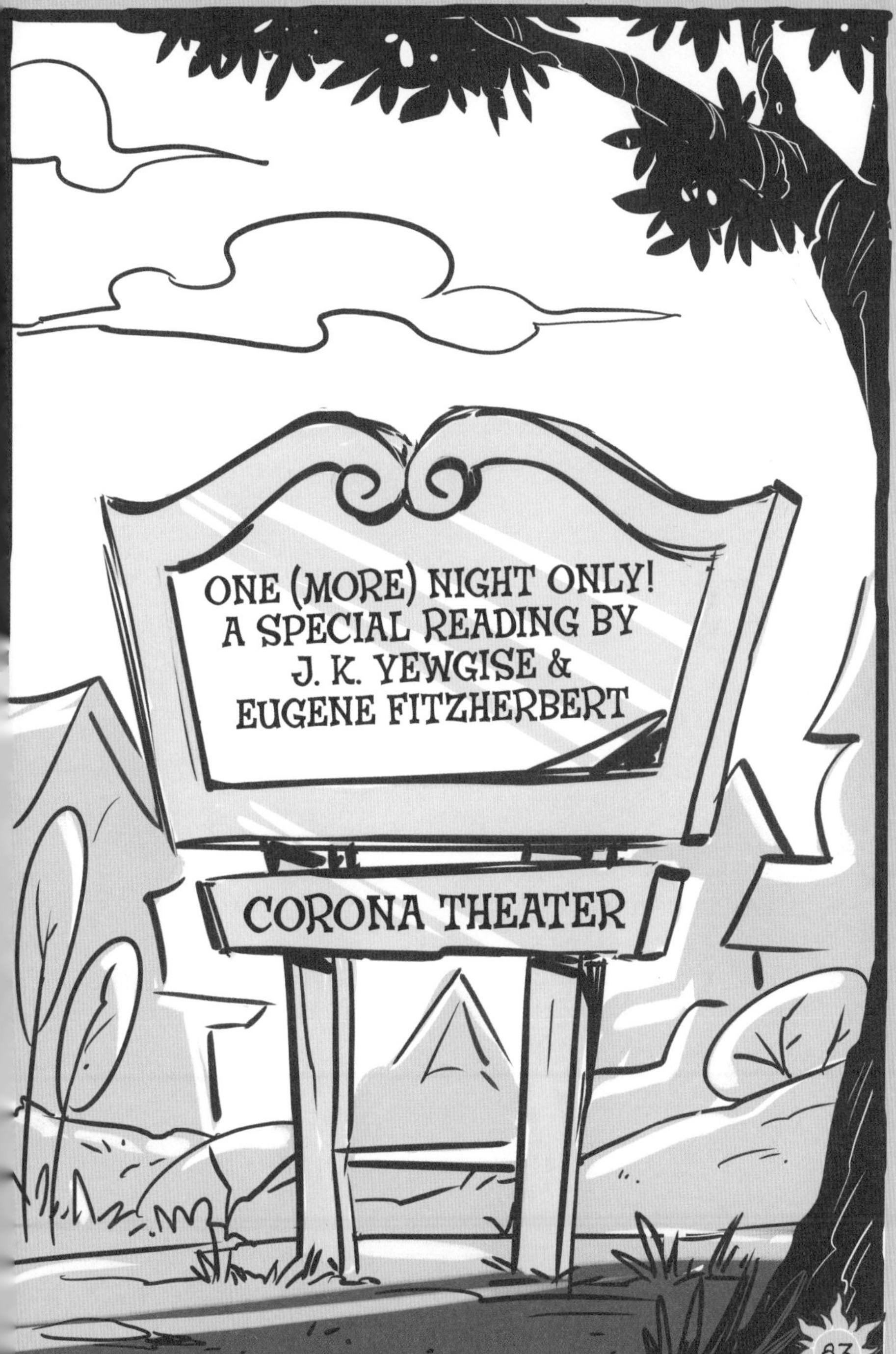
ONE (MORE) NIGHT ONLY!
A SPECIAL READING BY
J. K. YEWGISE &
EUGENE FITZHERBERT
CORONA THEATER

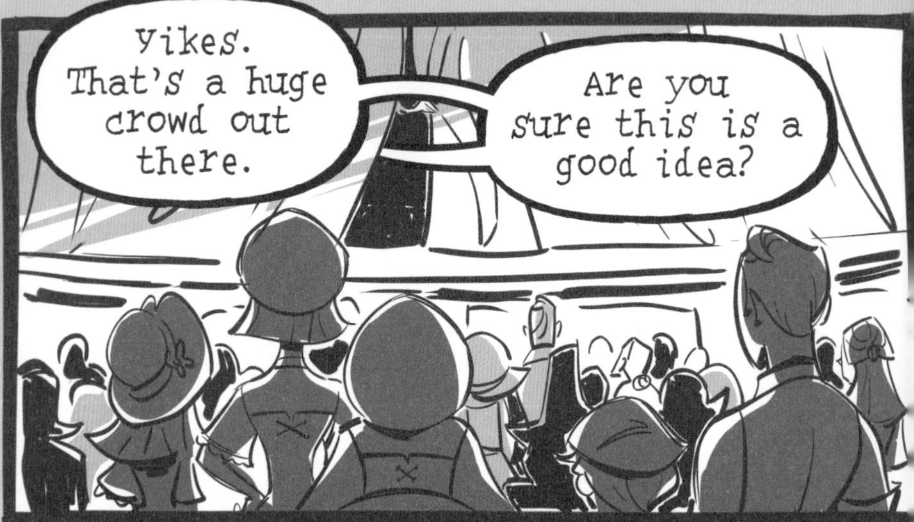
Yikes. That's a huge crowd out there.
Are you sure this is a good idea?
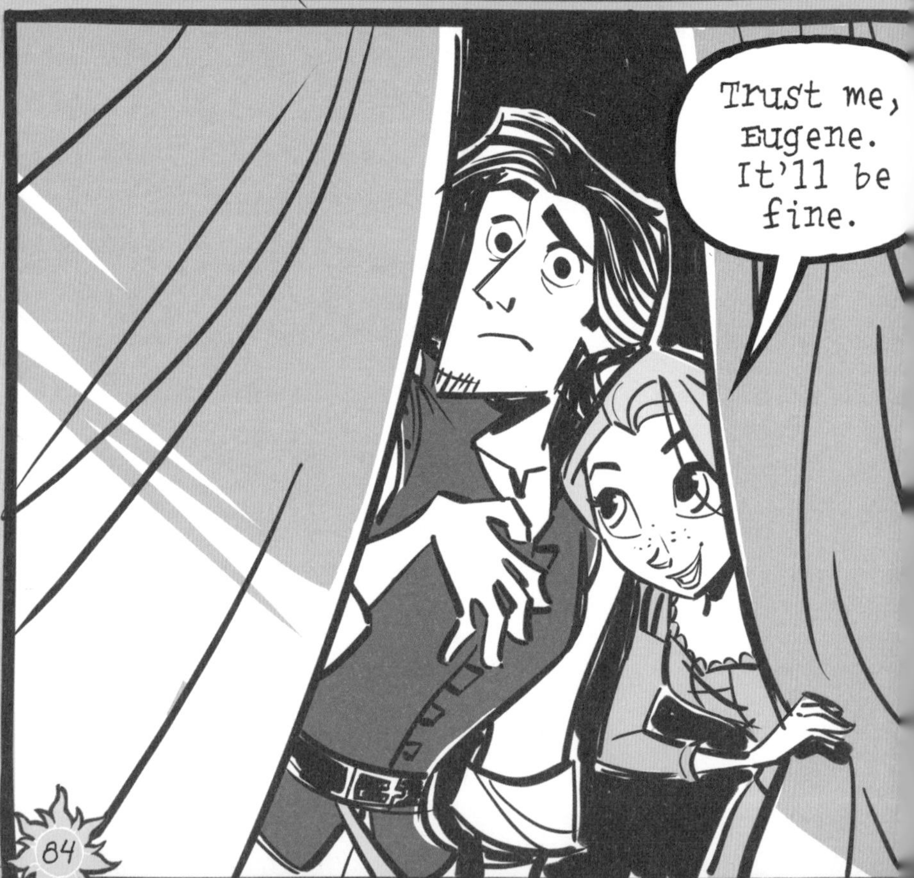
Trust me, Eugene. It'll be fine.

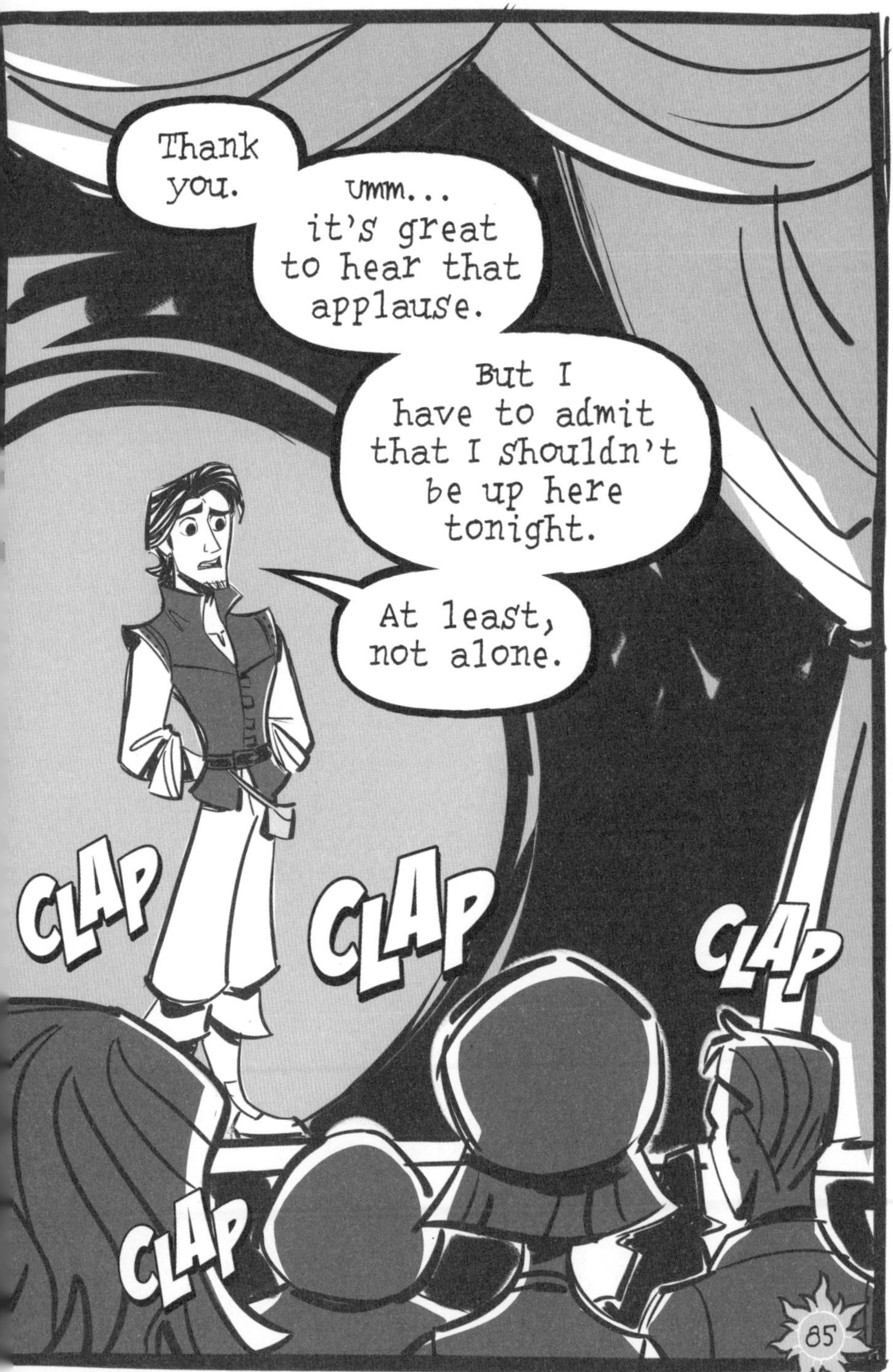
Thank you.
Umm... it's great to hear that applause.
But I have to admit that I shouldn't be up here tonight.
At least, not alone.
CLAP
CLAP
CLAP
CLAP

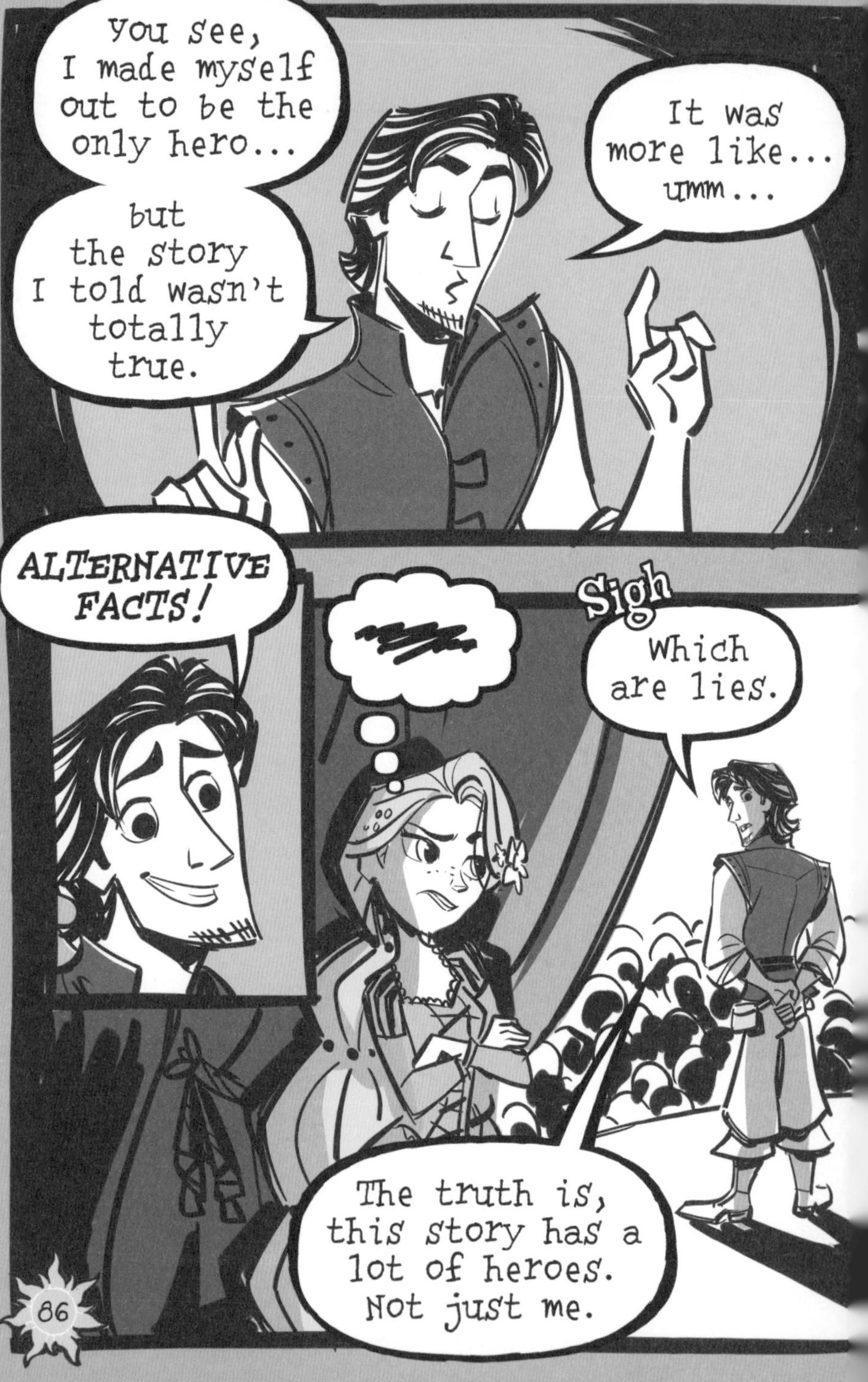
You see, I made myself out to be the only hero...
but the story I told wasn't totally true.
It was more like... umm...
ALTERNATIVE FACTS!
Sigh
Which are lies.
The truth is, this story has a lot of heroes. Not just me.

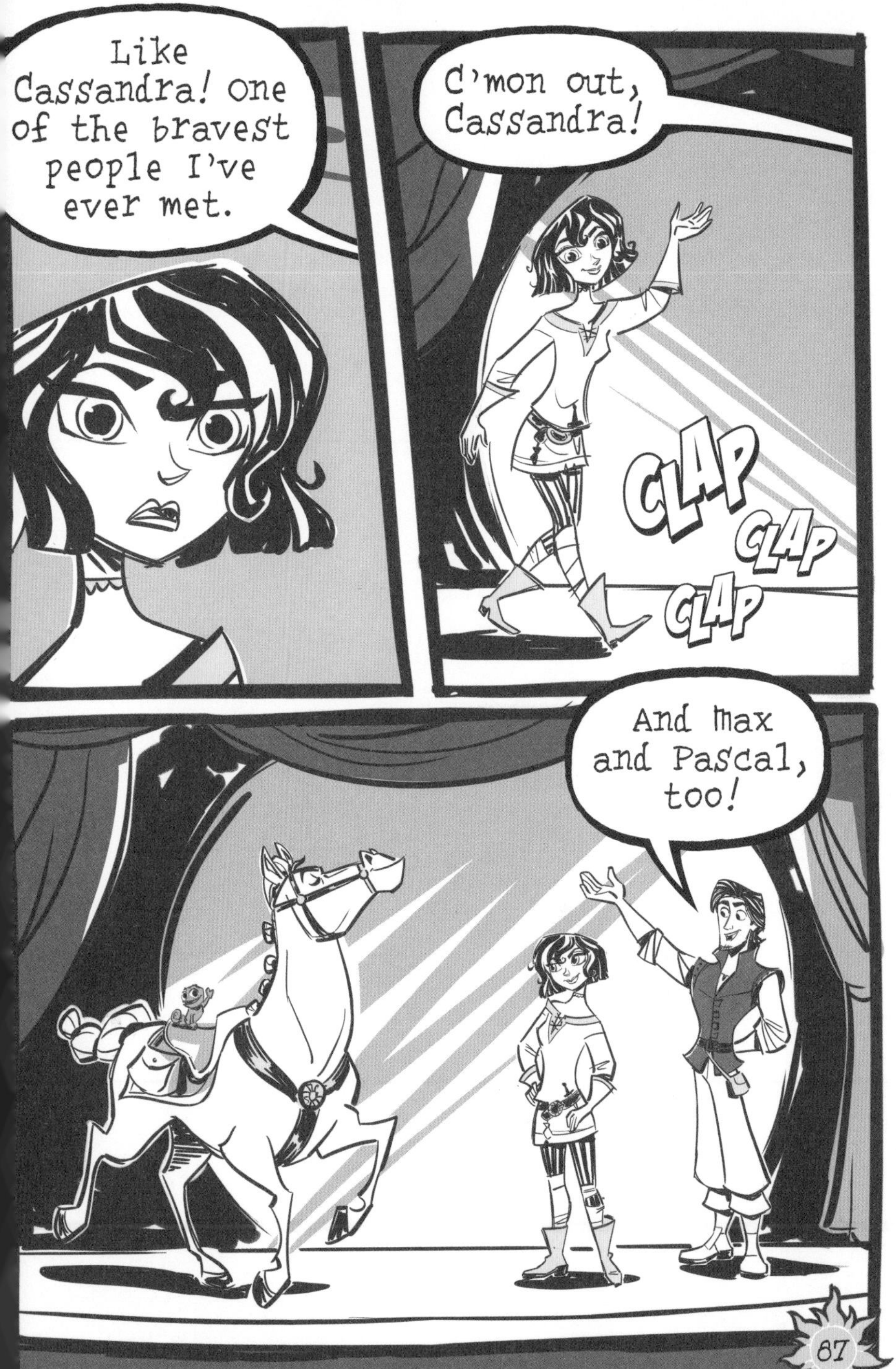
Like Cassandra! One of the bravest people I've ever met.
C'mon out, Cassandra!
CLAP
CLAP
CLAP
And Max and Pascal, too!

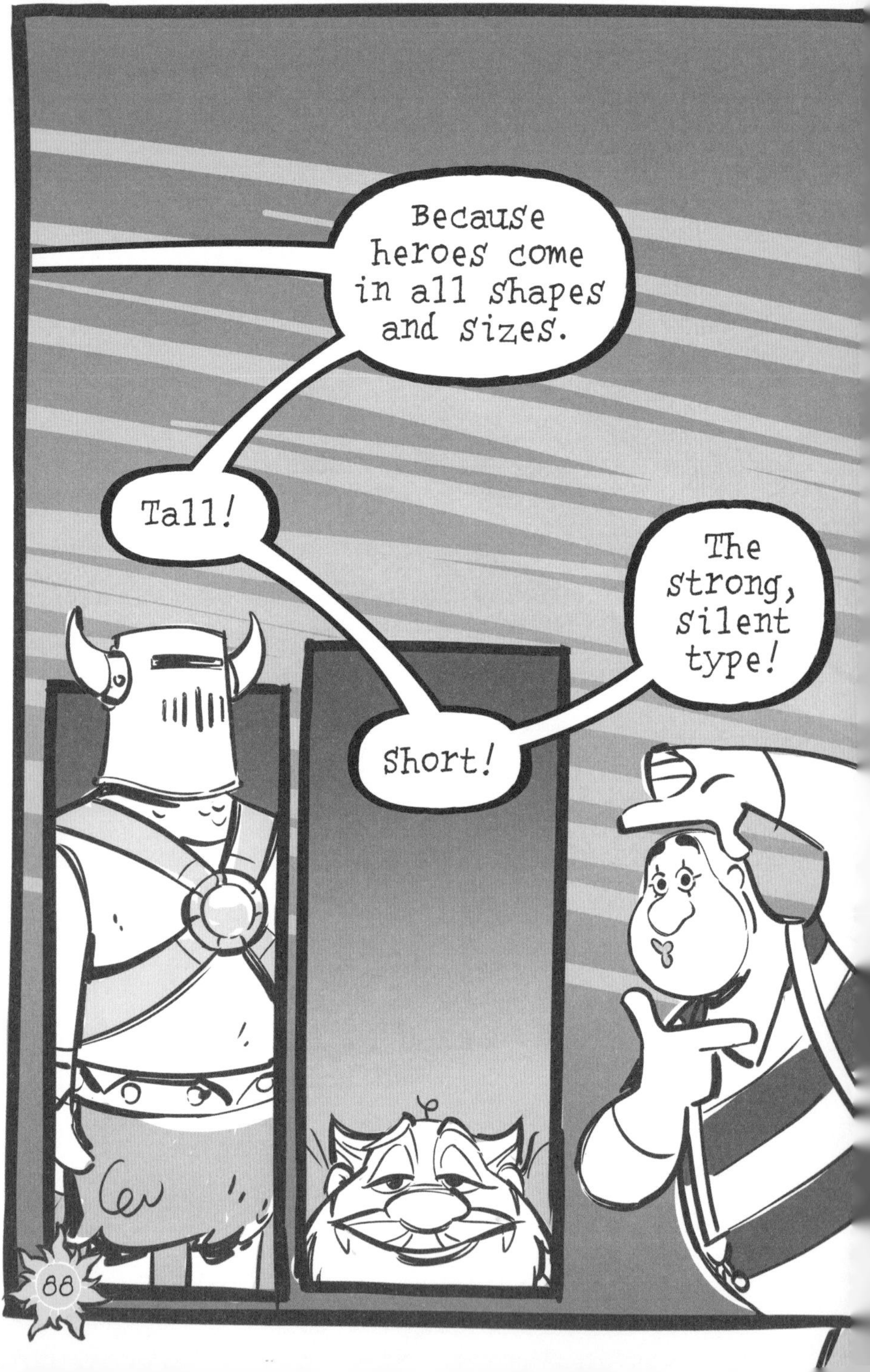
Because heroes come in all shapes and sizes.
Tall!
Short!
The strong, silent type!

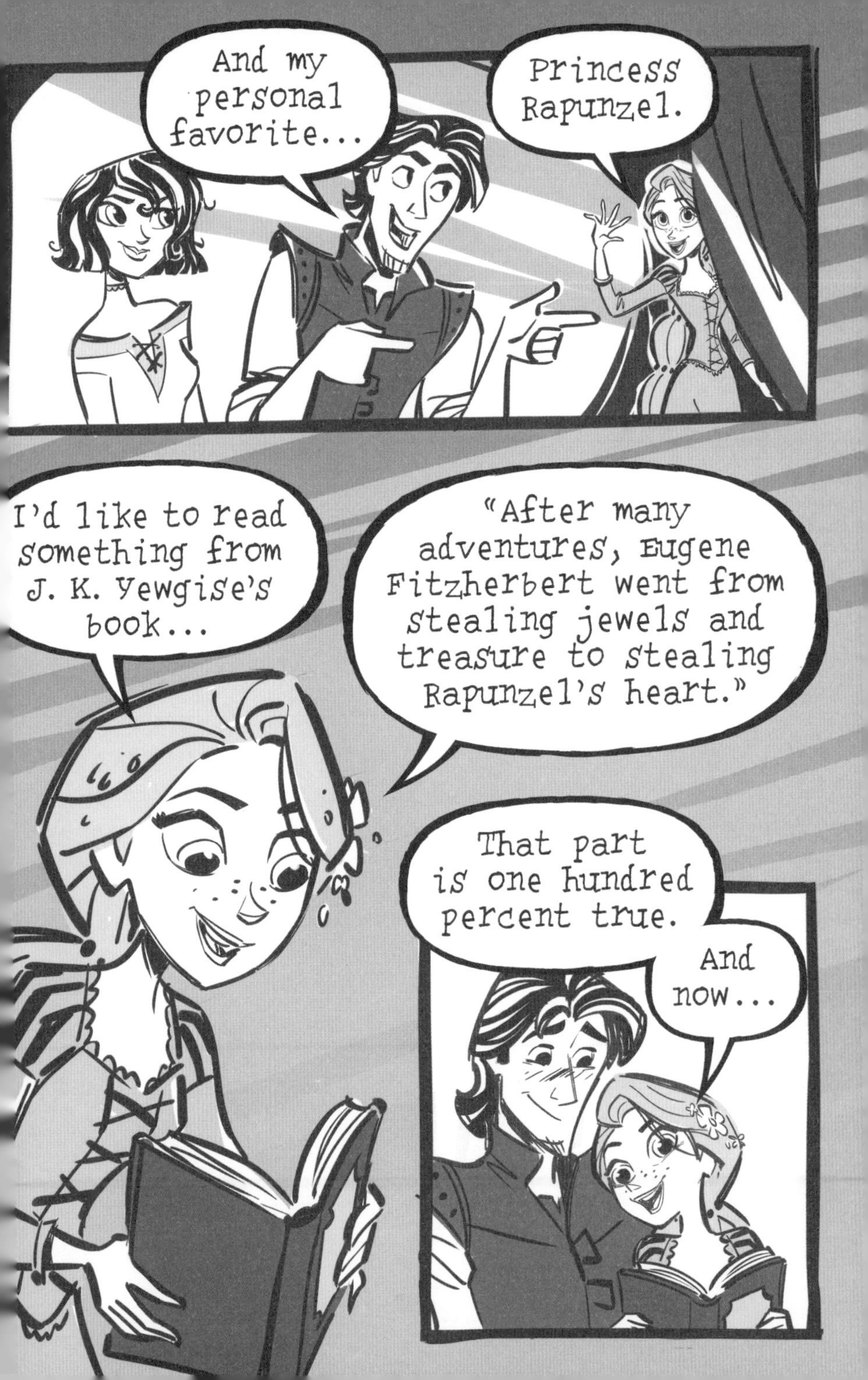
And my personal favorite...
Princess Rapunzel.
I'd like to read something from J. K. Yewgise's book...
"After many adventures, Eugene Fitzherbert went from stealing jewels and treasure to stealing Rapunzel's heart."
That part is one hundred percent true.
And now...

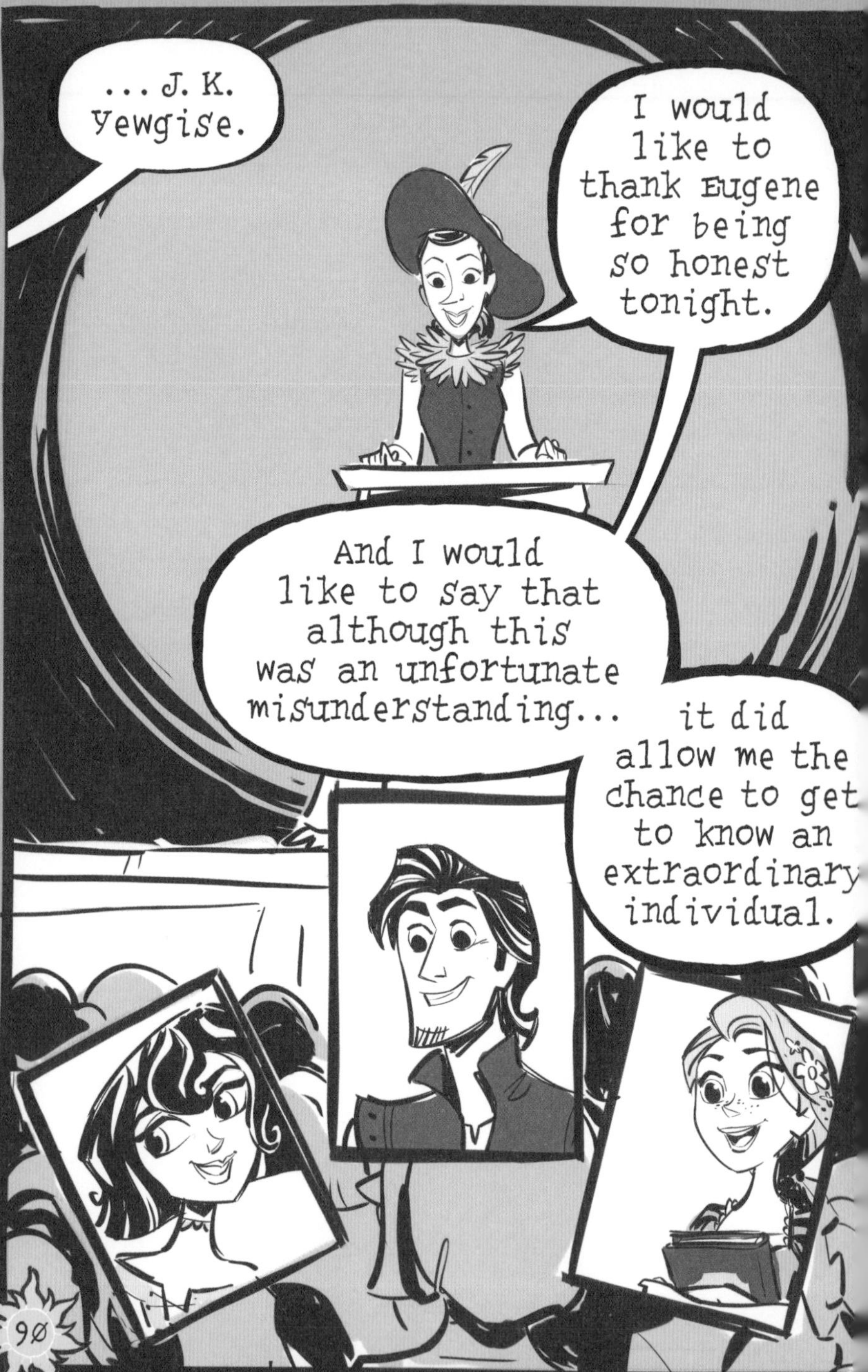
... J. K. yewgise.
I would like to thank Eugene for being so honest tonight.
And I would like to say that although this was an unfortunate misunderstanding...
it did allow me the chance to get to know an extraordinary individual.

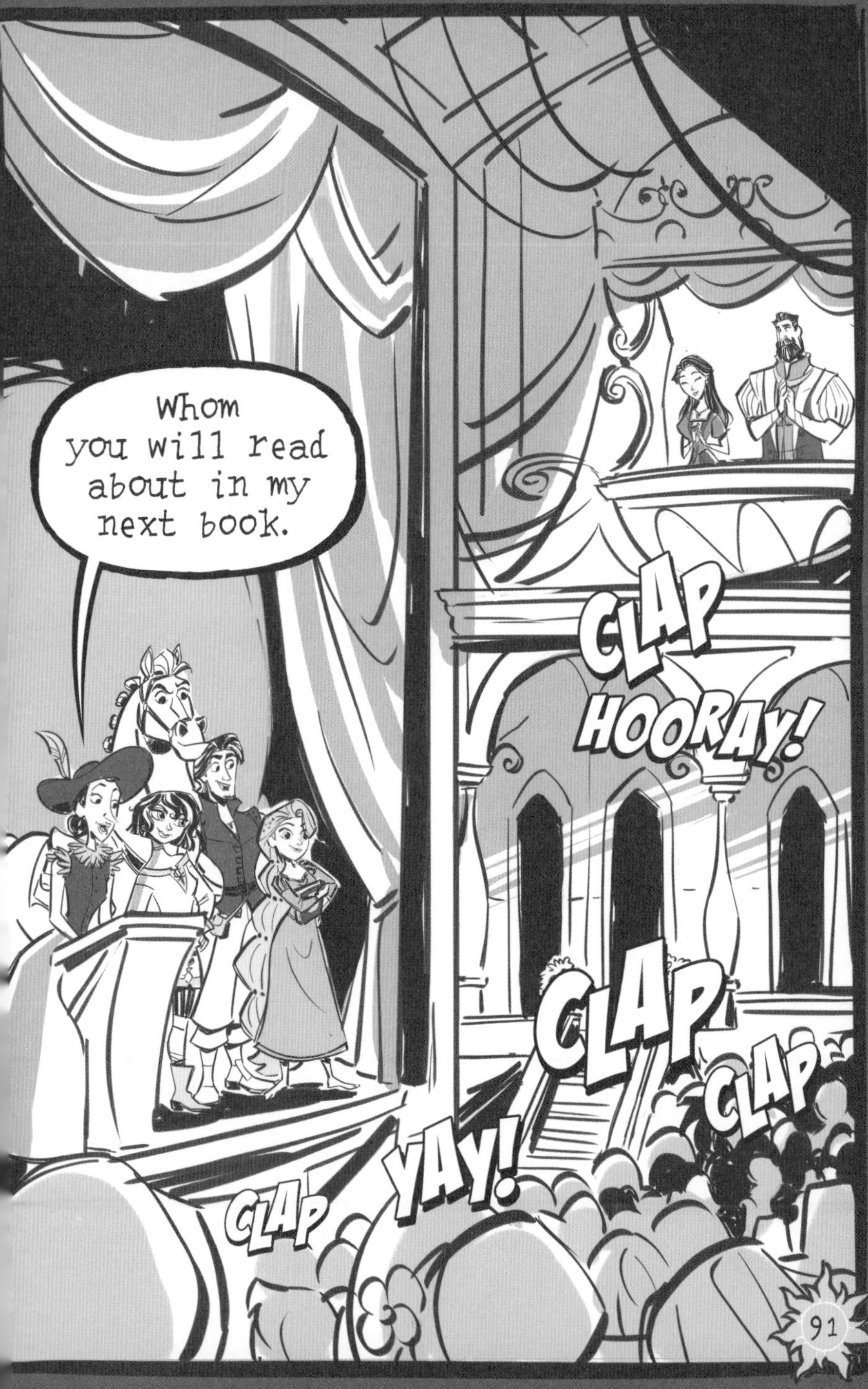
Whom you will read about in my next book.
CLAP
HOORAY!
CLAP
CLAP
YAY!
CLAP

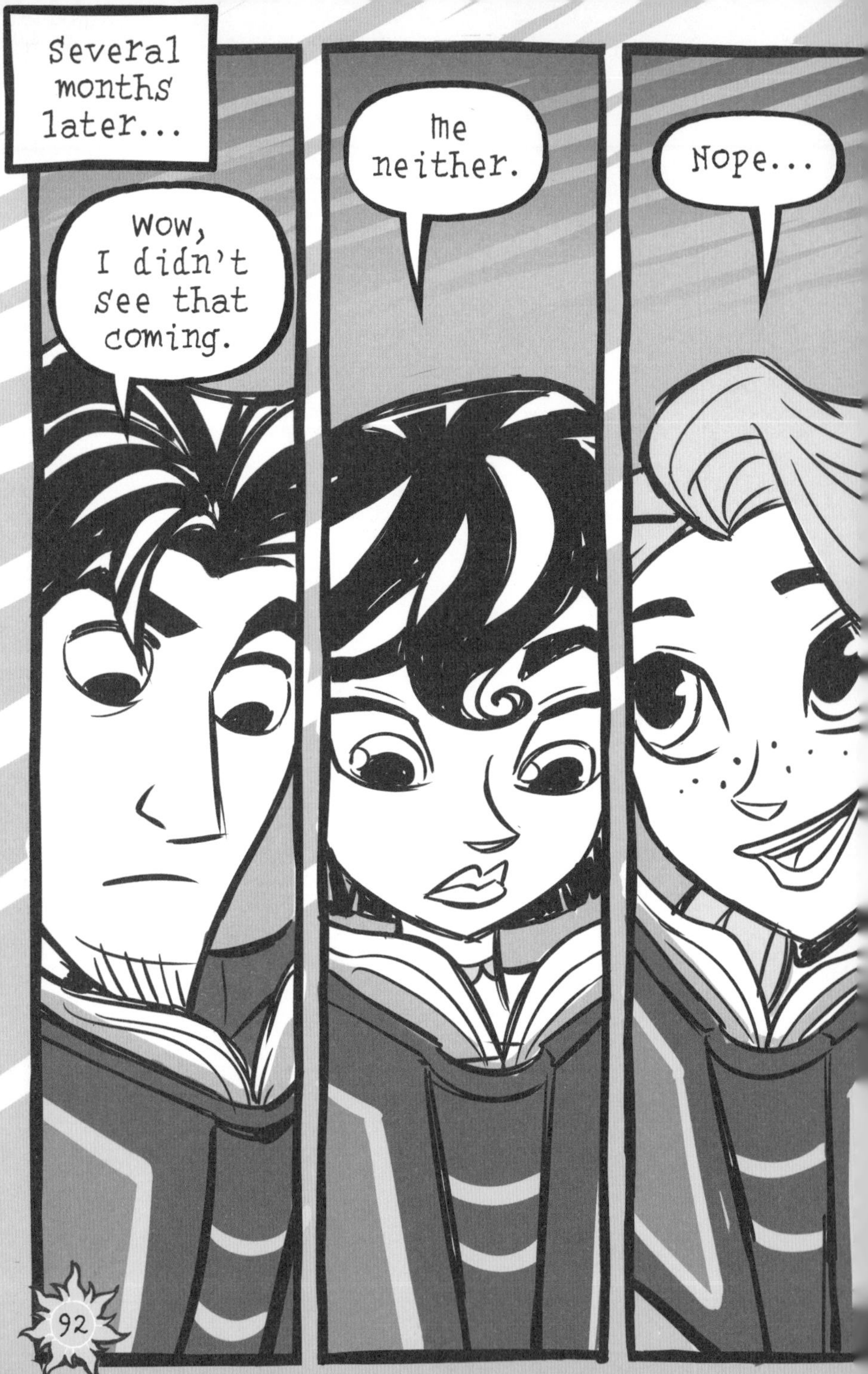
Several months later...
Wow, I didn't see that coming.
Me neither.
Nope...

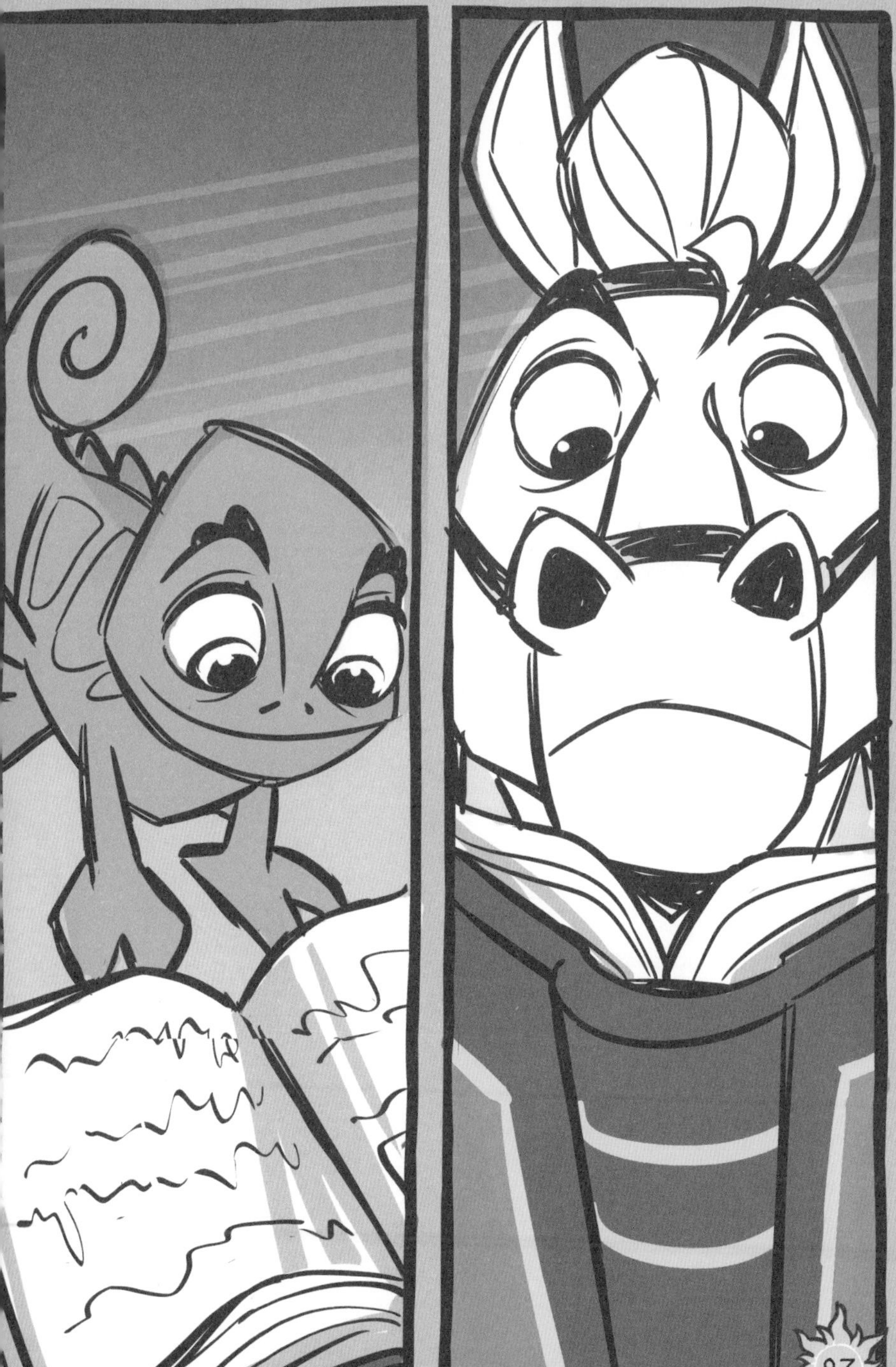

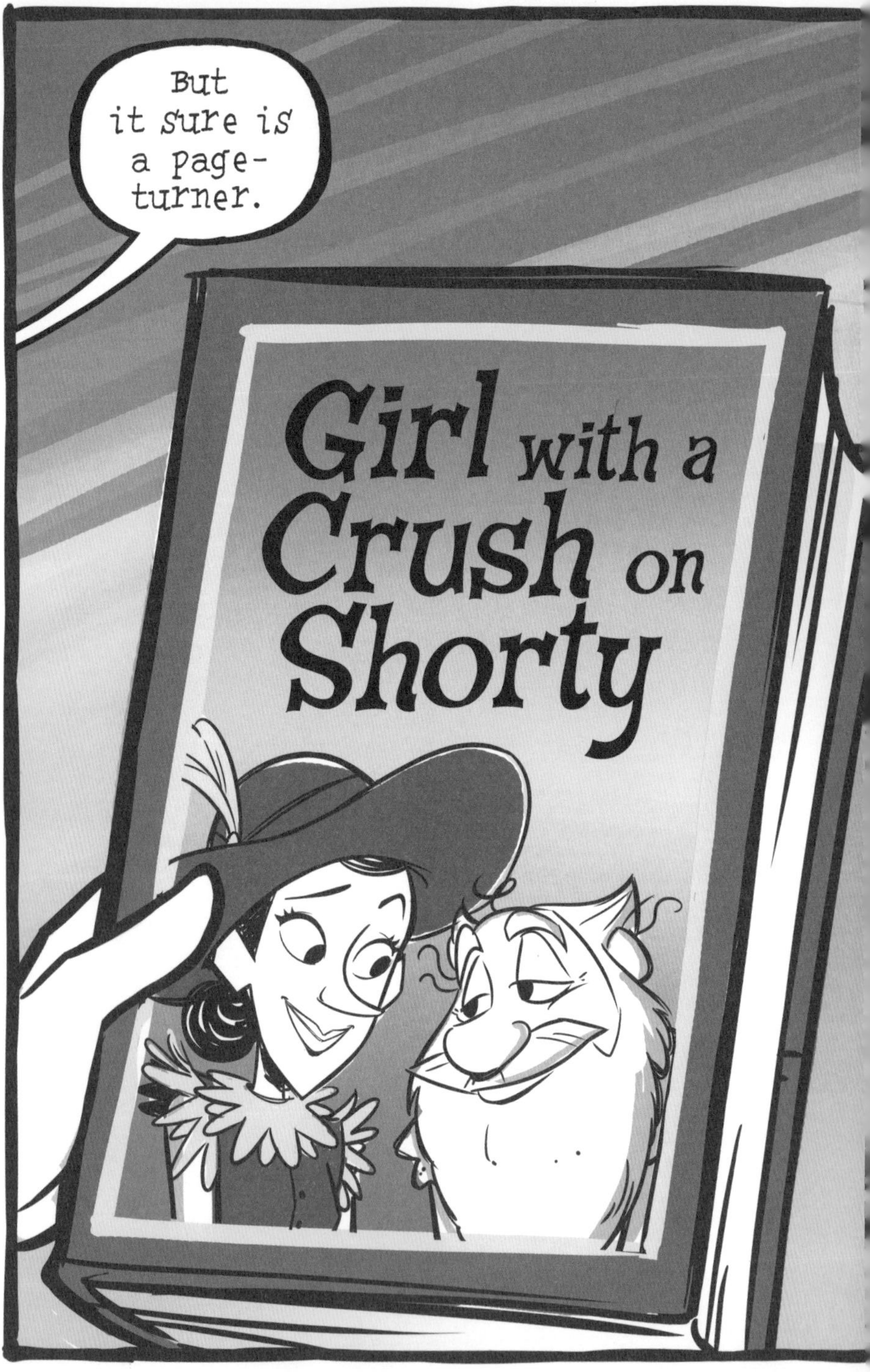
But it sure is a page-turner.
Girl with a Crush on Shorty